In Desolate Corners, Shadows Crouch

Published in 2012 by FeedARead Publishing

British Library C.I.P.
A CIP catalogue record for this title is available from the British Library.

Kriss Nichol was born in the North-East of England and, amongst other things, worked as a teacher for sixteen years before retiring to South-West Scotland. She lives in a converted stable block and writes poetry as well as prose. This is her first novel.

By the time Grace was sectioned she'd been hearing voices for over forty years. Circumstances leading up to the sectioning began way before she was born, but recent events were gathering momentum in that first week of May

Monday 5 May

11.00 a.m.

The Shambles, near Druridge Bay, Northumberland

Good. Nothing's moved. Nothing's been touched.

After this morning's shopping you're tired and anxious. The log cabin is quiet so you relax your shoulders a little but keep your ears cocked, ready to detect any sound, any indication of another presence. Quietly removing a roll of red ribbon from one of the kitchen drawers, you go back into the utility room. Your senses are still on alert, but experience has taught you that you need to keep up the appearance of normality, going about your everyday business.

-Now, where to put it? Round the handlebars? The saddle? Through a wheel? No. It needs something else.-

Your temples are still throbbing, still alert, as you go back into the kitchen and put the kettle on. Green tea helps you relax. You shake your head trying to get the thoughts and voices to unscramble, but they whizz around regardless. You sit down, put your hands on your brow and try to concentrate.

-What were you doing? What were you looking for? It doesn't matter. Don't force it, it'll come …-

11.20 a.m.

Looking at the clock on the kitchen wall you realize how long you've been sitting here. The tea's cold.

-What had you been doing?-

Oh, yes, the bike. Looking for one of those bows you saved. You save everything, whether you want to or not.

A little dizzy and disorientated you struggle to your feet. Using the bench tops for support, you make your way across the kitchen to the hallway where the dizziness ebbs and flows as the pressure in your temples and the back of your head pulsates, finally evaporating, leaving your head an echo chamber. You listen to the screaming silence around you and feel again the subliminal tap on your shoulder.

-You're being watched -

Your mouth opens and closes but nothing falls out for several minutes, until you hear your chest grinding. Gasps and sobs erode your ribs, there is a churning, then screeches and shrieks vomit upwards, spilling onto your feet and the wooden floor…

11.30 a.m.
Merry Farm, near Alston, Cumbria

On the other side of the country Gary Hindmarsh is feeling good. Another customer wants a bespoke kitchen and he has been down to the warehouse to have a word with Scott, the storeman. However, their conversation is interrupted by the phone in the office. He really must get someone in to do reception work now the business, which he runs from home, is taking off at last. Gary grabs the handset on its seventh ring.

'Hello?'

'Hello, son. How're you doing?'

Gary's whole face beams. At nearly six foot, with a broad frame and muscular arms, he could look intimidating, but his pale blue eyes, which light up when he smiles, are disarming.

'Dad! Great. You?'

'Not so bad, son. So, have you thought about it then?'

Gary's brow furrows. 'It's a great idea, Dad, but I still don't think—'

'Australia's where the work is. And

you'll love the lifestyle. Our Jason's having a great time—'

'It's not that… I've met somebody.'

'Oh, God, not again. Who is it now?'

'She's special, Dad.'

'They're always special.'

'You don't understand—'

'I understand Sharon was special—till she got rid of the baby. What's this one—'

'Dad, let's not go there,' Gary interrupts, struggling to control himself. 'Jayne's different. Like I said, she's special, a bit older than me—'

'How much older?'

'Just a few years. She's got kids.'

'Kids!' his dad shouts. 'Oh, God. Here's your mother.'

Gary exhales heavily.

'Hello, son,' his mam's voice breathes into his ear.

He can hear his dad muttering in the background, then his mam speaks again,

'So you've met someone? With children? How many?'

'Two. A boy, eight, and a little girl, nearly three.'

'What about the father? Where's he in all this?'

This isn't going to be easy but he's rehearsed this part. 'Adam's dad never had any contact and Claire's dad left just after she was born.'

'Doesn't it make you wonder why they left and why she's latched onto you?'

Gary grits his teeth. 'I knew you'd be like this, Mam.'

'That's not fair, Gary.' Her voice starts to quiver and Gary quickly backs down.

'Look, Mam, I'm sorry. I promise I'll think about it. Okay?'

She sniffs. 'Okay. Your dad could do with your help; he's not getting any younger. We have to contract out all the joinery work.'

'I know, Mam. I will think about it. Promise. Now look, I've got to go and this'll be costing you a fortune. Talk soon, okay?'

'Okay, son. Love you.'

'Love you too. Bye.'

3.46 p.m.
The Rise, Nenthead

The kitchen is a study in chaos. Jayne Freeman, a slim redhead with short spiky hair, has just returned from picking the children up from school and is about to hang a second load of washing out when Lizzie Marshall arrives. The women have known each other since school and their children are playing happily in the garden, the noise of their squeals easily heard through the open window.

'Coffee?' Jayne asks as Lizzie plonks her shopping down beside the lounge door.

'You're a life-saver. Thanks for picking John up.The sales are on in The Lanes—I've never seen Carlisle so busy. Can I hide these here until the coast's clear?'

At five foot seven Lizzie is three inches taller than Jayne, has long dark hair and still, despite all her dieting since John was born, has a persistent roll of flesh that at the moment is resting on the top of her hipster jeans.

'What did you get him?' asks Jayne.

Lizzie goes to one of the bags and pulls out a frothy set of baby-pink underwear—thong, bra, camisole with detachable suspenders—edged with caribou fur. The women scream girlishly as Lizzie holds them up to herself.

'You can't wear them! You'll never be able to wash them.'

'They won't be on long enough to get dirty—unless thoughts can soil them.'

Jayne nearly chokes. 'My God! He'll have a heart attack. And you! You've never been experimental in all the years I've known you.'

'Mid-life crisis. I might not have a toy boy like Gary, but Derek's always wanting to be more adventurous. Well, he's going to get a new woman before he starts looking for one.'

The women chuckle until the kettle pops and Jayne makes two cups of instant coffee, which they carry into the lounge.

'So what's lover boy up to tonight?' asks Lizzie, settling herself in an armchair.

'I've no idea. I want a night off—having multiple orgasms seven days a week can age you.'

Lizzie looks shocked. 'You don't!'

'What?'

'Have multiple orgasms. Do you?'

Jayne creases up and holds her stomach, laughter shaking her shoulders.

'Of course not. Well, maybe once. Lizzie, you're priceless.'

'Oh you. I never know what to believe with you. I read in one of those magazines in the dentist—'

Jayne resumes her laughing till tears roll down her cheeks. 'Never believe everything you read, Lizzie. Trust me, it's all bollocks.'

'Why aren't you seeing him, then?'

'I dunno. I just want some time to myself. He's a bit sort of…intense.'

'Isn't that good?'

Jayne considers her friend's question.

'Not this early in a relationship. Anyway, I just want some fun. After Sandy, I don't think I'll ever really trust anyone again.'

Lizzie nods then asks, 'Have you heard from him lately?'

'No, nothing. He'll pop up again when he wants something. He always does.'

'Well, don't give him anything,' Lizzie warns, frowning.

'Easier said than done,' Jayne replies with a seductive smirk.

'I'm not talking about sex. I just don't get it. You could have anyone you wanted—'

Jayne interrupts her with a snort of derision,

'—what on earth do you see in him?'

'No idea, apart from the fact he's got a big willy and knows what to do with it.' She starts to laugh but sees her friend's face and changes the subject. 'When do you want me to look after John for your night of the big seduction?'

'A week Friday? Is that okay?' asks Lizzie.

'Course. Fancy a bikky?'

'Not on your life. I've only a week and a half to get this old bod into shape. I don't want to look all spare tyres when we start trying out new positions.'

This is followed by further laughter until they are exhausted and fall back onto more mundane topics.

8.30 p.m.

That evening Gary calls round. He's picked up a bouquet of mixed flowers from the Co-op in Alston and thrusts them under Jayne's nose as soon as she opens the door. Aware of the effect seeing him has on her, she's determined not to give in.

'Gary, I told you—'

'I know, but I was passing and thought you might like to watch a DVD or something.' Putting his free arm around her he guides her into the kitchen and starts looking for a vase.

She is not pleased. 'Gary, I want to wash my hair and do my nails.'

'You look great. Your hair doesn't need washing and you can do your nails another time.' He gently draws her towards him. 'What about tomorrow? I'm working late—you can do them then.'

' But I'd planned to do them tonight.'

'Ah, come on. I'm here now.' He beams at her, pulling her closer.

She stands her ground.

'Why don't we snuggle down on the settee now the kids have gone to bed?' he asks leaning into her, nibbling her neck. She relaxes a little so he puts the flowers onto the bench before manoeuvring her up against it and grinding himself into her groin, still kissing her neck. He moves upwards, licking an ear. She shudders slightly as she speaks.

'You bastard. Okay, but you can't stay. The kids—'

'Fine by me. I need an early start.'

10.27 p.m.
The Shambles

You sit quietly on the bed, a photograph album resting in your lap. The noises in your head have stilled and you feel drained, but peaceful. The brown leather cover of the album has seen better days and the thick khaki pages it holds are loose now. Small diagonal slits secure the photographs and postcards that have for so long been trapped inside. Just like you.

Your right hand absently strokes one of the photographs, a sepia study of Dad, a handsome man in a studio portrait pose looking straight at the camera. His hair is thick and dark, cut severely short at the sides, and on top it is parted in the middle, slicked down. Underneath the photo a paper label is glued indicating the place and date written in cursive lettering, ink from the fountain pen fading to green. You look for any indication in his eyes.

-Did he know what was going on? Did he never suspect, even when his own mother told him?-

Looking at another photograph, of his wedding day, you fail to see what the attraction in Mother was.

-What power did she have? Where was it housed? In her eyes? Her mouth? Head? Hands?-

You've been doing this for years and are still no nearer understanding. And then you hear it.

A soft wail resonates inside your chest, growing slowly louder until you shut the album and return it to a shelf in the bookcase.

-It's late. Go to bed-

You inhale through your nose, hold the breath for several seconds and then exhale from your mouth, willing all tension to release, to flow out into the universe in the shape of golden stars, preventing negative energies from hurting anyone else. You repeat this process several times, visualising peace and gold flowing through you from the crown of your head, reaching every cell of your physical body. You ask for white light to protect you whilst asleep and for good measure visualise a cloak of iridescent blue held at arm's length around you, then close your eyes and wait for sleep.

Tuesday 6 May

5.00 a.m.
The Rise, Nenthead

Gary closes the bedroom door and after a couple of minutes Jayne hears his car start up as he leaves. Last night he suggested taking her to Paris to celebrate her birthday and she was thrilled, but this morning she feels a little unsettled. She shouldn't have given in like that. She curses her body for letting her down again, then smiles at the memory of their lovemaking. For all his intensity Jayne likes him a lot. He's honest, hard-working and reliable; the complete opposite to Sandy. Yet there are a lot of similarities when it comes to lovemaking. Both are imaginative and able to be tender as well as passionate and rough. Quite how rough Gary will be she is yet to discover, and she tingles at the thought of their trip to Paris. She could really let herself go, with no kids to wake up or worry about. She laughs. Poor Gary, he doesn't know what he's let himself in for.

8.30 a.m.
The Shambles

You're confused. You're sitting at the kitchen table but don't know why. Something has brought your attention to the moment but you're disorientated. Finally you recognise the sound. That's the phone ringing.

-Why is it ringing? Should it be ringing?-

You can't quite remember, but you're drawn to answer it.

'Hello Mam.'

It's Jaynie again. You're the only one who calls her that. She hates it, but old habits die hard.

'Mam? You okay?' Her question sounds innocent but what will they make of it?

Carefully you reply, 'Fine.'

'About the weekend—Gary wants to take me to Paris for my birthday. Can you have the kids for me at yours?'

-Is this a trick question? Call her bluff-

'Yes, dear.'

'You're sure you don't mind?'

-What's the correct answer?-

You know the phone's tapped, but you also want to reassure Jaynie. It's her first weekend away with her new man so you don't want her to worry. But why's she asking these questions over the phone?

'What time will you be getting here?' You shouldn't have asked that. You're playing right into their hands, providing them with vital information.

'About four. We've got to be at the airport for about six, six thirty. Mam, are you sure it's okay?'

'Of course.' It's going well. You can do this. You just need to focus and you'll be fine. 'See you Friday.'

The receiver clicks as you put it down. You wait exactly thirty seconds then pick it up again. It's their static; you'd recognize it anywhere. They're still out there, listening, plotting. The wall buckles a little as you lean against it, resting your body for a while. You recognize the signs - they've poisoned the tea again. It's a good job you only had a few sips. They mustn't know it's affecting you, so you straighten the wall, smoothing it back carefully, making sure it's returned to its correct position, then go upstairs to lie down. The bike can wait.

8.35 a.m.

The Rise

As soon as she puts the phone down Jayne feels a

niggling concern. Her mother has always been strange but today she sounds ... what? Different? More vague than usual? Re-running the conversation Jayne can't quite put her finger on it. Perhaps she's imagining it? Or perhaps Grace is just a bit nervous about having the children for the whole weekend at her house. It is a big responsibility... No, it'll be fine, she persuades herself.

Jayne remembers last night, the feel of Gary's mouth, his teeth and his hands, and there's that familiar buzz in the pit of her stomach again. Her pelvic floor muscles clench involuntarily. Not only is this a great opportunity for a wonderful, no holds barred, shagging weekend, it's also something just for her, and not for any of the roles she plays. It'll be great!

Her thoughts are interrupted by squeals from above and the arrival of Lizzie and John at the front door. Shouting up the stairs she calls to the children, 'Hurry up, Adam, John's here. Bring Claire's coat with you. Come on, we're going to be late.'

The children thunder downstairs, Adam in the lead. He throws Claire's coat at his mam as he pushes past her and through the door to see John. Claire follows in his wake but is caught by Jayne who struggles to put the child's coat on.

'Hold still, Claire. They won't go without you,' but the little girl is not convinced and she wriggles free from her mother's grasp.

'Claire!' Jayne is exasperated, but watching the boys make a fuss of her daughter she shrugs, picks up her keys and follows them all out into the street, closing the door behind her. The three children run ahead. Catching up to Lizzie, Jayne notices her friend looks unhappy so she asks her what is wrong.

'Derek's hours have been cut and I don't see how we can manage,' Lizzie confides.

'What'll you do? You've not worked since John was born.'

'I know.' Lizzie looks tired.

'What about Citizen's Advice? They might be better at advising you about what you're entitled to. Apparently there's loads of people entitled to benefits and don't know about it.'

'I'll do that.' Lizzie bites her fingernail absentmindedly. 'God, I hate this scratting round for enough to live on. Derek's lived here all his life and never been short of work, but now...'

'It's the same everywhere. Look at Gary. He set up his own business because there wasn't the work anywhere else.'

'I thought it was because his folks went to Australia.'

'That was part of it but—'

The boys are hitting each other with their bags and Claire is knocked over by mistake but picks herself up and joins back in with the rough and tumble.

'Adam! Be careful!' Jayne yells.

Adam looks at his mam and nods, then races in front, the other two children following close behind.

Turning her attention back to her friend Jayne continues, 'It was mainly because back then he found getting skilled work round here too difficult. He hit lucky really, just as incomers bought up all the old properties and wanted renovations. Now things have slowed for him too.'

'He hasn't got anything Derek can do, has he?'

Jayne laughs. 'I don't think there's much call for farm labouring in customised kitchens, but I'll ask.'

'Derek's good with his hands—'

'So you said,' says Jayne, laughing suggestively.

Lizzie's not amused. 'Be serious! You always have to turn things smutty.'

'Sorry,' Jayne apologises. 'I'll ask Gary. Of course I will.'

The women link arms just before they arrive at the school gates and wave the boys off after planting kisses on their reluctant heads. Only Claire is privileged to a hug and kiss from Adam before he and John join their friends. A whistle is heard, then all the children line up in classes behind their teacher, file in order through the doors and the school day begins.

11.10 a.m.
Schoolyard, Nenthead

Adam and John surge out of the double doors. Adam is small for his age and John is tall so they look like there is three years' difference between them. A shout stops them in their tracks as they're cautioned by one of the playtime staff to be careful and slow down. They obey until they get past the corner of the building, then Adam pushes John and the game of Tag begins. Soon several other boys have joined the game but Amanda Kitson wants to play too and wails when the boys tell her to go away. She attracts the attention of Mr Harvey, who comes to see what the matter is.

'All right, Amanda. What's the problem?'

'Please, sir,' she sniffs, wiping her nose on the sleeve of her cardigan, 'they won't let me play with them,' and turns towards the boys, smirking.

'I'm sure they will, won't you, boys?'

'But sir,' Adam starts to protest, 'she's a girl.'

'Very observant, Adam. So what's the problem?'

'She always wants to win. And when she's on she cries when she can't catch us. She's soppy.'

Amanda starts to cry again.

'I don't think that's very nice of you, Adam. Now, boys, let her play or you can all help me pick up litter.'

'Yes, sir,' they mumble in unison. Amanda looks triumphant.

'Amanda?'

'Yes, sir.'

'If you want to play with the boys then stop that silliness and play the game properly. Now, who's on?'

Adam tags Amanda, says, 'She is!' and they all scatter, leaving Amanda with a very cross look on her face.

2.25 p.m.
Druridge Bay

The path has been worn away by sheep and drifts of sand cling to the thick marram grass that stabs at your bare feet.

-You've forgotten your shoes again. No matter, just be careful-

You love the freedom of nakedness, the exhilaration of skin exposed to the air. Whenever Mother was out you'd pull your clothes off and dance, allowing the disturbed air to whisper over your body. Later, when you were older, you'd imagine it was Brendan's hands caressing you. But she caught you once and your skin burnt with her hands, not Brendan's. After that you taught yourself to be always alert.

The sand is deeper now as you approach the beach. Digging your feet in you propel yourself forward and feel the grittiness between the toes. Overhead birds are wheeling but your attention is concentrated on the lone figure near the shore. He's dressed in a parka with the hood up and you stop, feeling your heart pounding.

-It's far too warm to be dressed like that!-

Panic seizes you as he turns, then he's gone. Disappeared. You look and look but he's nowhere to be seen. The day disintegrates.

-Get back home. Now. -

4.27 p.m.
The Rise

Adam bursts through the back door, panting. His trainers and tracksuit bottoms are covered in mud, his face is red and his dark blond hair is sticking to his head. He's accompanied by John, who's similarly dressed and equally hot and sticky.

'Can I go to John's?' Adam asks, breathlessly.

'It's nearly teatime,' Jayne replies.

'Oh, Mam,' he whines.

'What's so special that won't wait?' Jayne asks.

'We're going to play his new computer game and—'

At that moment Claire joins them. She's covered in mud from head to toe and looking very pleased with herself.

'Oh my God!' Jayne exclaims, then bursts out laughing. 'What have you lot been up to?'

'Nothing,' Adam answers, assuming an innocent expression.

'Thems buried me,' Claire announces, her face beaming.

Jayne is shocked. A fist in her stomach closes. 'Adam! What have I told you? She's only little. You have to be careful with her when you play.'

'It just happened. We were playing and then... she... kind of fell and we…Can I go to John's please?'

'I want you back here in an hour. It'll take me that long to get her cleaned up.'

Adam gives out a whoop of '*Yes*!' and scuttles out the door. Claire moves to go with him.

'Oh no you don't,' says Jayne as she grabs her daughter. 'It's the bath for you, my little monster,' and she whisks her upstairs ignoring the wails of protest.

4.52 p.m.
Alston
Gary pulls up outside the post office and parks the car. He needs some Euros and a birthday card. Inside he checks the display carousel and chooses one 'To My Love' with the perfect verse inside. He wants everything to be perfect, especially at the hotel. He has already bought a couple of packs of rose petals and incense sticks but wants something for her to open. Underwear? Of course! She gets her 'good' stuff from Anne Summers—he's going to have fun checking that out online.

10.41 p.m.
The Shambles
-What time is it? It's dark outside—is it early morning or night-time?-

You struggle to see the clock but your eyes can't focus properly. It needs a new battery so the digital front is no longer luminous but the pad at the top still works. You press it and the strange mechanical voice informs you,

'It's ten forty-one p.m.'

You reach for the light switch but then decide against it.

-Use your night eyes. Concentrate -

You close your eyes and focus your energies onto the inside of your eyeballs, then lift the lids. It works. You can see the furniture in your room, the closed curtains, your bookcase and clothes spread on the floor, dropped there before you fell into bed. Rising carefully you swing your legs out of bed and feel the warmth of the varnished wood beneath your feet. It's solid today.

Making your way steadily to the patio windows facing east, you move out onto one of the balconies, automatically using your antennae to check for disturbances of energy as you edge your way forward. Pulling the curtains aside, along with the voile drapes underneath, you look out onto a clear, star-filled sky, but something on the wind has an edge to it, as if even the dark is anxious.

Metal wind-chimes in the garden tinkle in an invisible breeze as the moon casts its light onto them and solid, silvery beams are reflected upwards.

-Good. That'll hold them for a while, until the sun comes up.-

Opening the glass doors you hear an owl hoot a greeting. You observe its silent grace as it glides through the trees on sentry duty at the perimeter of your land. Beyond, the sea crashes onto the shore and the sound of surf stirs you. Something hovers just beyond comprehension and you wrestle in vain to bring it to its knees. You sniff the air but smell only salt, wind, and earth.

Downstairs you move easily, barefoot. Radiating your energy outwards you check for breaches in security, but all seems well. The workroom is still, devoid of any energy but your own. You inhale the familiar smells of paint and turps, pine and varnish, as you meditate cross-legged on the floor. Turning your thoughts inside yourself, you empty your mind, waiting for inspiration for the new commission, a series of images to be used for a publicity campaign on behalf of SHELTER. It comes. You breathe it in, digest and store it, before flicking on the light switch. You reach for your sketchpad and let the breath of creativity flow.

Wednesday 7 May

11.24 a.m.
Carlisle

Jayne gets off the bus at the Courts with Claire and makes her way to The Lanes, hoping to find a couple of dresses for her Paris trip. Claire is happily playing, avoiding the cracks, but it is slowing them down. Jayne is about to tell her to keep up but the sight of Claire's curls bouncing and the concentration on her little face make Jayne change her mind. It is sunny and the bus back is not till 2.20 p.m. so she has plenty time to shop. What does it matter if Claire wants to bounce along jumping from paving stone to paving stone?

'Mammy, you too,' Claire orders. Jayne obliges, feeling a lightness in her neck and shoulders. She smiles at her daughter.

12.07 p.m.
The Shambles

The hot noon sun beats down like volcanic lava spit on the cabin roof, but here in the workroom it's cool. A strange picture is taking shape on the canvas in front of you. Usually you work to a sketch, but you're so compelled to get it all down you've used the 'wet-on-wet' method of painting with oils, managing all the elements of the painting—tone, composition, shape, form and colour—at the same time.

The figure that dominates the foreground reminds you of the man on the beach with no face. You've painted him first in burnt and raw umber, adding black later. There's water swirling in the background and for this you've used grey, with flecks of white added later to show the crests. The man is stooping to the left whilst reaching out towards you with a clenched right fist. His other is clasping what looks like a red hoop, which is attached to the ankle of a child, who has a mix of yellow ochre and white for her hair.

-Where have these images come from?-

You shudder, take the picture off the easel, prop it against the wall and cover it with a piece of old curtain.

Setting up a new canvas, you take deep breaths until your heart rate is back to normal. You can work with acrylics now. Relaxing into the task, you lose yourself again until something draws you back. The shape is all wrong. You listen to the canvas but its whispers aren't any help at all, so you wash your brushes in Zest-It and decide to get cleaned up.

Your naked body is splashed with drops of paint so you use the downstairs shower then climb the stairs to your bedroom, stopping periodically to check all is well. A large white cotton kaftan is on the bed. Pulling its soft fabric over your head, you make your way back down to the kitchen. As you enter you sense something happened here yesterday, or was it the day before? You're confused and struggle to remember.

-What was it?-

Remnants of flimsy images trail, then clear. The bike. Claire's birthday present. A red ribbon.

-Of course, that's it. -

Pleased with yourself, you resolve to see to it after lunch. But then you hear them, scratching on your soul, demanding to be let in and your fear rises up, like a wild thing in a storm turning up at the shore with a wet face.

1.14 p.m.

The Almond Tree, Whitley Bay

Sue Johnson sips her cappuccino with her closest friend, Cassie Kennedy, who is vacantly looking out of the window. Cassie's face in profile is stunning, like a

Greek statue in its perfection. They've been friends for years and jealousy has never reared its ugly head between them. The other kids used to call them Laurel and Hardy at school but instead of feeling the nickname to be offensive, Sue thought it was hilarious.

'Out with it,' Sue asks.

'With what?'

Sue puts the cup down on the saucer. 'You know perfectly well. You've hardly spoken a word since we got here. What's wrong? Have I done something to upset you?'

Cassie looks guiltily at her then says, 'Don't be daft. Of course not.'

'Then what the hell's wrong with you?'

'Nothing, I just don't feel like talking.'

Sue laughs but it comes out a snort. 'That'll be a first. You've a mouth bigger than Tynemouth, you.'

'Charming! But couldn't you think of something more original?—my gran used to say that.'

'Not on the spur of the moment, no. Anyway, old clichés are the new wit.'

Cassie stares at her.

'You know, like "brown is the new black"?'

Cassie doesn't respond to that. Instead, she says, 'There's nothing wrong. It's just, well… I've been thinking.'

'Wow! That must be a shock for the brain cells. No wonder they've shut down. Overloaded the circuits, have you?'

Cassie begins to chuckle. 'No, cheeky bugger, I've just been thinking. You're nearly thirty—'

Now it's Sue's turn to be a bit cross. 'Don't remind me.'

'—and I'll be thirty next year.'

Sue returns to her sarcasm. ‘The woman’s a mathematical genius! That’s what comes of being a year younger than me. Well done! Fancy going to uni to study maths or quantum physics?’

‘That’s it! I’m not saying another word.’ Cassie folds her arms across her chest and gazes back out of the window.

There’s a few seconds of silence until Sue tries to jolly Cassie along with, ‘Huffy aren’t we? I wonder why? Menstruating perhaps? Hangover? No?’ Sue affects a pirate voice speaking to an imaginary parrot on her shoulder: ‘Well, shiver me timbers, me hearty, looks like we’ll have to apologise.’ The ‘parrot’ replies, ‘Go on then, apologise.’

Cassie’s not amused. ‘Can you stop mucking about for one minute. I knew you’d make fun of me. You always trivialise—’

But Sue’s not to be quietened. ‘Oooooooooooo trivialise. That’s a big word for you,’ she says, slightly too loudly.

Suddenly Cassie stands up, knocking the table. ‘Look, I don’t need this right now, okay. I’ll see you later, or something.’

She tries to leave but Sue grabs her hand and speaks gently to her: ‘I’m sorry, Cassie, I never did know when to shut up. Sit down. Please. I’ll put my sensible head on and you can tell Auntie Sue everything.’

For a moment Cassie hovers, indecisive, then she sits down again.

‘I could bloody strangle you sometimes, you know that?’

‘Yeah, but you won’t.’

‘And why not?’

‘’Cause you’d have no one to tell all your dirty secrets to. Come on. What’s really wrong?’

‘It’s just…I don’t know…I just feel like…like time’s passing me by. Here I am, nearly thirty, no man, no kids, nothing.’

‘Think positive. No one to hurt you, mess you about, leave you.’

‘And no one to love me either. Look, I’m not like you. I want somebody in my life. I want kids. I want what everyone else wants.’ Cassie sounds on the verge of tears.

Sue looks critically at her friend, then says, ‘Well you’ll not get it moping round with that ugly miserable face, will you? C’mon, cheer up,’ but Cassie just looks out the window, at a young girl pushing a child in a buggy. Sue softens and admits, ‘Look, despite what you think, I do know how you feel. But there’s worse things than not having a bloke, I can assure you—you want to see some of the people I work with!’ Sue finishes off her coffee and wipes her mouth. ‘Are you finished? I’ll get these, then I’m taking you home. I’ll run the bath, light your candles and put in some of this aromatherapy oil I’ve just bought.’

Cassie smiles and follows her friend to the till.

3.19 p.m.
Merry Farm

Gary’s busy. He’s re-organising appointments and apologising to clients. Most have been fine about the changes, but Mrs Pierce has been a right bitch and wanted a discount, of all things. Bloody cheek! He told her she was quite at liberty to get someone else to fit the utility room, so she backed down. But he knows that when he goes to do the job there’ll be no cups of tea or pieces of cake for him; he’d better remember to take a flask.

Those tasks done, he makes himself a cup of instant coffee, sits back and thinks of Jayne. He ordered some sexy underwear—nothing too erotic, mind—and wonders how he's going to surprise her with them. He paid for express delivery for them to arrive tomorrow and can't wait to see them. He had to guess at the size but he thinks it'll be okay. After all, they won't be on long.

Still pondering about the surprise, he picks up a copy of *Cosmopolitan*. He struggled to understand girls in his early teens and found women's magazines provided information that made sense to him. His dad laughed at him, but he wasn't put off. He's also read John Gray's '*Men are from Mars, Women are from Venus*'.

He flicks through to the back of the magazine where he spots, in amongst the ads for breast augmentation, an advert for male escorts. That's it! Well, not an escort, a stripper. He'll hire a stripper dressed as a flight attendant to give Jayne the surprise package. Perfect! He grabs a copy of the local directory.

4.55 p.m.
The Rise

Adam and Claire have been playing in the sink, washing dishes from a dolls' tea party they've just had on the lawn, when a neighbour brings a parcel for Jayne that was left at the wrong address. Excitedly Jayne undoes the string, releasing the contents onto the table in an explosion of colour. There are three T-shirts, several pairs of knickers and seven pairs of ankle socks. Nestling amongst the soft fabric is a home-made envelope and inside this a painted card from Grace wishing Claire a happy third birthday. It isn't Claire's birthday till July. Grace must've got Jayne's and Claire's birthdays mixed up.

Jayne reads the card again, then whirls on her heels and heads for the telephone. She takes a deep breath, lets it go, then picks up the handset, which she holds for a few seconds before changing her mind and replacing it on the cradle. She stands there for a while, unconsciously twisting her hair round a finger. Eventually she starts to dial, but replaces it again quickly and walks out of the room into the lounge.

Through the open window sounds of machinery waft in along with smells of earth and cement. A large bedroom extension is being built directly behind her house and Jayne realises she'll need an extension herself soon, now the kids are getting older. She lets herself be comforted by the sounds and smells, but anxiety niggles at her. She'll have to phone Gary to call it off, but what can she say? My mother's got the birthdays mixed up? That's hardly a reason, is it? Taking another deep breath she tries to release her fears, mentally intoning, 'Everything's happening perfectly,' as she exhales.

In the kitchen, Adam turns to his sister.

'Come on, let's get some toys from the garden. We can take them to Grandma's and play with them there.'

The little girl responds with nodding, shaking her honey-blonde, shoulder-length curls. She takes Adam's outstretched hand and follows him into the garden where they collect an assortment of toys and pile them at the back door. Adam looks pleased with himself but Jayne tells him to put them back and come inside for tea. He starts to protest but sees Jayne's face and thinks better of it.

'Don't worry, Grandma's got loads to play with,' he whispers when he sees Claire's crestfallen face. 'There's books and paints. And there's the beach and the dunes. And her garden.'

Claire's face brightens and Adam leads her indoors to help her wash her hands.

7.32 p.m.
The Shambles

Opening the back door you step outside and inhale the fragrances of grass, trees, earth and sea. The wind-chimes are silent in the still air and a peace has descended as you stand motionless, melting into the surroundings. The light is fading fast and in the twilight gloom the sculptures stand on sentry duty. You needed to secure a perimeter of protection, so meticulously positioned each sculpture for maximum effect; you're safe outside as long as it's within the boundaries of this garden. Yet you must stay vigilant—it's not beyond their powers to break through your defences.

A barn owl hoots and two bats swoop across the garden, playfully executing their aerial acrobatics from tree to tree. But still you don't move. You've taken root in the doorway, your root systems driving down into the earth, grounding you. There's a coldness in your bare feet but when you try to wriggle your toes you find they've turned to wood. You start to panic, but then tell yourself it's safe now, this is how it was meant to be. There's nothing to worry about. The owl hoots again and your skin tingles.

8.28 p.m.

You're still in the doorway when something breaks inside. The tap roots start to shrivel and you feel the pull upwards, like that delicious pain when you breastfed Jaynie; it releases you from your position. Suddenly you feel cold, exhausted and thirsty.

-Green tea. That's the answer-

Making your way back into the kitchen you pour water into the kettle, after first checking that the filter plumbed into your cold water pipe is still intact.

-Can't be too careful these days-

On the wall is a calendar. Normally you score out the days on the calendar but you can't remember whether you did it yesterday or not. You need to know which day it is because the children are coming on Friday—it's the first time you've seen them since February—and you have to be ready mentally as well as physically. They'll use the children to breach your defences. There's so much to do to secure the place with white light and crystals, to deflect any negative energies seeping through. You must rest now and re-charge your powers. You're going to need every ounce of strength you possess to get the children safely through this.

10.15 p.m.
The Rise

Gary and Jayne are in bed, relaxing in a post-coital glow. Gary gave up smoking when he started seeing Jayne but has never stopped craving them at certain times. This is one of them. It's a good job he's staying the night because the temptation to go to the pub right now and buy a pack is almost overwhelming. He looks at Jayne's face in profile and feels a surge of love. He wouldn't do anything to jeopardise this. Not after Sharon. He couldn't go through that pain again. This has to work.

Jayne shifts slightly and curls towards him, covering his thighs with her leg, snuggling her head onto his chest. He's learning to fall asleep in this position even though it's not a natural one for him. He's more a foetal curler, so 'spoons' is his favourite sleeping position with a partner. But sleep isn't something that Jayne seems to have in mind as she gently cups his balls in her hand and starts massaging them in time to the thrusts she makes against his thigh with her pubic bone. He feels the slightest of stirrings in his penis and not for the first time thanks his lucky stars he has decent powers of recovery.

Thursday 8 May

6.14 a.m.

The Rise

Oh, God, is that the time? Normally Gary leaves just after five but with the double session last night he's overslept. He shakes Jayne's shoulder and she rolls over without waking. Kissing her back he slips out of bed and reaches for his clothes. He can't find his socks. Bugger. He'll have to get them another time.

Picking up his shoes he tiptoes downstairs and into the kitchen to find his keys, accidentally overturning a pot of wooden utensils. Shit, shit, shit! He puts it back into position as quietly as he can and is replacing the contents when he's aware of a quiet padding of footsteps down the stairs. He holds his breath but it's no use. Adam walks into the kitchen.

'Hey, mate. What're you doin' up this early?' Gary asks him.

Adam rubs his eyes. His hair is tousled and his face is puffy with sleep. 'I heard a noise. Where's Mam?'

'She's still asleep. Why don't you go back and get some sleep too, until it's time to get up for school?'

Adam yawns. 'Are you having breakfast?'

'No, I've got to get home and get changed for work. Go on now. Back upstairs. And don't wake your sister, okay?'

Adam nods and makes his way back upstairs but stops when Gary opens the front door.

'See you later?' Adam asks.

Jayne appears at the top of the stairs pulling a large T-shirt over her head. Gary nods to her. 'I'll ring your mam first. Make sure it's okay. Off you go now.'

'Bye, Gary'

'Bye,' Jayne echoes, holding out an arm to Adam wrapping it round his shoulders as she leads him back to bed.

Closing the door, Gary feels warm and protective. If this works out, it'll be his family; he'll be a dad after all.

10.30 a.m.

Jayne's upset.

'So what did Adam say?' asks Lizzie, sipping her mug of instant de-caff. Jayne offers her a Blue Riband, which she resists.

'Nothing, that's the whole point,' Jayne answers, rather more aggressively than the situation warrants.

Lizzie frowns. 'I don't understand.'

Jayne takes a deep breath before continuing. 'Adam didn't say anything because he likes Gary.'

'And?'

'And I don't want him getting too attached, in case it doesn't work out.'

Lizzie puts her mug on the worktop and looks at her friend. Jayne's face shows worry lines on the forehead and round the eyes. She's still very attractive, even without make-up.

'If it doesn't work out! Jayne, give the bloke a chance. Try being positive, instead of all this doom and gloom stuff. What's really worrying you?'

'I don't know. He's young—'

'Lucky you! He adores you.'

'I know. And that's a problem too. I don't know if I feel the same way about him. I like him, I respect him, he's great in bed, but—'

'But what?'

Jayne struggles to articulate her feelings. 'I guess I just want some fun. Not all this forever after stuff. If it happens, then it happens, but it's far too soon to be thinking of the future. I want to provide a stable home for the kids, something I never had but—'

'Don't you think Gary would be a stable influence?' interrupts Lizzie

'I don't want him to be. *I* want to be the stable influence, I don't want to rely on a man to do it for me. That's where I went wrong with Sandy. I thought he'd give me what I needed. Then what does he do? Bugger off as soon as Claire's born and leaves us all in the shit.'

'But Gary's not like that.'

'I know. And that's what I like about him. But I'm not ready for anything permanent yet and I feel I'm getting hijacked into it.'

'How?'

'Because he's so... so... bloody perfect! He's everything a woman could wish for.'

Lizzie bursts out laughing. 'And that's a problem?'

'Yes, I suppose it is.' Jayne looks out of the window at the new buds on the trees and the last of the spring flowers in the borders. 'Something keeps nagging at me, like something I've forgotten. I try to remember—it's there, just beneath the surface—but I can't get to it.'

'I think it's called fear,' offers Lizzie. 'There are no guarantees in anyone's life, Jayne. We have to take chances and hope it all comes out right in the end. If it doesn't we learn from it and move on.'

'I know all that; we've read the same books, remember? No, it's not that, it's something else.'

'Well, until you figure it out, why don't you just relax and enjoy him. See where it goes and worry about it when it happens?'

Jayne laughs. 'Where would I be without you, eh?'

'No doubt in the gutter,' replies Lizzie.

2.11 p.m.
Chapel Street, Alston
Gary turns off the radio before taking a break and heading out into the garden. He's fitting a kitchen in one of the newly renovated houses in an area behind the main street in the centre of Alston. He could murder a fag right now, but he remembers Jayne and the kids, so he resolves to get more patches from the chemist when he finishes here. Thinking about Jayne has brought his thoughts back to this morning and Adam's acceptance of him being there. Jayne always insists Gary leaves early so the children don't know he's been there all night, but now Adam's seen him…That must change things, surely? The kids like him, Jayne likes him, so what's to stop the relationship moving up a notch? Maybe Sandy.

Gary's well versed about Sandy. He's never really met the guy, but it's common knowledge now how badly he treated Jayne. Feeling the tension in his neck Gary forces himself to relax. He's not a fighter, but if Sandy ever comes back here… Suddenly he really needs to hammer something, preferably Sandy's head, then the moment passes and he laughs. Jayne doesn't like violence so he'll have to keep those dark thoughts to himself. Anyway, the man's long gone now, in prison by all accounts. Good. The longer he's away the better. It'll give Jayne a chance to heal, to trust that all men aren't bastards. And Gary's just the guy to show her, starting with Paris. Smiling to himself he returns to the kitchen and turns the radio back on.

6.10 p.m.
Eldon Square, Newcastle upon Tyne
Sue Johnson is on a mission for a new outfit.

‘How’re you getting on? Need any help?’ a voice asks from outside the curtain

‘I’m fine, thanks,’ Sue responds as she struggles out of the red sleeveless dress, which rubs under her armpits and feels like Clingfilm. She needs a bigger size. Or perhaps a different style? Selecting a cream one from the five she’s taken into the cubicle, she unzips it and pulls it over her head, banging the sides of the cubicle with her elbows. Damn. They’re making cubicles smaller these days. This dress isn’t as tight as the last but it does nothing for her. She has long, natural chestnut-coloured hair into which she’s had red low-lights put to complement her lightly tanned skin. The dress, however, seems to drain her, leaving her looking like a slab of marble.

She has no more success with any of the others so she dresses and returns them to the assistant who’s ten sizes too small and shouldn’t be working in Evans at all! The party’s only just over a week away and there’s not enough time for a diet, so she heads for the nearest coffee shop and orders a large piece of banoffee pie and a mega cup of cappuccino. If it’s too late for a diet then these won’t make any difference the other way.

Feeling a little guilty now she’s finished the last dregs of the cappuccino and licked the chocolate from the spoon, she makes her way out of the shopping centre to the Metro, then walks the short distance home.

8.47p.m.

Flat 16, Coglin Mews, Royal Quays,Tyne and Wear

Sue’s flat is in the residential area of Royal Quays, overlooking the marina. Her colour scheme is cream and chocolate brown throughout, with ash-coloured laminate flooring and matching kitchen units with chrome handles and fittings. She's pleased with her investment. From her balcony she can see the red 'Tyne Anew' sculpture lit up. There's an unusually warm breeze coming off the North Sea and it carries the sounds of voices and laughter. The converted ferry boat, *The Duke of Northumberland*, is also lit up, its coloured bulbs reflected, dancing, in the water. There's a party on board. She can hear the music, see the couples. It's her party next week.

-Stop being maudlin. Get your lippy on and get out there, girl. What're you doing here on a nice night like this? - she asks herself.

Pausing to put on her lipstick she looks into the mirror and sees lovely brandy-coloured eyes with their long, silky lashes. She's got good skin, everyone says so, and her face, although perhaps a bit too round, has no wrinkles, not even round her eyes. Her hair tumbles onto her shoulders and the red lowlights catch the artificial light and burn brazenly. She tips her head forward, allowing the hair to hang down, sprays it with hairspray then flicks it back in an upward movement to add volume, which she primps with her fingers.

-Not bad, not bad. Darren Taylor, eat your heart out!-

She grabs a wrap and stuffs it into her bag. Just in case. Well, you never know, do you? It's the same with condoms. She always keeps a pack for emergencies, but lately the emergencies have been other people's, not hers. Sharon's was the last. They'd been out in town and met some blokes who were up on business. At least, that's what they'd said. There were three of them; Sam, Patrick and Mark. Sharon got off with Mark and hadn't come prepared, so Sue had given her the emergency supply. Patrick, the one Sue had fancied, said he was married and left before they went clubbing. Sam disappeared around 1.00 a.m., probably either drunk or with someone else, so she had to get the taxi home on her own—the story of her life these days.

9.08 p.m.

Lounge Bar, Duke of Northumberland, Royal Quays

Sue walks confidently up the gang plank; Cassie's working tonight.

'Back again? Can't you keep away from the place?' asks Cassie as Sue enters the bar.

'Just checking everything's all right for next week,' Sue says with a smile.

'Would I let you down?'

'No, it's just.....I'm going up to town later. Thought I'd check everything's okay and maybe have a couple before I head off.'

'Cranberry and vodka?'

'Thanks. Make it a double.'

Sue takes her drink out on deck and sits on one of the wrought-iron chairs. The breeze is warm and soothing this side so she relaxes into it closing her eyes, letting the breeze flutter over her skin. She's there for several minutes before she hears someone ask,

'Anyone sitting here?'

Startled, she looks up. Male, slightly balding, close-shaved head, yellow summer shirt, Diesel jeans, tanned arms carrying a pint of lager and round, reddish face. Not bad.

'Not really. No.'

He's youngish looking but she's not a good judge of ages. He sits down and asks, 'On your own, are you?'

'Waiting for some friends, thanks.'

She turns and faces out towards the marina. She's never seen him here before. Perhaps he has a boat docked somewhere. Curious, she ventures, 'Are you from round here?'

'A long time ago. I've been looking at some properties nearby so decided to have a drink before setting off back home.'

'And where's that? Home, I mean.'

'A hotel at the moment. The Copthorn. I've just come back from working in Saudi so I've been looking for somewhere to live. What about you?'

'I live just over there.' She twists round in her seat, indicating with her arm. 'The one with the blue chairs on the balcony.'

'Nice.'

'Thanks.'

She turns back to face him and there's a pause.

'On your own, are you?' she asks, tying to sound casual and failing miserably

He nods. 'What about you?'

'I'm meeting some friends in town later. Just thought I'd pop in for a drink as I'm early.' Another silence. 'Lovely evening, isn't it? I love the warm breezes at this time of night. It's really unusual for this time of year, isn't it? Git must be global warming or something. It's supposed to be a bad thing, but anything that gets rid of that icy wind off the North Sea can't be bad. You could almost imagine you're abroad on holiday.' She cringes as she hears herself prattle on. She only does it when she's nervous.

'Have you got any holiday plans for this year yet?' he asks, once he can get a word in.

'Mmm. I went to Namibia last month with a couple of friends. It's not too hot that time of year. It was fantastic; the best holiday ever.'

'What did you get up to? I wouldn't have thought all that sand and desert would've been your sort of thing.'

'And just what's my kind of thing?' She moves her body in closer towards him, looks down into her drink, then back up into his eyes, challenging him.

'Wild party nights in Ibiza or jet setting in St. Tropez?' he suggests. 'I was told that the Marina girls are always up for it—fun, I mean.' He holds her gaze and throws back his own challenge by licking the rim of his glass.

'I'm not a "Marina girl" as you put it. I live here—subtle difference.' The tone of her voice hardens a little.

'I can see that. No offence intended,' he placates.

She relaxes again but there's an awkward silence while they sip their drinks, until he ventures, 'What's it like to live here?' He's looking directly into her eyes and she shifts her position on the seat.

'I like it. It's got great views and walks, isn't far from shops or public transport and there's plenty going on. It depends what you like, really.'

'I'm looking for an investment, somewhere to rent out when I'm away.'

'They're still finishing off building houses at the back of the Marina,' she indicates with her arm, 'and after the credit crunch they started offering all sorts of good deals. I was lucky and got in when things were rock bottom. Then the area got popular and the flat went up nearly ten thousand pounds before I moved in and another ten thousand since, so if you're wanting to buy, you'd better get in fast.'

'What kind of flat have you got? Two or three bedrooms?'

'Three.' She hesitates. Nothing ventured, so they say. 'Would you like to see it? If you're not in a rush or anything?'

'No rush, but what about your friends?'

'Who?'

'The friends you're meeting?'

'Oh, they won't mind. I'll catch up with them later. They're just some people from work.'

'And where's that? Where d'you work?'

'Morpeth.'

'What as?'

'A nurse.'

'Not at the loony bin?' He chuckles.

She bristles and stiffens slightly before replying, 'I work with people who have mental health problems, yes.'

'Sorry. I didn't mean anything by it.' He holds his hands out in front of him, palms facing her. 'I've been away a while, that's all—haven't really caught up with being 'p.c.' yet.' He gestures for her hand, which, after a couple of seconds, she relinquishes into his. He raises her hand to his lips then brushes it gently with a kiss as he gives it a squeeze. 'Howay, don't be huffy. I didn't mean to upset you. I'd love to see your flat. In fact, I'd love to see more of you.' His eyes burn into hers. He kisses the back of her hand again and she feels her clitoris tingle.

She giggles. It's getting better by the minute. She can feel the warm moisture of her genitals as she stands up and takes her bag from the table.

'Are you coming then?' she asks.

'Not until you want me to,' he replies suggestively.

Friday 9 May

12.29 p.m.
A69, Bardon Mill, near Haydon Bridge, Northumberland

In the car the children play quietly in the back with their toys and Claire's soon asleep, lulled by the rhythm of the engine and the Vangelis CD Jayne brought. It's hot and sticky, even with the windows open, and Adam complains he's thirsty. Gary's making good time so they stop at The Little Chef. Jayne lifts Claire from the safety seat and manoeuvres her into a position across her shoulders. She inhales deeply into Claire's neck and as Adam watches he can smell the scent of warm skin, white chocolate and baby shampoo as surely as if he was breathing her himself.

As they all cross the car park Claire nestles against her mother's body, until the afternoon sun nudges her awake. The petal-soft skin of her bare arms brushes against Jayne's face as she struggles to see where they're going and to locate Adam who's behind, walking with Gary. Mounting the steps to the automatic doors, Adam sees them reflected in the glass. They look good together. Just like a real family.

1.33 p.m.
A69, Westerhope

Nearing the turn-off for the A I Jayne starts to fiddle with her hair and earrings.

'Is anything wrong?' asks Gary

'Of course not,' Jayne reassures.

They're silent for a while then Jayne turns to Gary. 'Don't take any—my mother. She's a little odd.'

'You told me already. Is that what's bothering you?'

'I s'pose so.' Silence, then she continues, 'When I was a kid… I never took anyone home.'

This is interesting. Adam's never heard this before, so he closes his eyes and pretends to be asleep.

'Why?'

'Oh, her hair, her clothes. She didn't wear shoes. Sometimes she didn't wear clothes.'

'You're joking?'

'No. She paints naked.'

Adam nearly laughs aloud. He and Claire have seen Grandma many times and it always makes them laugh to see her like that. She doesn't mind though. She laughs with them.

'Wow. Remind me to ask to see her working,' Gary teases.

Jayne, laughing, aims a playful swipe at his arm. 'Stop it. I'm serious. It was awful. She was always covered in either paint or soil.'

'Soil?'

'From gardening.'

There's a pause, then Adam hears the indicator clicking and the car moves out to overtake something. He opens his eyes. It's a milk lorry.

'She didn't behave like a mother. I was ashamed of her, I suppose. We lived in Ireland for a few years when I was born…'

'Why was that? Did your dad live there?'

'My dad? No. At least I don't think so. I never knew my dad. Or even who he was. She said I was her love child. I always took that to mean he was married or something. Anyway, that's when she started painting. But you know, even when I was little, I could always sense something. Of things not quite right, you know? She's never had any friends.'

'That can't have been easy for her.'

'She'd never let me play on a swing, we never had locks on the doors, and she wouldn't let me out of her sight. I used to pray it was because she loved me.'

'Wasn't it?'

Jayne sweeps back a few strands of hair from her cheek, pushing them behind her ear. Her voice is smaller this time.

'Gary, sometimes she's not... well. Not ill, exactly, but—'

'Are you having second thoughts?'

'No! No, of course not. It's just... I hope the kids'll be okay.'

'Why wouldn't they be? It's only for a weekend?'

2.18 p.m.
The Shambles

The car scrunches on the track leading up to the house, waking Adam who looks around excitedly. It was winter the last time they were here and now the air is filled with the smell of flowers, moisture and cut grass. Jayne gets out of the car to open the gate and allow the green Mondeo through, then closes it again.

The log cabin is impressive. It has two balconies, one at each end of the bedroom that runs the length of the upper floor. Most of the downstairs walls are glazed and patio doors at the back lead out to raised decking, on which is situated a large swing, a set of table and chairs, and numerous potted plants. In the roof are photovoltaic and solar panels, as well as Velux windows, and in the garden windmills, metal sculptures and wind chimes tinkle in the early evening breeze. Wild flowers surround the cabin, there is a pebbled area at the front where large cacti protrude, and at the back is an orchard and vegetable garden. Everything is orderly and cared for.

Grace greets them barefoot, her curly red hair tamed, tied back in a large grip, and she wears a long, russet-coloured crinkled cheesecloth skirt topped with a loose tunic in the same colour Her eyes are a startling deep grey. In the background Adam can hear the sea.

'Come in—let's get a good look at you,' Grace says as she holds open the door. Jayne slips off her sandals and Adam and Claire tug at the laces of their trainers. Gary bends down to undo his own, then lines them up alongside the others in the porch.

Everyone is ushered inside. The living area is wood panelled with an open fireplace in the centre. Huge canvas paintings of livid purples, aquamarine and scorched pink are set into the panelled walls and there are deep pile rugs on the floor. The children scamper in, careful to avoid the papers and drawings that are strewn haphazardly over them.

'What're you up to, Mam?' Jayne asks, indicating the papers. 'A new project?'

'Another commission. It's to do with natural objects and the light they reflect. Have you eaten? I've some salad.' She scoops the papers up and places them in a draughtsman's drawer beside a large desk, which is in one corner of the airy room.

'Thanks, we're fine. We stopped off at The Little Chef. The children will probably want something later, though.'

'Right,' Grace replies. Turning to Claire she asks, 'And how's my precious? Why don't you put this in the utility for grandma?' She hands her a tea towel. 'Adam—go help her.'

Adam takes the smaller child's hand and leads her to the utility room. Inside is a child's red bicycle, festooned in red ribbons and balloons.

'Mammy, Mammy!' Claire squeals. 'Come look.'

Jayne and Gary rush to the doorway.

'Mam, you shouldn't,' Jayne admonishes.

'Don't spoil it. Please.' There's a strangeness to that last word; Adam looks up at his mother and sees her eyes prick before she turns away.

5.25 p.m.

You and the children wave at the receding green Mondeo as it turns round the corner of the track. You're relieved. Now you can blur your outline and rub away the definition of your body. It's harder to pinpoint your position that way. Gary seems nice, but you're not fooled. You have to be on your guard because you never know. The invisible thread you wound round Jaynie before she left will keep you connected this weekend and you concentrate on sending her positive energy and white light. Suddenly you see water, a splash, and something red disappearing, but as soon as the image presents itself, it's gone. You're shaking.

Turning to the children you detect anxiety on their faces. 'Come on, let's play something. What would you like to do?'

Brighter now, sunny faces transmit positive energy back to you.

'Paint,' suggests Adam.

'And what about you, my sweet? Would you like to paint too?' You read the answer in the dove-grey eyes and slight, shy nod of the head. 'Okay. Let's go to the workshop.' You lead the way through the utility to the back of the garage where a section has been walled off to create another room, airy and light. You carefully avoid the line of fire from the Pakua mirror and open the door. Beyond the crystals and prisms the benches are covered in old bones, fossils, horns, a ram's skull, various vases and pottery. Several lengths of fabric, chicken wire, paint, canvas, wood, dried flowers, driftwood, branches and brushes are stored in open red plastic boxes and the smell of sandalwood incense, Zest-It, paint and clay is reassuring. This room has a calming effect upon you. It is your sanctuary. There are no bugs or transmitters here.

Lifting up some of the lengths of fabric from the bench a toolbox is exposed. Peeling back the lid you reveal pastels, gouache, pencils, chalk, tubes of paint, sponges and cloths; the smell of wood shavings reaches your nostrils. You hold the box out to the children.

'Cool! Thanks.' Adam dives in and selects a few pastels and a square cloth whilst Claire looks from the box back up to you.

'And what would you like?'

She selects a pencil. You give Adam some paper and he climbs onto a stool, clearing a space on the bench before laying his paper out. Scooping up the girl-child you sit her on another stool and feel her vibrations resonate inside you. Her soft hair, like wisps of candyfloss, is breathed into your mouth; you carefully remove the silky strands when you have her seated. Adam is concentrating on his picture of cars, his tongue protruding slightly from one of the corners of his mouth. Claire takes her paper rather reluctantly and tilts her head up to look at you. Gently guiding her hand in yours you help her draw. The energy between you flows slowly, peacefully, and your muscles relax, although your antennae remain on guard. Even here, you can never relax completely. Soon she is drawing by herself, the squiggles, dots and lines signalling a strange encrypted code.

\- The painting!-

You can feel its presence radiating from behind the old curtain you threw over it. Standing so close to Claire you feel caught in a cross-fire of energy thrown out by her and the picture. You must get rid of it, yet something nags at you. It's important somehow but you can't get it to surface enough to understand. Move it into the outhouse till you know what it all means.

6.07 p.m.

Newcastle Airport, check in area

Jayne and Gary arrive in plenty of time for their flight and join the queue of people waiting to check in. Gary tells Jayne he needs the toilet and leaves her with all the luggage. He's back in a couple of minutes, looking pleased with himself.

'What've you been up to?' asks Jayne.

'What makes you ask that?' he responds.

'Just the look on your face. You're like Adam when he's scored a goal.'

Gary tries not to look smug but doesn't succeed. 'You'll just have to wait and see, won't you,' is all he'll say.

The queue moves quite quickly and it's not long before their luggage is weighed and they are given boarding passes. As they make their way to the security clearance area they're approached by a security guard.

'I'm sorry sir, madam, but there's a problem with your passports. Can you come with me please?'

Jayne looks at Gary who shrugs his shoulders.

'It won't take long,' the guard assures and leads them off to a quiet corner of the airport where another guard waits.

Suddenly music blares from a cassette player and Jayne is horrified to see the first 'guard' stripping off his clothes down to a g-string and gyrating to the sound of Tom Jones singing 'Kiss'. It's only seconds before security are attracted to the noise and the bogus guards are ushered out of the airport. Jayne is left speechless, holding a parcel tied up in ribbons with a red rose.

'Go on, open it,' Gary encourages.

'If you don't mind, I'll wait till we get to the hotel,' Jayne replies, feeling embarrassed. 'It seems a pity to spoil it.'

'I hope you like it,' Gary says, disappointed, but his excitement soon returns as he steers her towards the security clearance area and the smiling faces of passers-by.

8.13 p.m.
The Shambles

They've exhausted you. Taking them upstairs you run a bath. The children play excitedly, splashing each other with sponges until Claire starts to cry and Adam teases her about being a cry-baby. You lift her out of the water and wrap her in a large, turquoise-blue towel. Adam, freed from the tap end of the bath, stretches out and dives onto his soft, brown belly. There's been a freak hot spell and both children are suntanned. Adam's white bottom is fleetingly covered by the backwash of water that then moves in the opposite direction and splashes onto you and Claire, who squeals in mock horror. The unexpected noise shears something inside and your sensors detect a shift in the energy in the room. You hold your breath, but keep snuggling Claire into the towel as you steady yourself against dizziness and images of water and shrieking birds.

Carrying her to your room, you put her down gently on the bed. It's safer here. You're going to sleep in the spare room but first you have to check it out and cleanse it of negativity. You've already removed all the ordinary mirrors from inside the house – you did that months ago - but you need to check they haven't brought any back in.

‘Stay here a minute, sweetheart,’ you tell her. Closing your eyes, you send out radar signals across the room. Nothing. Turning your head slightly, you shift the angle of your sweep until it has checked every square inch. Still you detect nothing. Remaining on alert, you return to the bathroom and instruct Adam to wash properly and you’ll be back to dry him in a minute. You cross the landing and enter the spare room.

The electricity points are all blocked up with childproof plugs but the energy feels wrong. Perhaps it’s the toilets. Checking both the bathroom and downstairs toilet you see the seats are down and the washbasins have their plugs inserted. What can it be? Adam is still happily playing in the bath and you hear Claire’s footsteps move from your room back into the bathroom; giggling and splashing sounds can now be heard.

Turning your attention back to the spare room, you suddenly feel it. It’s the curtains. You closed them very precisely before putting the children in the bath but now they meet slightly off-centre. Someone’s been in here. Maybe this is where they gain entry.

Quickly now, you go back into the bathroom and get Adam out, then carry Claire back into your room followed by Adam, whom you ask to close the door. Their bag of clothes is on the floor so you extract a pink pair of pyjamas for Claire and Adam dresses himself in a pair of red jersey shorts.

‘You can sleep in Grandma’s bed tonight. Would you like that?’

‘Yes!’ they chorus. They scamper into bed, pulling the duvet up over their heads but you stop their game and give them books to read, warning them to go to sleep before you’ve counted to three hundred. They settle down to read whilst you tidy up the bathroom and search for signs of intruders.

When you are finished you check on the children and wind a protective covering of white light round them, securing the threads to the door handle before retiring to the spare room. After lighting candles and incense sticks you lie on top of the bed, fully clothed, and softly repeat your protective mantra out loud, over and over, 'Hush. Hush,' feeling the sound in waves, cresting and crashing, until the darkness outside drains away and the pressure in your head dissipates.

Saturday 10 May

5.00 a.m.
The Shambles

You rise and shower, exfoliating your skin of the debris that has collected during the night. Magnetic particles are sluiced down the plughole and your skin starts to feel energized again, despite the lack of sleep. You radiate positive energy and your protective aura is repaired. Replacing the plastic cup over the drain in the shower tray to prevent entry, you then wrap yourself in a large, white towelling robe. Turning your head from side to side, you check your antennae are operational. Moving downstairs to the kitchen you pause on every third step to detect signs of movement.

Outside the kitchen door you stand, stock still, eyes closed, and focus your energies, sending them through the door. You see walls, benches, and appliances; you sweep them clean with blasts of energy before opening the door and entering the room. The bread is almost ready and the warm, yeasty smell greets you. Taking a jug of filtered water from the fridge you fill the kettle and perform the ritual of making green tea, then place the teapot, cup and saucer on a tray. You perform another mental sweep before carrying the tray to the bottom of the stairs, where you hesitate. You sense the presence of an entity and falter slightly.

-The children!-

Gathering all your strength, you channel your white light upstairs and wrap the children securely in it, afraid the previous protection has been breached. Next, you clear the staircase and gingerly climb the stairs. On every fifth step you take an extra deep breath, filling the stomach first, then the chest cavity, and on the out breath, you send caustic heat to cleanse your path. At the top, you do another sweep before entering your bedroom.

The children are safe, their breathing regular. There's no sign of an entity. You see the wisps of dreams exhaled through their mouths and skin and marvel at their innocence and beauty. Careful not to disturb them you carry the tray across the room, open first the heavy terracotta-coloured cotton curtains then pull aside the flimsy cream voile swathes. A patio door leads to the balcony and you set the tray down on the table there. Returning to your room you locate a patchwork quilt and carry it outside, closing the door behind you. The sun has already risen but there is still a chill in the air, so you snuggle yourself in the quilt and breathe in its familiar smells.

7.06 a.m.

Adam wakes. His fair hair is tousled and there are crystals of sleep in the corners of his eyes, which he rubs away with the back of his hand. The curtains are slightly open and Adam can see his grandma sitting outside on the balcony in a large cane chair, the magic quilt wrapped round her legs. He knows the story of the quilt, how it was made with scraps from his mam's old dresses. Grandma said it has magical powers to make you well, and she's right. It really does. He'd had a temperature the last time they'd all stayed and it had made him well again. John Waites doesn't believed him but Adam knows it's true.

Grace is sitting perfectly still, eyes closed, facing the sun. Adam watches her for a while, then turns his attention to the fluffy head on the pillow next to him. Claire's still asleep, her small mouth open in a perfect 'O', her left arm resting on the pillow. The cream duvet's been cast aside and her chubby brown legs lie on top of it. Her fine hair's matted and frizzed at the back of her head where she's rubbed it into the pillow.

At some point during the night the book she was reading slid from the bed and lies open on the floor along with several others. Swinging his legs carefully over the duvet, Adam slides out and tiptoes round to Claire's side to retrieve one of the books. His mission completed, he returns to bed and settles down to read. Claire stirs, shuffling onto her back, but she doesn't wake. Adam turns the pages, reading the words, feeling quite pleased with himself. English isn't his best subject.

He finishes in no time, so looks round for another. There are lots of books in a bookcase to the left of the bed but Grace keeps the children's books in the spare room, beside the toys, which she stores in a large wicker basket that used to belong to her mother, Emily Jayne. That's who his mam is named after. Grace tells them lots of stories about her mother, particularly about when Grace was little. They had a huge tree in their garden and Grace had a rope swing her dad made, but she had an accident and he took it down. Adam has seen the scar on his grandma's head where she had all the stitches put in. The hair doesn't grow properly there and the scar is puckered in a couple of places. Grandma lets him run his finger along it but Claire doesn't want to. Grandma keeps photographs in a large leather album along with some letters tied with ribbons. They could look at the album anytime they wanted, but they aren't allowed to touch the letters.

'So you're awake now, are you?'

Adam turns to look at Grace who beckons him to join her on the balcony. The air's fresh and clean, with a tang of salt. He shivers a little, despite the sunshine, so Grace wraps him in the patchwork quilt and draws him up onto her lap. Grace circles him with her arms and snuggles him close, breathing onto the back of his suntanned neck. It tickles, so he wriggles a little.

'What do you want to do today?' Grace asks.

Before he can respond Claire makes her presence known by whimpering at finding herself alone in the futon bed.

'Let's go see Claire,' Grace suggests and Adam shuffles off her knee onto the wooden boards of the balcony. 'It's okay, petalpops, we're coming.'

By this time Claire's sitting up, arms outstretched. Grace scoops her up in an arc so that her legs fly up into the air and Claire squeals with excitement.

'What would you like to do—have breakfast here on the balcony, or downstairs in the kitchen?'

'We always have it in the kitchen. Mam puts the TV on for us.'

'Sorry. I don't have one any more.'

'Why?'

'Because people can use them to watch you.'

'Why?'

'Because they do.'

'Why?'

Grace ignores him and asks, 'Balcony or kitchen?'

'Balcony. We can see the sea from here. We never see the sea at home.'

Grace laughs. 'That's because you don't live near it.'

'I wish we did.'

'Okay. Balcony it is. Is that all right with you, sweetheart?'

A nod.

'Right. Fruit or cereal?' This she addresses to Adam but a small voice to her left replies.

'Both.'

Grace laughs.

‘So you’ve found your tongue at last. Come on, let’s fill a tray.’ She leads the children downstairs holding Adam’s hand, balancing Claire on her hip, counting in multiples of three, pausing on every third step.

Outside the kitchen door she stops. The children look for an explanation but she has her eyes closed and seems to be concentrating, so they wait patiently. Her eyes open then she pushes the door and they enter the kitchen to the smell of freshly baked bread. Grace looks tense so they stay quiet until she turns to them and asks, ‘Banana, orange or kiwi?’

They reply, ‘Banana,’ in stereo.

‘Muesli or porridge?’

‘Haven’t you got CoCo Pops?’ asks Adam.

‘No.’

‘Rice Crispies?’

‘Sorry.’

‘Just a banana then.’

‘What about you, Claire?’

‘Same-same.’

Grace takes the bread out of the bread-maker and starts to slice it. She then pulls out a tray and starts to load it with their breakfast. Holding up the chocolate spread both children nod enthusiastically. She goes to the fridge and opens a container of freshly squeezed apple, pear and ginger juice, asking the children if they would like some. Adam smells it, then turns away. Claire’s reaching forward to smell it when Adam calls her name. She looks at him, just in time to see him blow a huge snot bubble from his left nostril. He opens his mouth and shows her a mouthful of half masticated bread, which he further rolls round on his tongue pretending to eat with his mouth open. Claire gags slightly and cries, which makes him laugh, spraying the soft, chewed-up bread all over the bench.

'Adam, that's disgusting,' Grace admonishes, but he only laughs louder.

'Not funny, Adam,' Claire warns and brings her little fist back to punch him.

'Now, now,' Grace soothes. 'Let's take this upstairs to eat on the balcony, eh? And no more silliness from you, Adam, okay?'

'Okay, Grandma. I promise.'

Claire reaches for Adam's hand. He squeezes it and leads her back upstairs behind Grace who's carrying their breakfasts on a tray. They count together in fives as they climb the wooden stairs to return to the balcony and the sounds of seagulls.

8.23 a.m.

An hour later, the sun, which had been so promising during breakfast, is hiding behind several layers of thick cloud. The air's warm and muggy and the children are quarrelsome. Claire wants to try out her bike so Grace carries it outside while Adam wheels his mountain bike out of the garage. Grace produces two cycle helmets, which the children put on. After a few minor adjustments they're ready.

'Stay on the track, Adam.'

'Okay.'

'Do you need a hand, sweetheart?' asks Grace as Claire struggles to manoeuvre herself onto the saddle. The stabilizers are lower than the wheels so a shift in weight causes the bike to rock from side to side.

'You won't fall, my darlin'—the stabilizers'll stop that. Here, I'll help.'

Grace holds the back of the saddle and centralizes the point of gravity. She explains to Claire what's going to happen and why, then, holding the child securely, tips the bike from one side to the other, reassuring her, until Claire relaxes a little. Claire starts to pedal, with Grace running alongside offering encouragement. She pushes harder and harder, faster and faster, her mouth a picture of concentration, until finally Grace lets go of the bike and she's on her own. It's several seconds before Claire turns her head to look for Grace who's no longer alongside and she wobbles, but then regains her posture and smiles, showing perfectly formed milk teeth.

Adam returns. Claire's managing a lot better but still looks under-confident and insecure so he parks his bike and offers to show her it's safe. Grace lifts the child off to let Adam mount. He pedals furiously, keeping the bike upright and off the stabilizers.

'Watch this!' he demands, leaning to the left to make the bike tip. Claire screams in alarm but the stabilizer blocks his fall. He laughs, turning his head, grinning at his sister.

'Not funny,' she warns, her brow wrinkling in a frown, but he cycles towards her and she skitters away from the advancing bicycle.

'See, you won't fall. It's great. Just get up a bit of speed and you'll be okay.' He brakes too hard, skidding, which sends a small shower of stones upwards, striking Claire who starts to cry.

'Stop being a cry-baby. I didn't do it on purpose,' shouts Adam, crossly.

Grace comforts Claire and carries her over to a seat to see if there's any damage, then turns to Adam.

'That was very silly and not something I expected from you. What if it had hit her eye?'

'I didn't—' he starts to protest then seeing Grace's face he says rather sheepishly, 'sorry, Claire.'

'That's better,' approves Grace.

The sky's been steadily darkening and a wind has now blown up. Small spots of rain stipple Grace's red silk blouse and jeans. Claire looks up as the spots turn into large drops and she shields her eyes. A black cloud blows towards them so Grace suggests they go inside. A rumbling of thunder is heard as Grace puts the bikes back into the garage.

Up in her bedroom the static in the air and the pressure of the advancing storm is tangible. Grace holds her head in her hands and tries to massage the temples.

'Stay here please, I need to lie down. Adam, look after your sister for a few minutes, will you, sweetheart?'

She gets into bed and covers herself with the duvet as the children look at each other.

8.27 a.m.
Hotel Citron, Place du Marcel, Paris

Jayne opens her eyes and for a moment doesn't know where she is. It's hot. The doors to the balcony are open but it feels like the city has no breath. She needs to shower but her legs are tangled in Gary's, and Jayne doesn't want to wake him.

Gary lies face down on the bed. He's shiny with sweat, which rises up in beads on his back and neck, looking as if someone has just painted them there. His uneven tan bears the outlines of several T-shirts and pairs of shorts, and there is a tattoo, a Celtic design, on his left shoulder, extending all the way down his arm in jags.

Bending down Jayne licks his scar delicately, her tongue shimmering over the tissue, catching beads of salt sweat on its journey. He stirs and turns over, enabling her to disentangle her limbs and slide out of bed. The sheet slides with her, exposing his erect penis, nestling against his stomach in all its morning glory, cushioned in its pubic hair. She replaces the sheet and goes into the bathroom.

The marble tiles are cold on her feet as she stands a moment examining herself in the large mirror. Sucking her stomach in she turns from side to side, appraising herself, letting it sag back as she turns the cold shower on. Stepping into its jets, the icy needles take her breath away and she pulls back a little before plunging in, surrendering to the temperature.

In a few moments Jayne is joined by another body, sliding into hers from behind. His hands are rough, rasping slightly on her skin as he soaps her. He scratches her back and she arches it, pushing her buttocks towards him. He lifts her up, spreading her legs. The cascading water makes entry easy, along with her body fluids. Her senses heightened, Jayne's aware of the condom smelling of lubricant as he enters. They change position so that she's facing him and he lifts her by the buttocks, re-entering her. She struggles to get a foothold on the tiles as soap gets in her eyes and she starts thrashing round, trying to ease the stinging. Gary carries her out of the shower and they fall onto the bed. He wipes her eyes with the sheet; it smells of sex and rose petals from the previous night.

Rolling over, Jayne assumes a dominant position and smothers his face with kisses, until he rolls her over again and she's back underneath him. Using his arms to raise himself, Gary escapes her lips to watch her and his movements slowly gather momentum. Jayne tastes blood in the back of her throat as he rides her; time stands still and her heart feels it's going to burst out of her chest. She can't breathe, can't take in any air and feels like she's drowning in her own heat. Her arms and legs are rigid for a few seconds, then she groans, a low cry from deep within. She hovers for an instant then collapses, her skeleton turning to jelly.

10.04 a.m.
Rue des Champs, Paris

They leave the hotel just after ten, marvelling at the warmth, the colours of flowers in pots on the pavements and the dappled sunlight between the trees. Closing her eyes Jayne feels the scented air on her skin and breathes deeply, surrendering to her environment. It's as if she's melting into the landscape, like one of Dali's clocks. Only the gentle pressure of Gary's hand on hers keeps her from disappearing altogether. They're on their way to the Orangerie to see Monet's Lily paintings and are surrounded by pavement cafes when Gary asks if she fancies a coffee.

'Where?'

'How about here?' he says as he slides a chair out towards her.

'Perfect.' she replies. And it is.

11.01 a.m.
Musee d l'Orangerie, Paris

Sitting on circular vinyl seats they look in awe at Monet's paintings. They'd walked the gardens and terraces but decided to shelter from the heat in the air-conditioned rooms. The vinyl makes Jayne sweat but absorbed by the huge canvases of water lilies, the colours so amazingly delicate, Jayne almost forgets where she is. She closes her eyes, retaining the picture on her eyeballs as she breathes in, sensing the long grasses, smells of paint and pondweed, ignoring the memories of Ireland they conjure up.

11.33 a.m.
The Shambles
The red bicycle's parked alongside Adam's mountain bike, in front of Grace's sit-up-and-beg, which has a front basket and twin panniers draped over the back wheel. Inside are waterproofs, bottles of filtered water, fruit, small cartons of fruit juice and individual packets of fruit and nuts. Claire's trying to mount her bike and looking to Grace for help but Grace is busy performing her exit rituals. Adam laughs at his sister as she stomps her foot and makes panting noises.

'You sound like a horse.'

'Do not.'

'Do too.'

'Not.'

'Do.'

'Enough, please!' shouts Grace, her head throbbing.

Adam helps his sister climb onto the saddle and checks that her feet are on the pedals. He grasps the back of the saddle and gently pushes her forward until she gets the hang of pedalling again, then he watches her, the triumph in her eyes, as she cycles unaided.

Grace closes the garage door and checks round the house, trying doors and windows. Satisfied, she turns and joins the children. 'We're going along the track to the dunes, then I thought we'd cycle to the harbour and have fish and chips for lunch. What do you think?' she asks.

Both heads nod enthusiastically.

'Okay. Adam, you go in front and I'll follow Claire.'

'No. Me in front.'

'No, sweetheart, you stay in the middle. It's safer. What would I do if anything happened to you?'

'Okay. But me carry the bag.'

Grace retrieves a small blue and red backpack from the front basket and helps Claire put it on her back.

'Are we ready now?'

'Yes!' chorus the children as Adam cycles away in front.

'Wait!' Claire shouts at him and he turns mockingly, pulling a face, which sets her off in tears again.

'Cry-baby! Cry-baby!' he teases, but Grace snips at him, 'Adam, that's enough!'

He cycles away, eyes narrowed, mouth set.

1.27 p.m.
Eiffel Tower

This is their next stop. Jayne had been to Blackpool once, so thought she knew what to expect, but finds the sheer size of the tower and number of tourists overwhelming. They take the lift and are jostled by Japanese trying to catch themselves and each other on film and video. Jayne looks over to Gary and they smile simultaneously.

It's cooler up here on the higher levels but Jayne can feel the tower swaying slightly; she wants to get off. Gary squeezes her hand and shows her the Perspex outside, to stop suicides leaping from the top, telling her she's quite safe. The view of the city is amazing, but Jayne still feels discordant, jangling.

On their right is a little girl of maybe five or six years old, wearing a beautiful white and blue sundress with matching hat. The tops of her shoulders are peeling from sunburn and her mother still hasn't covered them. Jayne always slathers Adam and Claire in suncream, even when there's only a watery sun. She hopes Grace is looking after them properly and not letting them get burnt.

1.48 p.m.
Druridge Bay
It takes a long time to reach the dunes and Adam waits patiently for them, his bike propped up against a fence to keep the chain free of sand. Grace puts her own, then Claire's bike, next to Adam's and secures them to the fence with a thick metal chain and padlock. The tide's out, so the children amuse themselves building castles and dams, collecting shells, driftwood and seaweed.

3.47 p.m.
Waterfront, Paris
Gary takes lots of pictures then an American couple snaps one of them together in front of the tower holding ice creams. Jayne's is dripping through her fingers because it takes a long time before the shutter is pressed; each American is telling the other how to get it right and arguing about it. Gary takes her hand and licks the ice cream off, his tongue finding delicate places between the fingers. Jayne's whole body crackles with desire again.

They make their way along the embankment, past the open-air swimming pool to the boat landing where the river cruisers are moored. Jayne selects the brightest and they clamber on board. The water churned up by the boats is dark and brooding and river smells clog Jayne's nostrils. She leans back into Gary and closes her eyes. Her senses are heightened again and she can feel the rhythm of his heartbeat in time with her own. His warmth is like a cloak on her back and the thin fabric of her sleeveless dress is damp in the shape of his silhouette. Jayne drifts again, becoming one with sunshine, boat and the sounds of water and birds.

Suddenly, as they round a corner for the return journey, the colours of the breeze change. Jayne sees images of water churning, birds swooping menacingly and hears children scream. She feels a panic that is not yet hers and knows instinctively something is seriously wrong. For several minutes she's immobilised, whilst wave after wave of terror is channelled through her, until it becomes her own. As suddenly as it began, the spell is broken. Frantically looking around she can see only foreign tourists enjoying themselves and the smiling face of her lover.

'We've got to go back,' she tells Gary, her hysteria very close to the surface.

'We are, they've just turned the boat round.'

Trying to keep control she struggles to speak. 'No, we have to go home. Something's happened to the children. I know it.'

Gary tries to calm her, holding her tight so he can whisper in her ear. 'Stop shouting. We can't get off until the boat gets back to its berth.'

Jayne starts to shiver and tremble so Gary pulls her even closer and looks weakly at the other passengers who are staring. Jayne rests against him, quietly now, until they can get off the boat, then insists they return to the hotel. Gary doesn't argue.

4.10 p.m.
Amble Harbour

After the accident the ambulance crew and doctor are very kind. The doctor gives Grace a sedative to calm her down and to stop her banging her head against the wall, before helping her into the ambulance. The police take Adam away in their car and Grace keeps repeating Claire's name over and over and over, unable to stop until the doctor gives her a second shot. After that, the darkness comes and she can't say much of anything anymore.

Following her admission onto the ward Grace has a deep, drug-induced sleep. She's given more sedatives to prevent her from hurting herself, or anyone else, is placed on twenty-four-hour watch and the team are briefed about the circumstances of her sectioning.

6.32 p.m.
Hotel Citron

Back at the hotel Jayne can't settle. She phones Grace but no one answers.

'We'll have to phone the police.'

'For goodness sake, Jayne, don't you think you're carrying this a bit too far?'

She twists and twists a paper hankie until it shreds, then looks at the mess uncomprehendingly.

'They won't know where to contact me. I didn't even leave a number…'

'Hang on a minute. I don't understand this. A simple phone call will sort it out. But why do you think something's happened to them anyway?'

'I just *know*! You have to trust me on this. I have this feeling…'

But Gary's rational and doesn't understand any of this. He phones Grace's number, leaving a message for her to contact them. He tries to persuade Jayne that she's being silly and that they were all probably just out enjoying themselves. This tactic doesn't work and Jayne is still anxious, so in frustration he asks, 'Is this your roundabout way of pulling back, of keeping me out?'

'Of course not!'

'So what is it? Come on—what can possibly have happened in twenty-four hours?'

How do you explain something like this? Jayne checked everything before they left and there are no roads, ponds, discarded farm machinery, electrical appliances or any other potential death threats, so realistically, what could have gone wrong? But she *knows* and it feels like a million ants are crawling around just beneath the surface of her skin.

Sunday 11 May

8.52 a.m.

Fletcher Ward, St Julian's Hospital, Morpeth

Your eyes crack open and survey your surroundings. Your tongue is stuck to the roof of your mouth and your eyeballs have difficulty moving. Straight in front of you is a window but the curtains are closed. You see the outline of the window frame through the curtains; it must still be daylight. Inspecting the curtains, you take care not to move your eyeballs. They could be watching you from behind some microscopic hole they've drilled into the wall or door. Or perhaps they're behind those horrible curtains. You wouldn't be seen dead with them in your house. Whose place is this anyway?

Sweeping your eyes round the room you collect cobwebs on your eyelashes, but identify that the walls are devoid of wallpaper; they're painted instead. Quite a pretty blue, actually. It's more lilac than cornflower. What's the shade called? You try to recall the colour but your attention wanders.

There's a washbasin to the right of the window and a single wardrobe made from tacky Formica on the wall to your left. You wonder if anyone's inside but you really haven't got the energy to pursue any thought for long. Apart from the wardrobe and the bed the room is bare. Where are your things? Why are you here?

Sitting on your bed is Mother. She tells you to get out of bed, but you can't. Your arms and legs are paralysed, held down by the weight of the duvet covering you. She's angry again but hopefully she'll go away soon. You really can't be bothered with her right now. You close your eyes and drift…

8.59 a.m.
Mother's not smiling anymore. She's angry and shouting, her yells spinning your antennae out of synch. There's a huge weight on your chest and another pressing down on your head, crushing your skull, oozing your brains out of your ears. You try to scream but she's cut off your tongue and the blood is gushing everywhere, drowning you as she laughs. The door opens and she hides from the man dressed in jeans and sweatshirt. He opens your mouth and puts something in, gives you water to drink, ignoring the blood that splashes on his feet, staining his jeans, making puddles on the carpet. He says something you can't hear, then leaves and closes the door. Your eyeballs roll up inside and Mother disappears as you enter the dark.

9.15 a.m.
You open your eyes to the sound of curtains being drawn back

'Good morning Grace. My name's Sue and I'll be looking after you today.'

You stare at her, determined not to show you're afraid.

'Can you sit up Grace? The doctor's doing her rounds and she'll be in to speak to you soon. Is there anything you want? A drink of water perhaps?'

You just look at her. If you speak you might give vital information away. So you remain silent. Your head doesn't hurt so much but you're still very weak and your limbs are heavy. You stay where you are, hoping she'll go away, but she doesn't. She stays, looking at you, making notes. You close your eyes and see different shades of purple and blue, soft edges, mixing together like petrol rainbows on water. Water. That's important; it's the reason you're here, isn't it?

You struggle to remember and the colours change, getting darker and more ominous, with ragged edges, jagged like shards of glass……………

10.04 a.m.

She's here again, sitting on the bottom of the bed.

'Hello, Mother.'

'Get up, you lazy cow.'

'Can't.'

'There's no such thing as can't. Get up!'

You struggle to lift the concrete duvet and hear your body try to help. There's the clicking of the neural messages, the whooshing of the release of chemicals into your bloodstream and the tensing of the muscle receptors as they try to catch the chemicals, but it's such an effort. Eventually you push the rock of your tomb away and manage to swing your legs out so that your feet are on firm ground.

She's moved. She's standing in front of the curtained window, the light behind creating a halo effect, but her eyes, black and brooding, devoid of any light, stare at you. Her lips are pursed, as always. You try to swivel round to face her but are knocked off the bed by a tidal wave of venom when she opens her mouth. She's laughing. Too loudly it seems, as someone puts a key into the lock and enters the room. It's that man again.

'Ah, you're awake. How're you feeling today?'

Mother dares you to tell, so you close your eyes. Memory, like a thick black rope, snakes round your neck, choking you.

'Come on, Grace. Look at me. How're you feeling today?'

It's another of those trick questions. What does Mother want you to say? You open your eyes to look for a clue, but she's moved again. You wish she'd keep still because it's making you dizzy trying to find her all the time.

She throws a barb at you and it snags your nightdress, dragging you off the bed. You collapse into a heap on the floor, curling up to protect your head and face, expecting her to lash your back. Nothing happens.

'Let's get you back into bed, eh?'

Strong arms help you up, then tuck you in, feel your brow, take your pulse, read your blood pressure.

'Well, everything seems to be normal.'

Mother suddenly rushes at you from behind the man. You can smell decomposition and the stench makes you gag.

'You've got to swallow it, Grace. It's for your own good. Come on, now. Stop fighting me.'

Water spills out the side of your mouth, runs down your neck, dribbling onto your nightdress which has suddenly grown too big. Far too big. You hear Mother laugh, then feel the poison enter your throat as you shrink, shrinking smaller and smaller, until at last, you disappear, back into the safety of the dark…

10.40a.m.

That's the sound of a bird. Opening your eyes you see sunlight streaming through a crack in the curtains. It makes a sign on the wall and you hear the bird again. It has a message for you but can't get in. It is imperative you get up and open a window and the urgency of the situation chokes you. Your breathing is laboured as one of Mother's metal bands tightens around your chest. Chains are strewn haphazardly over the top of you and rattle as you push them aside in order to lift the lid off this box you're in. The bird signals one last time but is frightened off by demonic laughter. You search with your eyes but can't discern where she's hiding. You call her name but she just laughs at you, then you realize you're standing. There's evidence of where she's been—cobwebs on the ceiling, dust on the wardrobe—but no clues as to where she is now. Perhaps the curtains? You grasp one with your hand but are unable to draw it aside. Suddenly you are zapped by electricity shrieking through your body, shooting into the floor, rooting you to the spot…

10.45 a.m.

'How long has she been standing there?'

'Just a few minutes. I've tried prising her hands off the curtain but she's clenching too tight.'

'Grace, this is Doctor Norman. You remember me, don't you? We met when you first came in. I'm going to hold your hand and help you back to bed, so I need you to let go of the curtain. All right?'

You feel a small, soft hand fit into your left hand and another tries to take your right hand off the curtain. The hand inside yours gives you a squeeze. It's like a child's. Like Claire's.

'Noooooooooo!' You scream but the hand's still there. 'Get away! Keep away! The water—'

'It's okay, Grace, it's okay. There's no water here. Look round. Where do you see the water?'

You can't answer, but you know it's there.

'Let go of the curtain, eh?'

'Come on, Grace. Let go.'

Your antennae has picked up a crackle. Your vision clears a little and you swivel your eyeballs round to get a better look at the two women. One is small, pretty, young, plump, wearing jeans, trainers and a Greenpeace tee-shirt. The other is older, taller, thinner, wearing a mint-green linen two-piece and beige sandals. Tuning in to them you are drawn to the younger woman and are almost blinded by the intensity of her aura. The older woman has more muted colours but with a darkness in her heart chakra.

'That's better. Come on, back into bed,' suggests the tall one.

You must do as she tells you, before her darkness seeps into you. You pull the covers up again, close your eyes but keep your antennae on alert. You need a shower and a detox to get rid of all the particles clogging you up so you can repair your aura protection. Perhaps the young one might help? You open your eyes to see where she is and connect with china blue. You try telepathy, but it's no use; you'll have to talk.

'Can I have a shower?'

'Not just yet,' the older one replies but you keep your eyes on China Blue. 'We need to discuss some things first. Is that all right?'

You nod, knowing the interrogation is about to start and look round the bedroom for Mother. She'll tell you what to say. If nothing else, she was good at that.

10.48a.m.
Charles de Gaul Airport, Paris

Jayne travels home alone, back to Newcastle airport. The airline is sympathetic but they can only provide one seat immediately, so Gary is travelling on a later flight. He takes Jayne to the airport and holds her hand but it's awkward and there isn't a lot to say. All Jayne can think of is the telephone call and what the woman had said. What must it feel like having to tell someone that? Was it all in a day's work? What is it like in those moments before someone answers? Perhaps there's a formula they use, but in those moments before the phone is picked up and the words take flight, are the people ever nervous in case they get it wrong?

Gary tries to hug her but she twists away. She doesn't want to be touched. Not by him, not by anyone. Ever again. He shouts something about not worrying, he'll be there soon, but Jayne doesn't turn round or acknowledge she's heard him. She can't see properly for the tears brimming up. She feels them dribble down her face, their warm wetness on her cheeks, but it isn't until they start running down her neck and into her cleavage that she wipes them away. Then they just stop.

On the plane Jayne sits upright, staring straight ahead, trying to concentrate on the pattern of the seat in front. It's blue with funny little squares of orange that merge together after a while. If she watches closely enough she can make them swim like square fish in a blue moquette sea. The cabin crew are asking questions about food or drink but Jayne just keeps staring at the seat in front for the duration of the flight.

When they land Jayne is taken off first. One of the cabin crew, a nice young girl with red fingernails, holds out her hand for Jayne and helps her stand up but it takes all Jayne's concentration just to put one foot in front of the other without her legs folding in on themselves.

'The police are waiting for you inside. You need to go through passport control then someone will meet you and take you to the hospital. I'm very sorry…'

Jayne's body moves but it doesn't seem to belong to her. She looks in her handbag for the passport and is surprised to see her hands. They don't look like hers at all. They don't even look as if they should be there, on the ends of those skinny arms. Perhaps if they'd had strings attached they would work better as all the shaking is making her drop things.

She's met by WPC June Turnbull and PC Manny Burgo, who drive Jayne to the hospital in Newcastle city centre. WPC Turnbull is kind and tries to explain the accident but Jayne can't take it all in. She sees the sunshine, the traffic, and people walking along the streets as if nothing's happened. They pass buses full of disembarking people, taxis, cyclists, cars and pedestrians. There are young men in shorts, some with no shirts on, elderly people sitting on benches, women with pushchairs, children in sandals, all going about their business. It seems so unreal. Like the weather this early in the year.

As they turn a corner the hospital comes into view. It's an old brick building with lots of new extensions. WPC Turnbull helps Jayne out and they make their way past the smokers at the front door, down corridors, past people in wheelchairs, on trolleys, carrying catheter bags, or buying flowers. Jayne's courage starts faltering. She feels claustrophobic and wants to run away, her heart beating faster and faster making breathing difficult. Then everything goes black for a few seconds and Jayne falls against the wall, banging her head. WPC Turnbull grabs her and holds her until she feels better and able to go on.

4.22 p.m.
Newcastle General Hospital, Ward 17

A young doctor in a white coat checks Jayne over and prescribes 'something to help'. He also writes a note for her GP, which he seals in a brown envelope and hands to Jayne. A nurse enters the room and the young doctor excuses himself whilst the nurse begins the paperwork, then they take her to the morgue to identify the body. Seeing that tiny body lying there Jayne pictures Claire terrified, struggling for air, her blonde curls bobbing about in the water as she twists her head back and forth. In the background she thinks she hears the screeching of gulls until she realises the sound is coming from her…

7.48 p.m.
The Rise

When Jayne and Adam get home the heat is oppressive in the house but she has no strength to open the windows. She knows she should have waited for Gary, but it seems irrelevant somehow. Jayne wanted to get home so the police kindly took them. They didn't really speak much on the journey and Adam slept a lot of the way, curled up on Jayne's lap. She marvelled that she never really noticed before, but Adam has angular bits that stick out, whereas Claire is—was—round and soft, still with a baby fluffiness Adam has lost. She held him loosely, afraid to pull him into her because she'd suffocate him, so great was her need to absorb him, to put him back inside her, keep him safe.

After putting the kettle on, Jayne sits down. There's a metallic taste in her mouth, weighing heavily. Adam keeps looking at her but words freeze on her tongue. She doesn't know what to say to him. He looks tired and confused but she is unable to comfort him. She feels in a different dimension, where everything she sees is through dimpled glass, everything she touches, through huge mittens.

'I tried to help, Mam, really I did. But no one listened.'

His little face pleads with Jayne but she needs to get away from him. 'Not now, Adam, I've got a headache.'

He looks crushed but she can't stop herself from getting up from the settee and making her way upstairs, leaving Adam alone in the sitting room.

The phone rings. It keeps on ringing until Adam picks it up. She hears the one-sided conversation.

'Hello?
-Yes.
-She's upstairs. I think she's asleep.
-No. Just Mam.
-'Course.'

The phone is put down and the television switched on.

11.51 p.m.

It's late when Gary arrives. Jayne hears his car pull up but doesn't want to lift herself off the bed. She tells Adam what to say and he shouts through the letterbox, 'Mam says she's too tired to talk.'

'Are you okay?' asks Gary.

'Yes, thanks.'

'Can you open the door?

'No, I can't reach.'

'I'll put the suitcases in the garage and I'll ring in the morning. Will you tell her that?'

'Uh uh.'

Jayne closes her eyes and turns over to face the wall. All the ties have snapped and are blowing in the wind.

The doctor at the hospital suggested I write about my feelings. He says it'll help but how can I describe the emptiness that has taken over and completely obliterates who I am, or who I used to be? Words aren't enough. They can never be enough, but for Adam's sake I am trying. If I didn't have him I don't know what I'd do.

I had to identify her body. She was cold, like the ice needles inside me. Her hair looked waxen and the skin had been rubbed off her left cheek, just below the eye. I wonder how that happened. Was it the sand? Or perhaps she hit the bike or the pier? It's important to know so I tried to ask someone, but my mouth kept opening and closing like some stupid fish out of water and the words swam away.

Everything was unreal. I felt lost inside and needed to get out. My bones had melted and the skin, which had held everything in so far, suddenly split and frayed, spilling everything on the floor. I didn't care; someone else would have to clean it up.

They told me they were bringing Adam and I remembered I had to take him home with me. I'd forgotten about him until then. They wanted to know if I needed them to contact anyone to pick us up, or if there was someone to stay the night and I told them about Gary. Then I panicked about my luggage until I remembered Gary was bringing it back. I hoped he'd remembered to put my make-up bag in the case. It was a birthday present from Lizzie and I couldn't bear the thought of losing that too. I started crying then and didn't think I'd ever be able to stop.

To think that while we were... she was...

Gary knows my weak spots. In the hotel I could smell his after-shave and feel the pressure of his teeth on my neck as we lay back on the bed. He murmured to me, more and more urgently, erotic words and phrases that turn me on. I could smell him, feel the sheer physicality of him and felt aroused again. A heat scorched me, the flames demanding, insistent. I fought, rolling him over, finding the zip of his shorts. I dragged them off to find his penis, erect and freed from his underwear. Skewering myself down onto it he looked surprised but didn't object until I tore at him, biting, scratching and screaming; he just managed to throw me off.

Later, we went downstairs. The restaurant had started to fill up and most of the tables were taken. We had to wait a couple of minutes and I felt wired. My nipples and clitoris tingled as we walked to our table and it was as if I was radiating thermo-nuclear energy from between my legs; I'm surprised no-one noticed. Gary walked behind me. He was quiet, subdued almost, whereas I felt fireworks shooting from the ends of my fingers and sparks from my toes in the open strapped shoes I was wearing. They were black stilettos, and I fantasized about standing on Gary's chest, puncturing his skin, until I looked at him and saw him avoid my eyes as we sat down. Then my bones liquefied and I felt ashamed. A cool breeze blew through my veins and it was over. The heat imploded and I was free.

Our table had a view of the Seine and we were making polite conversation about the weather and how dark the water was when I started shaking. There was a look of concern on Gary's face as he took my hand, gently rubbing my knuckles with his thumb. He asked if I was okay and I said something like, 'Someone's walking over my grave,' but it sounded hollow and corny, even to me. I apologised for hurting him and spoiling things. He looked at me awkwardly. I knew I'd shocked him, so suggested we pretend it never happened but he said, 'It did.' I told him we needed to talk and he nodded but I could feel the disconnection, his energy cutting off from mine, separating itself like a rogue strand of fuse wire. I couldn't earth myself, despite the power of the setting sun. The phone call came the next morning. They'd traced us from Gary's message on Mam's answer machine.

Monday 12 May

3.40 a.m.

Alston Moor

Johnny Medhurst is checking the traps. The air is cool, exquisite in its pre-dawn stillness. Grey light slithering through the trees sketches a subtle chiaroscuro landscape and the atmosphere is rich and thick like blood. In this area he has three traps: a spring snare; a baited spring snare; and a wire snare. Over the years he's learnt to use different kinds of snares to increase the probability of catching something and also to confuse his prey. Ever since he was a child he's been fascinated with wildlife, believing nature to be evidence of a higher power. His father tried to knock those ideas out of him long ago and very nearly succeeded, but it is here, in this place he now calls home, that he has evolved a tentative sort of inner peace and allowed nature to begin to heal him.

The first trap, a spring snare suitable for fox or rabbit, is located in a narrowing of the trail in a bottleneck created by rocky outcrops. He uses as many natural or recycled resources as he can to make the traps and this one has a wire noose supported by twigs. A length of string goes from the top of the noose to a wooden trigger bar driven into the ground. From the trigger bar a length of cord is attached to a sapling that has been pulled down and secured under tension. When game is unlucky enough to be caught the trigger bar disengages and the prey is lifted off the ground, keeping it safe from predators and preventing the animal from getting a foothold from which to struggle to escape. Unfortunately it has nothing in it today.

Moving in a straight line he comes to the clearing where he has set the second trap, a baited spring snare. The forest is brighter now and faint sounds of water scooting over stones dances in the air. This trap operates in a similar way to the first, except this time the noose is laid on the ground with bait strung above it, releasing the trigger when the bait is taken. There's nothing here either.

The lonely cry of a curlew reaches him as he moves further on to check the trap in an area to the right of the clearing. Here he has carefully placed a simple snare consisting of a wire noose supported by twigs anchored to a wooden stump. From his observations he's learnt that rabbits tend to sit in cover and watch the terrain first for danger signals. They wait till they're satisfied all is well before hopping along the track, so this snare is hidden in the grass, a hand's length from a fallen branch, to accommodate the hop.

His luck is in; a young rabbit's caught by the back legs. A well-aimed chop behind its ear with the edge of his hand kills it, then Johnny presses its belly to empty the bladder. He slits its throat and hangs it from a tree, collecting the blood in a plastic container he found, its lid he places carefully on the ground nearby. Johnny removes the wire from the rabbit's leg and re-sets the trap, taking care to secure the wire again in the carved twigs. He wears gloves, combat models, to eliminate as much human scent as possible. Although necessary, he doesn't like wires because they bite deep into the flesh of the leg, and rabbits, in an attempt to free themselves, often bite through the rest of their leg. Rope's no good; rabbits can easily chew their way through them.

He deftly skins and guts the rabbit, leaving the entrails on the trap line. This is to encourage more animals into the area and therefore into the traps. When the animal stops bleeding, Johnny places the lid on the container of blood and takes a length of plastic from an old orange survival bag he keeps in his pocket. He lays the rabbit and pelt on it, rolls it up, then puts it and the plastic container into his rucksack. He swings the sack easily onto his back, pressing on to check the rest of the traps. Only one, another spring snare, has been sprung. After dispatching this rabbit in the same way, he puts it with the other and slings the rucksack over his shoulder and onto his back.

Walking on, Johnny's attention is focussed on the ground; it's not long before he spots what he's looking for. Taking a small plastic self-sealing sandwich bag from his other pocket containing the bladder campion and nettles he picked earlier, he reaches down beside his feet and plucks some garlic leaves and their pungent, white flowers, making sure the bulbs don't come with them. These he places carefully in the bag with the other plants.

Further on, in a shaded area beside some ruins he spots brown cap mushrooms and fronds of fennel. These join beefsteak fungi in another bag in his pocket. He's going to enjoy the stew tonight; he has blood cakes and lichen syrup back at base to add to the flavour. He knows that nutritionally he must get more protein—rabbits can fill you up but the flesh lacks the fat and vitamins essential to humans. As a boy he always thought it strange when his dad told him of the trappers working for the Hudson Bay Company who starved to death despite eating lots of rabbits but not much else. Apparently, the body uses its own minerals to digest rabbits and these minerals are passed out of the body with waste. If not replaced, over time the end result is death.

There's a sharp nip of midges on his forehead and he swats at them. He wipes the sweat from his forehead with the back of a gloved hand, leaving streaks of blood and earth to mix with the dirt he had rubbed there before leaving. There's been a full moon and he hadn't wanted to be seen. Not that the old man objects to him catching the rabbits. No, Johnny just wants to be left alone. That's all he's ever wanted, but his dad just didn't get it. Thought he was a 'poof' and tried to 'toughen him up'. Said the army would make a man of him. Well it did that all right, just not the kind of man he was thinking of. Memories start to surface, of the Falklands, of prison, so Johnny tries to swat them away, just like he did with the midges.

He came here by sheer luck. Whilst in prison his old Major contacted him, offering him one of the tied cottages on the estate in return for help with the grouse. Johnny remembered the place from an exercise he'd done in the area, just after basic training. He'd been billeted with the Royal Engineers at Ripon and they'd gone there after training on the range at Warcop.

It hadn't taken him long to get everything together. He travelled for a couple of days, keeping to the forests and country roads, moving only at night, carrying everything he needed in his pockets, rucksack and a survival pouch attached to his belt. He'd been well trained, after all. There's probably still a warrant out for not reporting to his probation officer, but the Major won't grass him up.

The grouse thing didn't work out—it meant too much contact with people—so he moved out of the tied cottage and found a ruined house, once an old mine shop. He walked past it at first, but then he smelt something different about it. On further exploration he discovered it wasn't far from a labyrinth of old mine workings and passages. In the days of lead mining these passages had been used to link villages when snow cut them off. They carried bodies through them to get to the church for funerals; such was the grip of winter in those days that everything above ground froze and was impassable. But below ground it was more or less a constant 10-12°C, whatever the weather above. So he made the shop his temporary home by repairing the roof with saplings covered in mud and turf; some of the walls he rebuilt with dismantled stones. To the unobservant passer-by it was still derelict, but it provided him with shelter whilst he started on the tunnels.

Johnny was a B2 Grade Military Tunneller in Tunnel Troop 1st Fortress Squadron for eighteen months back in 1967 in Gibraltar, so it was easy for him to break through into the tunnels and move about wherever he wanted without anyone knowing. He also created a series of bolt holes for himself in case of an emergency. The main one is in an old chamber which used to house explosives. It is dry, encased in concrete and he keeps a bed, blankets made from hide, a couple of Premier carbide headlamps and several different kinds of supplies there, enough to survive a week if necessary. His other boltholes are in little hideaways in flues or disused chambers which he cleared of rock-fall. These are emergency resting places holding enough supplies for a few days.

Moving stealthily through the trees Johnny makes his way down to the river. The sun is up now, soaking everything in pale gold. He likes to sit here, listening, smelling. This is where he feels most alive, where he does most of his thinking. A fish plops and he allows himself a rare smile. He can stand in the river for hours without moving, letting the fish swim around his legs, never suspecting they'll soon be speared and barbecued for supper. It took nearly a year of practice before he could achieve that because the refraction of light through the water meant that he had to aim ahead of the fish, not at it. So not only does he have to be a good shot, he also has to predict the direction it will take.

When he first arrived he used hooks, but with a lot of time to spare he learnt how to guddle the fish, catching them with only his hands, then he progressed to the spear, relishing the absolute concentration needed for the job. For ease though, he likes to use spinners. He takes great pleasure in fashioning propeller shapes out of the aluminium cans he comes across on his forays further afield. He was lucky last week and found an ants' nest, which he then suspended over the river. When the ants fell into the water the fish came to the surface to eat them and were curious about the shiny objects dangling there. Unfortunately for them their curiosity was their downfall; he still has several dried fish stored at his base camp. This morning he is checking the nightlines and renewing the bait on the hooks with some of the guts from the five fish snagged on them. At this rate his stocks are going to be plentiful but he trained never to be complacent.

It feels good, this day. He stretches his arms upwards, towards the sun, and acknowledges something deep inside him, beyond the feral impulses that keep him alive. Perhaps his luck is changing. He sits for a while, just being. He doesn't really ask anything of himself these days, just does what has to be done to keep himself alive. And in that, at least, he finds a contentment of sorts.

9.15 a.m.
Fletcher Ward, St Julian's Hospital

Lying in this room you're aware of them. They've changed the sheets on your bed and you recognize China Blue's touch as she takes your temperature.

‘That’s fine Grace. Let me just fix those pillows for you.’

You can smell her perfume, humid in the air around your head. A door opens. Someone comes in.

‘Everything okay here?’ It’s a man’s voice.

‘Fine, Darren, thanks. Oh, by the way, have you managed to swap yet?’

‘Sorry?’

‘My party. Next week. You said you’d like to come but were on the wrong shift. Will anyone swap?’

‘Er, I don’t think so. To be honest, Sue, I kinda forgot. But I’ll see what I can do. See ya later.’

‘Fine.’

A door closes. You feel the vibrations change. China Blue is plumping up your pillows with a bit more gusto. She sighs, then takes your hand.

‘Oh, Grace. How’d you like to swap places for a bit? I could do with a nice coma at the moment.’ Her voice changes tone. ‘Come on, Grace, talk to me. You want to get better, don’t you? Get out of here? Come on, open your eyes.’

Her voice recedes and you slip a little. You smell yourself, naked in Brendan’s arms, your skin the slightly-smoked smell of hot summer days. There’s incense in the air, the vapours curling around the slap of wet bodies, filling your mouth. His hands burn your skin, leaving his brand, which you feel long after he dresses and buttons himself up. Silence clots around you as he leaves.

Time here is a slow, steady drip of minutes. Sometimes they sparkle, like dew on morning cobwebs, at others they’re like a bottomless dark lake. It starts off simply enough, slow and shallow, but drip by drip it ends up deep. And the worst thing is that you have no control over what breaks free and rises to the surface…

It's a muggy day, with the charged heat and humidity of a storm. Your fringe is damp and curly on your forehead and you're worried. Grandma has told you to stay clean, that at five years old you should take care with your appearance and that Mother will be looking to find fault, so you've hardly dared breathe all day.

The clock ticks on the mantelpiece, echoing in the stillness. Dad's taken the Austin Cambridge to the hospital to pick Mother up but he's been gone a long time.

'How much longer, Grandma?'

'How should I know!' she snips. She's a severe-looking woman with corned beef coloured legs from sitting too near the fire, and lined lips that look as though she's spent her life sucking lemons. She looks at the clock for the third time in the last five minutes, then rises and fills the kettle. She mutters to herself as much as to you, 'Not long. I've made us some nice scones, not that she'll appreciate it, but your father will. Why he's bothered with her…He should never have married her in the first place. Shameless she is. He should've left her there the first time, if you ask me. But no one ever asks me what I think. Your grandfather was just the same, never listened… Anyway, we'll have them with a nice cup of tea when they get here.'

She turns and looks at you. 'Now you just sit there and stay clean,' she adds sternly as she returns to the blanket she's crocheting.

You nod, look down at your dress and smooth it over your knees. You clasp your hands together and rest them in your lap like Grandma showed you. Tiny beads of sweat stand up on your neck and you feel dizzy, but the voices tell you not to move, to sit still. You look to see if Grandma has heard them but she's busy with her crochet work, grasping it tightly and muttering under her breath.

At last, there's the sound of a car engine. It stops outside the open back door and your heart leaps. Grandma puts the blanket away into a big red bag with the rest of the crochet squares, shushes you forward into the doorway, then out into the street. Dad's walked round to the passenger side and is helping Mother out. Other children have gathered and are peering into the car. Dad opens the door, bows and says in a funny voice, 'Your public awaits you, madam.'

'Jim, please, don't make a fuss,' Mother says in a tired voice. She's wearing a simple powder-blue shift dress and you can see the material dark under her arms with sweat.

'Make a fuss? I want the world to know, at last you're home—'

'Now, now, Jim. Let her get into the house and settle before you start all that malarkey,' Grandma warns him.

'Can't a man just be happy his wife's home?'

'Just let her get in,' orders Grandma.

Dad goes to assist her, but as Mother swings her legs out of the car and is helped into a standing position, you feel afraid. Grandma hovers nearby.

'Hello, Mam,' you whisper, eyes fixed on a tar bubble which has erupted with the heat. You feel her eyes on you.

'In you go,' Dad instructs, propelling Mother forwards, past you. 'Mam, put the kettle on and let's have a cup of tea. Are there any scones?'

'Of course there are. When have you ever known me to forget to make scones?' Grandma beams triumphantly.

Caught between Mother and Grandma, you feel the air crackle…

You hear, smell and feel life going on around you but it's all mixed up with other things. You pull up one memory and a lot of others are attached, brushing your face with their wings. Ones you don't want. Ones you didn't bargain for. So you try to come back to the room, to get away from the memories, to reach out, grab the voices and shake the silence off your back. But they're behind frosted glass and you're pinned down, hands and arms at your side.

2.09 p.m.
The Rise

Jayne and Lizzie are upstairs when they hear the front door open. Lizzie's putting some ironing away and Jayne's lying down, staring at the ceiling.

'I thought you locked the door,' Lizzie says, looking at Jayne who's sliding off the bed.

'I did.' Jayne moves to the top of the stairs and sees Sandy, grinning like a Cheshire cat. Caught off balance she grabs the handrail to steady herself.

'Still the same place for the key then.' He laughs.

'What do you want?' asks Lizzie, the tone in her voice unmistakable.

'I see Poison Ivy's still around then,' answers Sandy, combing thick, shoulder-length red hair from his face with long, bony fingers.

He goes into the kitchen and the sound of water filling the kettle reaches them.

'I'll swing for that bugger,' asserts Lizzie making her way forward but Jayne holds her back as they go downstairs.

'You'd better go home, Lizzie,' Jayne says as they reach the entrance hallway. 'I'm okay, I'll see what he wants.'

‘I’m staying right here. He can’t just come in here like this.’

‘I need to tell him about Claire,’ Jayne whispers but Sandy’s heard and pops his head round the door. Jayne notices he’s lost weight since the last time she saw him.

‘What’s wrong with Claire?’ he asks.

Lizzie surges forward but is stopped by Jayne.

‘Lizzie, please,’ Jayne implores, opening the door.

Lizzie hesitates then says, ‘Ring me if you need me. I’ll pick the kids up from school and come back then. You sure you’re okay with this bastard?’

‘Sure.’

Lizzie glares at Sandy who smirks at her as she leaves.

Jayne faces Sandy who tries to put an arm round her.

‘It’s been a long time—I’d forgotten how good you look, even without make-up,’ he murmurs as he tries to nibble her neck. Same old lies, same old Sandy. She knows what she looks like.

‘Stop it, Sandy! I’ve something to tell you, though God knows why I should even bother.’ Tears are very close to the surface again.

‘Don’t be like that, pet. I can’t bear it when you’re angry. I’m sorry I’ve been away, but I’m here now.’

‘And that’s okay, is it? What about the last three years? No word, not even a postcard. You’ve never even been back to see Claire—’ Her voice breaks.

Sandy pulls her into his chest and soothes, ‘Come on, it’s all right. That’s what I’m here for now.’ Unwillingly Jayne succumbs to his embrace until he adds, ‘Circumstances beyond my control took me away—’

This incenses her. ‘What circumstances? For almost three years? Liar!’

'Look, I made a few mistakes, all right? I borrowed money from the wrong sort of people, you know—'

'No, Sandy, I don't know. You weren't here to ask.'

'Like I said, I'm here now. Where is she? I've been dying to see her.'

Jayne crumples and sobs, her anger dissolving, leaking from her pores.

5.41 p.m.
Merry Farm

Gary's just got inside his house when the phone rings. It's Lizzie.

'Gary, Sandy's back.'

'What?' he yells, incredulously.

'Calm down. He came back this afternoon, strolled in as if he's just been to the shops. He's still there and she won't listen to me.'

'She won't even see me,' Gary says, his voice wobbling slightly with emotion. 'What on earth can she want with him, Lizzie, after how he's treated her?'

'I have no idea,' confesses Lizzie, 'but we've got to do something. She's not in a fit state to make rational judgements and he's the kind to prey on her vulnerability.'

Gary grips the phone in fury. 'I'll do anything, you know that.'

'We have to get her to see sense. I've tried, but she won't listen to me. Derek says I should leave well alone, but she's my best friend. I just can't do nothing.' Lizzie starts to cry.

'Don't cry, Lizzie. I'll see what I can do.'

She stops sobbing and takes a deep breath. 'Thanks, Gary. I'm sorry, I know this is hard on you too. See what you can do and I'll try to see her tomorrow. Maybe together…'

‘Yeah, maybe,’ he says putting the phone down. Fear clutches at him and he runs to the downstairs toilet to be sick.

6.37 p.m.
The Rise

Adam’s in his room when the doorbell rings. It rings a few times, then buzzes incessantly until Sandy opens the door. He creeps to the top of the stairs. It’s Gary.

‘Let me see her,’ Gary demands.

‘Push off!’ Sandy attempts to close the door but Gary’s foot is in the way.

‘You can’t stop me from seeing her.’ Gary clenches his fists but manages to stay calm.

Sandy sneers at him, ‘I just have, pal. She doesn’t want to see you so I suggest you fuck off now. Without a fuss.’

Gary hesitates, controlling his anger. ‘Let her tell me, then I’ll go, if that’s what she wants.’

‘I told you, she doesn’t want to see you. Can you blame her?’

‘What you on about?’ Gary’s momentarily taken aback and Sandy manages to manoeuvre Gary’s foot out of the doorway.

‘Insisting she left them with that crazy old cow,’ Sandy replies, nastily.

‘Hang on a minute.’ Gary’s temper is about to explode. ‘It wasn’t like that at all. I didn’t—’

‘Just fuck off.’

The door slams shut and Adam returns to his computer. The hollowness that has grown inside him since Claire’s death chills, like an empty house with the wind blowing through. Adam hears Sandy climb the stairs, then his door opens.

‘Hi, son, how’re you doin’?’

Adam doesn't look up. 'Who was that?'

'Nobody, son. Nobody.'

'Sounded like Gary.'

'No, it was just someone sellin' double glazing. What's that you're doin'?' Sandy bends towards the computer and looks over Adam's shoulder. Adam sighs. He feels worn out.

'Nothing. How long are you staying?'

'That depends.' Sandy shifts his balance and straightens up, ready to turn and leave the room.

'What about your job?' asks Adam.

This stops Sandy in mid-turn. 'I could try to get one here. Would you like that?' He looks towards Adam but the child remains facing his computer.

'Like last time, you mean?'

On the defensive now, Sandy asserts, 'No. Not like last time. A proper job—Hey, what did your mam tell you about last time?' Adam feels Sandy's eyes boring into the back of his head.

'Nothing. Just that you had to go away for a while, that's all.'

'Aye, right. That's what happened. But this time it's different.'

Adam swivels in his chair and faces his stepfather. He looks deeply into Sandy's eyes for several seconds then shakes his head, turns and looks away, out of the window, before returning to his computer game.

Tuesday 13 May

7.11 a.m.
St Julian's Hospital, Morpeth

Sue hums along to the radio as she drives. The traffic's not bad this time of the morning so she is able to take more notice of her surroundings. She likes to come this way, despite it being longer, because it's off the main street and she gets to breathe fresh air through the windows, along with the damp smells of pre-summer, earth and countryside, feeling them on her skin. Early blossom has started to fall, spiralling upwards in gusts of wind, then showering down gently to decorate hillocks along the roadside.

At the hospital, which is set back from the road in five acres of land, the lawns are neatly trimmed and hedges clipped. Gardening therapy seems to be very successful at the moment. They tried it out last year but there were only three takers; this year there have been fifteen so far.

Parking the car in its allotted bay she drags her handbag from the passenger seat and locks the doors, satisfied with the simultaneous metallic clunk of the central locking system and the peeping of the alarm. The air is crisp and the sunlight, reflected on the wet pathway, momentarily blinds her as she turns to walk to the entrance. The swish of her hips disturbs spiders' webs clinging to wooden posts as she manoeuvres her way around the car to the pathway leading to the secure entrance on the side of the building.

Inside, her sandals squeak on the polished vinyl tiles. She walks towards the staffroom where she changes into comfortable leather clogs and puts her lunch in the fridge. Checking the log to see if there have been any problems overnight or messages from the night staff, she then makes her way to the staff toilets. Well, you've got to be comfy before you start, haven't you?

8.15 a.m.

'How are you today, Grace?' asks Sue.

The hand-over was longer than usual. There had been two new admissions during the night who had to be heavily sedated and Dr Norman was off sick. Grace was still catatonic and there was a note about her medication.

The door opens and Harvey, dressed in blue striped pyjamas with the buttons fastened thought the wrong holes, demands, 'I want my slippers. Someone's stolen my slippers.'

Sue smiles at him. 'No one's stolen them, Harvey. Let's look in your room.'

'They're not there. Someone's stolen them,' he whines.

Patiently Sue suggests to him, 'Let's look anyway. Have you tried under the bed?'

A nod.

'In the wardrobe?'

'Yes.'

'Have you showered this morning?'

'Of course! I'm not dirty.'

'Of course you're not. But have you looked in the shower room?'

He says nothing.

'Come on, let's look in the shower room.'

She takes him by the arm and leads him out.

12.49 p.m.

It is lunchtime and Sue is in the staffroom with Lisa Bennetti, making herself a cup of coffee.

'What time should we be there?' Lisa asks.

‘Anytime after seven,’ answers Sue. ‘The food’s being served at nine but it’ll be good if people turn up sooner, rather than later.’

‘Have you asked Darren yet?’ asks Lisa.

‘Of course.’

‘And?’

‘And nothing. He’s on the wrong shift. Why? Do you fancy him or something?’ There’s an edge to Sue’s voice.

‘Of course not. I was just wondering, that’s all,’ responds Lisa, taking an arm and flicking her long dark hair over to the right side of her head. She has Italian parentage and her creamy olive skin is starting to darken with the sun.

Sue looks at her friend, dressed casually in jeans and a top, just short enough to show her flat stomach and belly ring. ‘Really?’ she asks.

‘Really,’ asserts Lisa. ‘Now, what’re you wearing? I’ve bought a new strappy thing but don’t want to look overdressed.’

‘Ha! That’ll be the day—there’s hardly any material in your clothes.’

‘You know what I mean. What are you wearing?’

Sue shifts uncomfortably in her seat. ‘I’ve not found anything yet. But if Darren’s not going, it doesn’t really matter, does it?’

‘Of course it does!’ Lisa slides her arm around Sue’s ample shoulders. ‘Dress for you, not for him. Wear what makes you feel good and sod the rest of them.’

‘That’s easy for you to say,’ Sue declares.

‘How?’

‘Oh, never mind.’ Sue shrugs. ‘You’re right. I’m going to be thirty so why not push the boat out. I can’t wait to get pissed and have a good dance. There’ll be spare blokes there—Chris and Andy are bringing some of their friends—and we may even get one or two gate-crashers, with a bit of luck.'

'That's my girl. Sod the lot!'

'Sod the lot!'

They raise their cups in mock salute, then collapse into fits of giggles.

1.35 p.m.

The room's hot and stuffy. There are four people squashed into it and the smell of perspiration is nauseating. Hilary Norman leans across the desk and opens a window but the noise of the lawnmower outside is too loud and she closes it again.

'Let's try to make this quick. Has anyone managed to contact the daughter yet?'

Sue volunteers, 'No, I've tried a few times, so has Darren, but it's only ever her answer machine now. We've left messages but she's not got back to us.'

'It says here that Grace connected with her eyes a few times. What happened?'

'Darren had put the CD player on for Harvey—he wanted his 60s music on again—so we were listening to that, having a laugh with him and dancing. I went in to see Grace and was singing along—"Heard it through the Grapevine", I think—when she opened her eyes. I spoke to her but apart from following me with her eyes there was nothing and at the end of the song she closed them again. I got Harvey to let me put the song back on but she didn't respond. That was about three o'clock or three-thirty, wasn't it?' Sue asks Darren. She can't help noticing his long eyelashes and forces herself to look away.

'About quarter past, I think,' Darren confirms, smiling benignly.

'Anyway, later on, about ten, I went to check again and her eyes were open, watching the door as I popped my head round. She watched me for a few seconds, then closed them. She seemed quite peaceful.'

'Thank you, Sue. That's good. Keep up the stimulation and let's see if we can get her back.'

Hilary Norman closes the file and picks up Harvey's.

2.34 p.m.

Back on the ward Sue pushes the medicine trolley into the corridor and begins to dispense the drugs into containers, which she then gives to the patients. That done, she locks the trolley away and checks on Grace. She changes the urine bottle and checks the bottle of clear liquid suspended by Grace's bed. After that it's blood pressure and pulse, which she writes down on Grace's chart. As she clips it to the bottom of the bed Grace stretches and rolls onto her back, assuming a star position. Sue hurriedly notes this on Grace's file, then watches for any more movement, but there is none. After a couple more minutes she strokes Grace's forehead and leaves the room.

2.35 p.m.

You feel the pressure in your head as it swells like a helium balloon, then pops as the memory surfaces…

You're seven years old, huddled in a corner in the dark, pressing your back against the walls. It feels like you've been there a long time but you're not sure. Closing your eyes you sense movements elsewhere and hear the faint cries of a baby. The voices keep telling you it'll be fine, that Dad will be home soon, but you don't believe them. For as long as you can remember they've spoken to you, whispering secrets, showing you things, but now you wish they'd go away and leave you alone. You don't want to listen any more, it gets you into too much trouble.

Footsteps approach and you brace yourself. A key clatters in the lock as it turns the levers, then the door opens. Light hurts your eyes, making them water, so you shield them with your hand. Mother stands in the doorway, the light from behind shining through the wisps of hair that rise from her head.

'Come here,' she demands.

The voice is not entirely unfriendly but the whispers in your head increase, making your ears feel like they'll explode. You know you must be careful.

Suddenly the wail of the baby changes its timbre and Mother turns her head in the direction of the noise, then back again. This time her voice is different.

'I said come here!' it yells.

You reluctantly leave the comfort of the corner and walk gingerly towards the light.

'You'll have to run and fetch the doctor. David's getting worse. Tell doctor he's got a temperature and I can't bring it down. Then go and get your dad. Well, what're you waiting for? Go on, run!'

Hardly believing your luck you run and run. Out of the house, down the street, along the main road up to the doctor's house, a large detached building overlooking the park. You have to stand on tiptoe to ring the bell, wait a few seconds, then ring it again. The sound echoes against the panelled walls in the hall and you feel it bounce back to you.

A stout woman in a too-tight brown cardigan opens the door.

'I'm really sorry, Mrs Allen, but Mam says David's getting worse. He's got a temperature she can't get down and can the doctor come quick?'

'He's not here right now, Grace, but as soon as he gets back I'll tell him. Has your mam tried a cold bath?'

'Dunno.'

'Tell her to strip him and put him in a cold bath. That usually does the trick, but Doctor Allen shouldn't be long.'

'Thanks, Mrs Allen.'

You're halfway down the street before she closes the door. You feel exhilarated, the wind in your hair, free for a while, at least. You run along the main road then turn left and ziz-zag through the lines of terraced houses until you reach the row at the bottom of the hill running adjacent to the railway line. At the back of these houses are several allotments growing a variety of vegetables and soft fruits. Leeks, cabbages and potatoes grow in neat rows and the canes from the runner beans and peas remind you of the graveyards in France you've seen in Dad's photograph album. Two of the allotments have chicken runs covered in wire and one has a pigeon loft. There's a cinder path between the allotments and the back yards and you race down this.

'Dad!Dad! Mam says to come quick. David's getting worse. She's sent for the doctor. She can't get his temperature down.'

Dad's been busy digging but he throws the spade down and reaches for his jacket.

'Go on then, I'm coming,' he urges. You turn on your heels and run back along the cinder path, then your legs start to wobble. You lean against the nearest wall as the whispering in your head gets louder, deafening you. You feel yourself choking, like when Mother's angry with you, then it's gone. Opening your eyes you look round. No one's there. Dad steps out into the lane so you pick up your feet and run ahead, back to the house where David's wailing feverishly.

'Did you do as I said?'

'Yes. Mrs Allen says she'll send Doctor Allen round as soon as he comes back and you're to put David into a cold bath.'

'Get the sink filled. I haven't forgotten that wet bed, so don't think you're getting away with it. Your dad will have something to say when he gets here. Now move yourself!'

You head back into the kitchen as Dad appears and Mother falls into his arms.

'I don't like the sound of his chest,' cries Mother.

Dad holds her as you turn on the tap. Suddenly you have a phrase in your head which you can't ignore, so you tell Dad, 'David's going to die.'

Dad tries to reassure you. 'No sweetheart, the doctor's going to make him well. Don't you worry,' but you know. And so does Mother. You can tell by her face that she's heard the voices too, although she won't admit it…

3.49 p.m.

'Doctor Norman's here to see you Grace. '

'How has she been today. Any movement?'

'Yes, she was a bit restless earlier and responded a bit with her eyes when I was talking to her, but it only lasted a few minutes, then she went back.'

'We'll see how she does over the weekend. I'm not in till Tuesday—I've a conference to attend—so Amit will be covering for me. Any problems, page him. All right?'

'Fine. Have a good weekend. Are you doing anything nice?'

'Not really, just spending time in the garden and trying to catch up with Tim. He's been lecturing in Israel and is due back this evening. We've a lot to talk about.' Her grey aura darkens and you feel her turmoil transmitting to you—there are divorce papers to sign. Adultery.

'You take care. Bye.'

'Bye.'

There's a warmth between them that didn't exist when you first arrived. You can feel it circulating in the room, settling on China Blue like dust. You try to lift your fingers to touch it, but they're pinned at your side. Then another memory floats to the surface…

The doctor is young and he's smiling. 'That's fine, Grace. You can get dressed now.' Turning to Mother he asks, 'How long has this been going on?'

'Since she was five. She does it deliberately you know, just to spite me.' Mother glares at you.

'What makes you say that, Mrs Watson?'

'She's naughty. She always has been. It's her grandma's fault, always spoiling her.'

'So why five?' he asks.

'Five?'

'You said she's been doing this since she was five. Did anything happen then to start it off?'

'I suppose when her grandma died.' Mother begins to look uncomfortable. You concentrate hard on looking at the floor.

'Was Grace close to her gran?'

'Not especially,' she sniffs.

'Anything else happen?'

'No. Why?' Mother asks, suspiciously.

'There doesn't seem to be any physical reason for this—'

'I told you, she does it to spite me. She smashes plates, throws them against the wall, has screaming tantrums. She harms herself as well—cuts, bruises, that sort of thing.'

'Is that right, Grace?'

You drag your eyes from the ground, look at Mother and nod.

'Why do you do it, Grace?' the doctor asks, gently.

'You'll not get any sense out of her,' Mother asserts.

You feel Mother's energy twist, satisfied, but challenging. You daren't look at her.

The doctor's voice is soft, reassuring. 'Grace, look at me. Why do you do these things?'

You hang your head and say nothing.

There's a pause, then Mother says, 'I told you. She's a wicked child and needs to be put somewhere—for her own good, of course. I can't cope any more since her father died.'

'Of course. I do sympathise. Why don't I have a word with her myself? In private?'

'Private? I don't think so. I don't think it'll do any good at all.'

'Let me be the judge of that, Mrs Watson. Could you wait outside please?'

'It won't do any—'

'Humour me and let me try,' he insists. 'It can't do any harm. If you wouldn't mind, Mrs Watson.' He starts to open the door for her. You feel her anger, simmering under the surface as she rises and walks across the room to the door.

'Dr. Jameson would never –'

'It won't take long.'

She wrenches the door open and walks stiffly out, closing it softly behind her.

You're shaking. You grip the sides of your seat to prevent yourself from falling. You feel sick.

‘Right, Grace, let’s start again, shall we? Is it true what your mother says, about you smashing things and hurting yourself?’

You shuffle, but don’t answer.

‘Is it?’

You nod, then stare at your feet.

‘Why do you do it?’

You can’t tell him the truth, so you continue to stare at your feet in red sandals, at the two T-bars and buckles. Your ankle socks are clean and white but one is higher up your ankle than the other. You reach down to correct this.

‘Come on, Grace, you must have a reason.’

‘Don’t remember,’ you mumble.

‘What, you don’t remember why you do those things or you don’t remember doing them?’

All these questions. You’re starting to sweat. You feel it on your top lip.

‘What don’t you remember, Grace?’

You glance at the closed door. ‘Can I see Mam, please?’

‘Of course you can. When we’re finished.’

‘I want to see my mam.’ You’re trembling.

‘I know, but this won’t take long.’

‘Please, I need my mam.’ You’ve started to wail now. She hates that. You’re agitated, unable to sit still. You keep looking at the door.

‘Okay, let’s talk about something else, shall we? When you wet the bed, does it happen as you’re waking up, or in your sleep?’

‘I don’t know… I can’t remember.’

‘How old are you now? Twelve? It’s a little bit old for this kind of thing so we need to find out what’s causing it, so we can sort it out. Do you understand?’

‘Can I see my mam now?’

Doctor Penninghame sighs, then writes on your file before opening the door and inviting Mother back in.

'I think I need to see Grace again when the tests come back so make an appointment for two weeks. Can you also write down each occasion that she wets the bed and any other behaviour which you think is relevant here—destroying things, mood swings, anything like that?'

'I've a lot to do,' Mother answers.

'A capable woman like you—I'm confident you'll manage, Mrs Watson. We'll be unable to do anything until we get a clear picture of her behaviour, and I'm sure you want us to help Grace as it'll make your life easier too, in the long run, won't it?'

'Of course, Doctor. Two weeks, you said.'

'Two weeks.'

Outside the building you begin to shake. You feel the first dribbles of urine leaking out, despite all efforts to control it. Mother yanks your arm and hisses in your ear, 'What did you tell him?' but before you can reply you feel a warm trickle running down your legs, into your ankle socks…

7.49 p.m.

Lounge Bar, Duke of Northumberland

Sue and Cassie are perched on bar stools.

'What colour streamers do you want?' Cassie asks. She's dressed in a black skimpy skirt and tight white top. Next to Sue, who has carried several boxes downstairs into the function room, she looks tiny.

'I found some purple and silver ones in Semi-Chem. They were in the sale; they'll be okay, won't they?'

''Course. How do you want them?'

'I thought we could put them in different shapes, like this,' she demonstrates, 'along the walls, then hang the rest from the ceiling. What d'ya think?'

'It's your party, have them wherever you want.' Cassie consults her pad. 'Any veggies?'

'God, I forgot to ask. I know of three for certain, actually one's vegan, but there's bound to be more. Why not do a lot of veggie stuff—you don't have to be veggie to like veggie food, and about ten without wheat, gluten or nuts.'

Cassie nods in silent agreement as Sue puts her glass down on top of the baby grand piano. The staff had been going to move it out of the room to give her more dancing space but she wants it to stay; she thinks it looks more romantic.

'What's your final numbers? Still thirty?'

Sue's brow furrows in a frown. 'Well no one's let me know they're not coming, so I guess so.' She brightens and suggests, 'We can always let some in on the night to make the numbers up, if we're short.'

'Okay, fine,' agrees Cassie. 'The cake's decorated and we've enough champagne. When d'you want us to bring it out?'

'When's best?' asks Sue.

'Depends. Are they getting a glass on arrival or d'you want it saving for the food at nine?'

'What about a bottle on each table when you serve the food?'

Cassie nods.

'I'll put some mints on each table—some people are right fussy about garlic these days. Is Dylan all right for the disco?'

'Yeah, but he says if you want to bring any special CDs for him to play he'll need them tomorrow to give him time to work out a sequence.'

Sue nods then adds, 'God, my stomach's playing up. I feel so nervous. I hope nothing goes wrong.'

'It'll be fine, you'll see. Stop worrying and just enjoy it. It's not every day you turn thirty.'

'Don't remind me. But you're right. And to celebrate that fact, let's have another.'

Cassie returns to the other side of the bar and pours them both another drink.

8.45 p.m.
Garrick's Fell

The sky has turned magnificent shades of fiery red and burnt orange laced through with crimson clouds as Johnny makes his way back home with his catch. He takes time out to watch the sky change, the backlight subtly shifting intensity and colour, catching the clouds and holding them hostage to its death throes. It's mild for the time of year and Johnny is soaked in sweat from cutting through heather and bracken. A good job he's not hunting as his prey would easily be able to smell him as well as pinpoint his position from the noise he's making. He sighs.

Sunset complete, he resumes his journey home. Some of the gamekeepers must be aware of his existence by now but he's safe as long as he's not caught off the Major's land. He never bothers the Major. The two men haven't exchanged more than a dozen words since he left the cottage, but he knows the Major understands why and why he refused help from ex-Service organisations like Combat Stress and the British Legion. The Major came across one of Johnny's traps one night, a few years ago, when Johnny was hiding amongst the undergrowth. He'd looked hard and long at the trap, snorted, nodded his head and left. After that Johnny saw him on two other occasions out in the woods, but Johnny doesn't like being around people, in case he goes out of control again.

Johnny hasn't seen him for a couple of months now, not since the last time he'd been up near the big house. He used to imagine what it must have been like in its heyday, bustling with family, servants and children. But then the dark thoughts, rages and shakes came back and he couldn't control himself; his bowels and bladder emptied. When it was over he ran away, ashamed. He's never been back.

Wednesday 14 May

6.32 a.m.

The Rise

It's the day of the funeral, and for the moment, the house is alive with silence, morning coiled tight, expectant. The curtains are closed and it's brooding and dark in the bedroom as Adam stares at the ceiling. The other single bed in the room is empty, the safety bumper still in place. For the last three nights he has crawled into that bed to inhale the body smell that belonged to Claire; Jayne hasn't removed the sheets yet. Adam covered his head with the duvet and lay face down in the pillows each night, but the previous night he got into his own bed and lay, rigid, just like now, staring at the ceiling, at the luminous stars his mam put there. He can hear the sounds of movement downstairs and the low hum of conversation interspersed with sobbing. He lets the sounds wash over him; in a few hours he has to say his final farewell to the little body lying downstairs in a box with brass handles. His eyes are dry; since Jayne collected him from the hospital he has been unable to cry.

The bedside clock registers 6.36 a.m. The room is hot, despite the open window. Adam rises, pulls the curtains apart and sits on the windowsill. Rainbows are dancing on the ceiling and walls as he spins a prism hanging at the window. He's done this every sunny morning since Claire moved out of her cot in his mother's room and into the single bed in his. She used to laugh, clapping her chubby hands, demanding, 'More! More!' or 'Again! Again!' This particular morning there is only silence in the room as the colours dance.

Looking down from the window he sees the garden littered with the toys he forgot to put away before they left for Grace's. He can still see Claire that day in the garden, excited and red-faced, puffing and chasing after him, then sitting down, huffy, because he wouldn't let her catch him. He loved to tease her, to watch her face get cross, then watch her stubbornness in not forgiving him until he'd begged and begged. After that, her face could change in a second and she'd be up, running away, making him catch her, him letting her think he couldn't.

The door opens and Sandy enters the room.

'How're you doin', son?'

Adam doesn't look at him.

'D'ya want any breakfast?'

'No.'

'Sure?'

There is silence as Adam returns his gaze to the garden.

'C'mon, you've gotta keep your strength up,' encourages Sandy.

'Where's Mam?'

'Downstairs. You comin' down?'

'Not yet.' Adam's voice sounds flat and tired.

'Can I sit down?' asks Sandy.

Adam shrugs and looks back at the spinning crystal.

'Are you staying again?'

'That's up to your mam. Right now, though, we've got to get her through today. You've got to be strong for her. A big lad. Okay?'

Adam nods. The sun disappears behind a cloud and the rainbows vanish.

9.55 a.m.

The man who stands on the step is holding a black top hat in his hand. Behind him an assistant is gathering the flowers from the back of the hearse. They are both wearing black tail-coats, black waistcoats, wing-collared shirts and black ties. The door opens and Sandy, tall, ginger-haired, in a charcoal-grey suit, white shirt and black tie, is framed there. He is wearing a black armband around his left arm and leads the men into the front room.

The room is dark, with a sickly-sweet smell in the air. Windows and curtains are closed so no light or fresh air intrudes. Two large candles are lit, one at each side of the small coffin mounted on a portable, collapsing table the funeral director erected when he brought the coffin in. Jayne insisted on having Claire home last night, despite entreaties from neighbours and friends to leave her in the Chapel of Rest. Other people have been there earlier, but they are now waiting outside in their cars to give the family some privacy.

Jayne reaches to hold Adam's hand but he moves out of the way.

'It's time now,' suggests Sandy.

'Not yet. Just a little longer,' Jayne wails.

Sandy swallows hard and grasps her shoulders. She looks into his eyes, then her body crumples against him.

'Say goodbye now, Jayne. It's time.' He speaks softly to her. She struggles, but then breathes a resigned sigh and bends over the small body, planting tears and saliva on the cold, white brow.

'What about you? Do you want to kiss your sister goodbye?' asks Sandy.

Adam looks up at him, then back to the coffin. He feels hot but his hands are freezing cold. He wants to scream, to drag Claire from the box and shake life into her, but his legs and arms are paralysed.

'Adam. Do you want to kiss your sister?' Sandy repeats.

Suddenly there is fire in his limbs and Adam tears himself away from the scene, runs up the stairs, collapsing onto Claire's bed, pounding it with his fists, his face white and dry.

10.15 a.m.
St Peter the Apostle Church, Alston

There are lines of people waiting as the funeral cortege pulls up and unloads its cargo. Jayne is flanked by Sandy on her left. Adam walks stiffly in front of her, her hands on his shoulders, but these are soon dropped as she breaks down again and has to be helped up the steps. He sees Gary escape from the ranks of people waiting and tries to help Jayne, but he is pushed aside by Sandy. Adam is feeling lost and vulnerable until Gary bends down, hugs him tight and whispers, 'You're doing fine. Not long now,' then leads him inside the church, settles him in the front pew beside Jayne and takes a pew further back. Jayne leans heavily on Sandy, her sobs echoing in the cold church. Adam clenches his fists.

An hour and a half later the green Mondeo pulls up outside Jayne's house. Adam and Gary have been silent during the journey but now they turn to look at each other.

'Are you coming in?' asks Adam.

'I don't think so… I don't think your mam wants me to. She's pretty upset right now and your dad…' His voice trails off leaving a heaviness hanging there.

'But I want you to.' Adam looks towards the house, 'It's awful in there.' His voice comes out a bit higher than normal and he bites his lip.

'I know, son, but right now isn't the best time. Maybe when your mam's better. Here... look… If you need me, just ring, Okay?' Gary hands him a business card. 'Don't forget now.'

Adam nods but won't meet Gary's eye. He opens the car door, slams it shut and walks away without looking back…

6.38 p.m.
Meldon Rigg

Johnny has improvised different methods of cooking. There's a hobo stove, which is a five gallon oil drum with holes punched in the sides for warmth and grilling food on top and a metal box oven, made from an old first aid box with a hinged lid that he uses for baking. These are all stashed neatly, away from view. At the moment as he is wrapping his fresh catch of fish in chickweed leaves and placing them on the hot embers of a campfire, above which stands a smoke tepee made from a triangle of sticks supporting a platform. He is ready to boil greens in an old catering sized tin of peach halves and hums tunelessly as he works.

The air is heavy, mixed with wood smoke. Overhead birds are wheeling, taking their night flight before bedding down and a cry from a vixen can be heard. Looking into the fire Johnny remembers his first camping trip with Harry, his father. He was seven at the time and Harry was having a 'dry' spell. Harry was good fun then, when he wasn't drunk, complaining, or being angry and unreasonable. It was the best holiday Johnny ever had, but for Harry it was downhill all the way after that. Johnny had always wanted kids but it hadn't worked out for him and it was too late now. He'd have made a good dad, much better than Harry, but there's no use pondering on the impossible. Life's not too bad now, all things considered.

11.52 p.m.
St Julian's Hospital
The dining room is in darkness as Sue enters to make herself a hot chocolate. She's covering for Angela and working an extra shift. She hates the graveyard shift but the consolation is that she'll be working with Darren, giving her time to work on him before the party. Flicking the light switch on she waits patiently for the fluorescent strip to light up. It takes three attempts before the tube is fully lit so she makes a mental note to write it in the log. It probably just needs a starter.

She still has nothing to wear for the party, which is only three days away now. Looking at her reflection in the glass window she turns sideways, first to the left, then to the right. She smoothes the baggy tee-shirt into the contours of her body and sighs. If only she was a couple of sizes smaller. The shops will be open at the end of the shift so she could go to town before she goes home. However, the thought of trailing round busy shops instead of falling into bed doesn't appeal at all. Perhaps she could just wear one of her black skirts with a new top, if she can find one? Who'll notice anyway? Darren hardly notices she's a woman so he's not likely to notice what she's wearing. But, you never know.

She tears herself away from the window and makes herself black coffee. She carries the mug carefully back to the staffroom just as Harvey is framed in the doorway. He's wearing only his pyjama top and his genitals dangle loosely between his legs.

'Go back to bed, Harvey,' Sue urges.

'The bed's wet. Someone's thrown water over me when I was in bed. I'm not going back there,' he complains.

'There's nobody there, Harvey. Just let me put this down and we'll go back together.'

'I need a drink of water.'

'Not now, Harvey. You know what happens when you drink after six o'clock.'

She opens the staffroom door and places the mug on a beer mat on the coffee table. Darren looks up from the car magazine he's reading.

'Harvey's wet the bed again. How come I get all the good jobs?' asks Sue.

'Just luck, I guess,' he replies, turning back to his magazine.

'Gee, thanks,' Sue replies sarcastically. She turns on her heel and closes the door behind her, accompanying Harvey to his bedroom in search of clean pyjama bottoms. She changes his sheets and settles him down, then makes her way back to the staffroom. Darren hasn't moved. Sue appraises him—five foot ten, short brown hair going bald at the crown, dressed in khaki Wrangler jeans and a bright yellow tee-shirt—and wonders what the attraction is.

'You're a man…' she starts.

'So they tell me,' Darren replies, still reading his magazine.

'What do you think I should wear to my party?'

At last she's got his attention and he looks up.

'How am I supposed to know? I don't know what clothes you've got.'

'No, but if I was to buy something new?' Careful, girl, not too pushy.

'I have no idea.' He's dismissive and returns to his magazine.

Sue tries another tack. 'Who's your ideal fantasy date?' That gets him.

'Madonna, Lady Gaga and Pink all rolled into one.'

'And what would you like this dream woman to wear?'

'Preferably nothing,' he says with a leer.

'You're absolutely no use at all… Why those women?' she asks.

'Fantastic bodies and unlimited, available sex without strings or repercussions. What more could a man want?'

'Love, kindness, loyalty, respect...'

'That's for a wife, not an ideal date,' Darren asserts.

'So you think about having a wife, do you?'

He laughs. 'Not if I can help it. I suppose someday I'll succumb to the need to have children, so I guess a wife would have to come into the equation somewhere— unless I could get away with doing a runner.' His eyes sparkle and she feels herself melting.

'You're so shallow, Darren Williams. So shallow.'

He smiles and turns back to his magazine. 'Maybe a strappy dress or something,' he comments without looking up. 'You've a nice cleavage as far as I can see, so show it.' He turns the page. 'And nothing fussy round your throat. Just a simple chain or something.' He turns another page, then laughs. 'Or better still, let your hair be your necklace; it'd look nice like that.' He holds the magazine up for her and she sees an advert for shampoo. The upper part of the woman is naked except for her long, brown, shiny hair, which is draped around her neck and over her body.

'Yeah, I'm sure. I can't quite see me greeting my guests dressed only in my hair. Have you got a Lady Godiva fetish or something?'

'Mmm, not arf!'

'Pervert.'

'I wish…'

Thursday 15 May

4.03 a.m.
Fletcher Ward

Sue checks on Grace. The sheets are smooth over Grace's body, which hasn't moved since the physiotherapist was in. Grace's hands are placed neatly across her stomach and Sue suddenly finds the whole picture disturbing, reminiscent of death, loss, and unbearable sorrow.

'Come on, Grace, let's untidy you a bit.' Sue moves Grace's hands and as she does so she feels just the slightest pressure from one of them.

'Are you trying to hold my hand, Grace?' she asks as she holds Grace's right hand in hers. 'You don't want to lie here all the time, do you? You want to get back home, to the beach and the dunes.' Then from nowhere she finds herself saying, 'I'll visit you if you want. Once you've left here it won't matter that you're a patient. All you have to do is get well.'

What is this sudden affinity she feels for this woman? She squeezes Grace's hand and she is rewarded with a very faint squeeze back.

7.45 a.m.
The Rise

Jayne and Adam sit in silence at the breakfast table, listening to sounds of Sandy upstairs getting dressed. Adam is in his school uniform but Jayne is still in her nightwear. She's not taking him to school, so why get dressed? He plays with his cereal and Jayne snaps at him.

'Don't do that! Eat it up.'

He doesn't look up and continues to play with his food.

'Adam, are you listening to me?' Jayne challenges.

He still doesn't look at her.

'For God's sake, Adam, this is difficult enough…Please. Eat your breakfast.'

'Why doesn't Gary come round?'

Jayne is taken aback. 'What?'

'Gary never comes round now. Why?'

'Look, Adam...it's grown-up stuff.'

He frowns and continues to stir his cereal. 'I like Gary. Why doesn't he come here anymore? Does he hate me too?'

'Nobody hates you, sweetheart. Whatever makes you think that?' asks Jayne, horrified.

Adam doesn't answer.

'Gary cares a lot about you. It's just that …you know how you and John sometimes fall out?'

He nods.

'Well, sometimes grown-ups fall out.

'What did you fall out about?' Adam asks.

Jayne tries to reassure him with, 'It's not because he doesn't like you, it's just, … it's difficult right now.'

But Adam is not to be deterred. 'So when can I see him?'

'I don't know, darlin'… we'll see.'

'Soon?' he insists.

'I don't know…we'll just have to see how it goes, eh?' Jayne suggests but Adam looks away and returns to playing with his cereal as Sandy calls from the hallway,

'I've got to see a man about a dog – be back later.' They hear the front door open, then close.

Adam's gone to school and the empty house ticks like a time bomb. Tick, tick, tick. Energy has left my body and my limbs feel too heavy to move. It's easy to sit but Lizzie will be here in a while and I want to

get the dishes done. I've been having counselling—her idea—and I have to set myself three tasks a day that are achievable. Today's are: cook, or make, meals for me and Adam (Sandy gets his own now); wash and dry the dishes; write in a journal. I can just about make the meals but eating them is a chore for both of us. The dishes shouldn't really be a problem but they're still in the sink and ... I remember a quote from King Lear—'I can't heave my heart into my mouth'—well, I can't heave mine into a bloody journal. What can I say? I don't have the words for this right now.

10.44 a.m.
Merry Farm

Gary's in agony. If only he hadn't turned to look at the phone when it rang, he would have been okay. Instead, now there's a gaping gash in his hand where he struck himself with the chisel.

'Damn! Damn! Damn'! He hurls the chisel away in disgust and wants to howl like a child. Now blood is all over Mrs Marshall's wood and he'll have to give her a discount if he can't get it off.

Running into the kitchen he leaves a trail of blood splashes behind him. The cold tap is difficult to turn—another job to do—but he manages and plunges his hand underneath the icy stream. It stings. He sees the cut is deep and needs a stitch or two but he's reluctant to go to the hospital. There's so much work to catch up with, and what if Jayne rings? Buggeration. He has to stop the bleeding somehow. Maybe a tea-towel? And water. Lots of cold water.

He's watched from the corner of the room by a white puppy who quickly scrambles across the floor to attack the laces on his boots. Despite everything, Gary has to smile.

He reaches his good hand down and strokes the dog, a pedigree husky pup that he bought because Adam wanted a dog. Jayne was against the idea but he had hoped to change her mind and thought that if he did all the looking after and grooming, she would come round eventually. It made sense to keep the dog at his house for the hairs, paw prints and other mess, until she got used to the idea of extending her family to include not just the dog, but him too. He collected the pup just after the funeral, but then Jayne wouldn't return his calls so he hadn't been able to show the pup to Adam.

'Hey, Kumar. Feeling a bit neglected, are you? I know the feeling.'

1.21 p.m.
Alston Moor

It has been raining for the last ten hours but the water, which is a good two inches deeper in the entrance, has not penetrated here. Johnny is replenishing his supplies and taking some of the older stuff back home for cooking. He worked in the kitchens in prison after a 'back to work' type of course in food safety. It is about the only thing he found useful in there.

Picking out several pieces of dried fish, some blood cakes and a dried wood pigeon, he stuffs them into his rucksack. On the way back he intends to pick some fresh chickweed, garlic mustard, hairy bittercress, charlock and dandelion leaves for a salad. He may be poor but he eats well. Alan always used to laugh at him when he tried out new dishes. Roger didn't. He was glad of the variety, but Alan…best not to think about Alan. Or the past. Keep it locked away so it can't do any more harm.

4.10 p.m.
The Rise

Jayne has just made herself a drink when the phone rings. Picking it up she takes it to the kitchen table and doodles on an unopened envelope. Adam, just in from school, is framed in the doorway so she turns her back to him. He goes into the living room and there's the sound of the television being switched on.

'Hello?'

'Mrs Freeman?' a woman asks.

'Yes.'

'It's Sue Johnson. I'm—'

'I know who you are.' Jayne feels her neck muscles tighten.

'I've left a couple of messages—'

'What d'you want?' Jayne interrupts.

'Your mother would like to see you, if that's possible.'

There's silence for a few seconds then Jayne erupts, 'No, it's not!' Her throat hurts as she tries to control the yell.

'It really would help—'

'Who? Who would it help?' Jayne asks, nastily.

'Mrs Freeman, your mother's ill.' The voice is patient and controlled, despite Jayne's vehemence.

'I know that.' The woman's stupid. She has no idea.

'I think I explained it before—' Sue starts.

'It doesn't make any difference,' Jayne interrupts but Sue continues,

'—she really is very ill and her relationship with you—'

'That's an excuse, is it? Jayne hurls at her.

'Mrs Freeman—'

'How would you feel?' Jayne's raging now, finally giving vent.

‘I’m not saying—’

‘Then just what are you saying?’ Jayne grips her fingers in a fist, unaware of the nails digging into her palm.

‘Look, she’s asking to see you, that’s all. It’s crucial to her recovery—’

Jayne finally snaps. ‘What about my recovery? What about Adam’s? And Claire? What about her?’

‘I realize how hard this must be for you—’

The anger is passing. More calmly she says, ‘Do you? I doubt it,’ her voice like cold steel.

‘Mrs Freeman, your mother isn’t responding as well as we’d hoped. Your co-operation would help her enormously.’

‘She can fuck off and die for all I care!’

Slamming the phone down Jayne throws the pencil across the room. Bloody woman! Then she feels it coming up, like heartburn. It sticks in her chest, making breathing difficult. Jayne is shaking, so she bends her head, resting it on the table, unable to hold the sobs in. The sound of the television in the next room gets louder.

9.59 p.m.
Merry Farm
Gary is drunk. He’s had several cans of Special Brew and is feeling decidedly sorry for himself. His hand still throbs and he’s angry now. She never contacted him. He could be lying in a pool of blood and what would she care? What has he ever done to her other than try to give her whatever she wants? That’s his trouble, isn’t it? Too bloody soft! It happens all the time, doesn’t it, someone always taking advantage of his good nature? Well, no more. He’s not putting up with it any more. He’ll show her.

Flinging open the front door he suddenly remembers his keys and staggers back into the kitchen for them, vaguely aware of the fact he shouldn't drive, but who cares? If he kills himself, it'll serve her right. Fishing in the drawer he retrieves the keys and lurches out, slamming the door behind him.

10.12p.m.
The Rise
'Go away, Gary. Sleep it off,' Jayne orders. She's standing inside the front door.

'Open the door! Just open the bloody door!' he demands.

'Stop shouting! You'll wake Adam,' hisses Jayne through the door.

'Open the bloody door! I'm warning you,' he threatens, moving back, ready to charge at it. He unbalances and falls heavily on his side. The makeshift bandage he's wrapped round his injured hand is soaked in blood again. He cries out in pain, then, defeated, he pushes himself into a sitting position, rests his head on his knees and cries. Jayne opens the door and looks down at him, pityingly.

'Look, Gary, I can't let you in, in that state. Go home and sleep it off.'.

But Gary is still angry. 'You won't let me in, but you let that bastard in. After all he did to you!' He struggles to his feet again. 'So what's he got that I haven't? A bigger cock?' he asks, swaying a little with the effort of trying to remain upright. He gives in to gravity and slides back down into a sitting position.

Jayne's pity evaporates. 'Gary, that's pathetic. Go home before Sandy gets back.'

'Why isn't he here with you? I wouldn't leave you on your own...'

‘I’m not standing here arguing with you.’ Jayne moves to close the door but stops. She bends down and touches his shoulder. He tries to look up at her but his eyes can’t focus properly and his neck feels disconnected from his body.

‘Don’t you understand? I just can’t see you right now. It’s too raw.’

He doesn’t answer. She shakes him. ‘I’ll phone a taxi.’

‘Fuck off with your taxi! I don’t want a fucking taxi! I can manage,’ he yells, struggling to his feet. He staggers getting back into the car, then drives away.

Bloody Gary! Adam’s asleep now but his breathing’s irregular and he’s restless. Poor Adam has nightmares most nights, drenching him in sweat, and it takes me a long time to settle him back down. Sometimes he wets the bed. He’s nearly nine and hasn’t done that since he was three, but the doctor says it’ll get better in time.

Time. You think you have so much of it when you’re young. I remember in Ireland how time dragged. I couldn’t wait for the holidays to be over so I could go back to school, even though they bullied me and called me names. It was just to get back to being with people. I couldn’t bear the isolation at home. I thought it would help Adam getting back to school but if anything, the nightmares have got worse. So I sit here on Claire’s bed and watch, storing up my time with him, waiting. I can only do this at night. During the day I can’t help him at all.

Friday 16 May

7.25 a.m.
The Rise

'Time to get up, Adam.'

He stirs and rolls over, snuggling into his pillow. He's in the comfort zone, that twilight land that's between asleep and awake, where nightmares dissolve and reality hasn't yet kicked in.

'C'mon, sweetheart. Wakey, wakey, lemon shakey. You don't want to be late.'

He shrugs sleep off and opens eyes gummed a little with dried yellow crystals, which he wipes with the backs of his hands. Sitting up he yawns, then swings his legs over the side of the bed and moves automatically towards the door before turning round. Looking at the faint damp patch on the bottom sheet and pillow, he feels his crotch and looks bewildered.

'I'm dry, Mam, but the bed's wet.'

'You must've had another bad dream, sweetheart; it's sweat.' Jayne attempts a joke, 'Your skin's been leaking.' She smiles weakly and suggests, 'Go and get your shower. I'll change the sheets. Your clothes are over there.' She points to the pile in the corner on a stool. 'Hurry up now. Breakfast's laid.'

He wanders off to the bathroom and she can't help remembering how different everything is. Claire would've woken him up by bouncing on him and he'd have chased her, then splashed her from the shower as she peeped in and out round the bathroom door, using it as a shield. Jayne used to yell at them… Suddenly the sheet's too heavy; she'll have to do it later.

When Sandy came back, despite everything, I suppose I was grateful. I thought that it would be good for Adam to have at least someone around who could see to him. I was worse than useless. To give him his dues, Sandy was helpful at first. He answered the phone, kept people away and talked to the hospital when they phoned about Mam. He cooked meals for Adam and sat with me when I was shaking. But I couldn't bear him in bed with me, not after Gary, and I slept on top of Clare's bed. Sandy was spending most of the time out, looking for work he said, so the rows started again.

He didn't leave because we weren't sleeping together. No, his past came back again this morning in the shape of a leggy redhead, so he left, just like he had after Claire was born. Except this time, I saw him go. I don't miss him, but it was different then. Claire was so small, only three weeks old, and I felt I'd never be able to cope with two children on my own, but Adam saved me. He helped with his baby sister, feeding her, changing her, singing to her when she was crying. Come to think of it, he probably did more with her than I did. Poor lamb. To be saddled with me as a mother.

I remember once, it was last Bonfire Night and it was my turn to have the party. All the families in our close get together every year in someone's garden and we take turns hosting the party. Everyone decides beforehand what they'll bring and I was doing the toffee apples and baked potatoes. I was stressed to death trying to get everything ready and tidy before people arrived. Claire was toddling all over the place and followed Adam like his shadow. He was putting his toys away as I'd asked him to and she kept pulling them back out, wanting to play. I was getting more and more frustrated and I shouted at her. She started crying and sat down sobbing, her little head bent forward over her legs—how do babies do that?—and Adam picked her up and carried her to the settee where he cuddled her and sang nursery rhymes. She soon stopped howling and he made a game with her of tidying up. Later he said to me, 'She's only little, Mam. Don't shout at her, she doesn't understand.'

Now it's me who doesn't understand.

9.10 a.m.

'Hi there,' Lizzie says brightly as Jayne opens the door. 'How's things?'

'Not bad. About the same,' Jayne lies. She's not sure how to tell her about Sandy.

Lizzie follows Jayne into the kitchen, not looking at the dishes in the sink. 'Look, about tonight. The big seduction. Let's make it another time. To be honest, it's the last thing on my mind right now.'

'Sorry, I'd forgotten.' Jayne automatically reaches for the kettle but Lizzie stops her.

'I can't stop for coffee. I'm off to an interview.'

'Where at?'

'The estate office. I've got to be there for half eleven so just wanted to know if I can get you anything at the shops when I come back?'

'Oh...uh...don't think so.'

'Adam's got his trip on Wednesday. Did you need anything for his packed lunch? I'm getting John some of those little packets of lunchbox things—cheese and fruit—d'you want any for Adam?'

'Oh, God, I've forgotten. I've got a mind like a sieve—Mam always used to say that...About herself, not me...' And then Jayne cries.

Lizzie hugs her and passes a tissue from the box on the bench. Taking a deep breath, Jayne blows into it.

'Good luck with the interview,' she manages between sobs.

'Are you okay? Is Sandy around?' asks Lizzie.

‘I’m fine. Really. Christ, where does all this stuff come from? I must be waterlogged or something. You’ll come back and I’ll be all shrivelled up with this lot leaking out of me.’ Jayne manages a smile, which is returned. She follows Lizzie to the door.

10.31 a.m.
Merry Farm

Gary throws up ceremoniously in the toilet. This is his first experience of projectile vomiting and if he didn’t feel so bad he’d be impressed. His head pounds like a jackhammer, his skull and his eyeballs feel like the controls. Every time he moves them he has another bout of sickness accompanied by the pounding. Never again.

At last the sickness subsides, his stomach muscles relax and he staggers back into bed. He can hear Kumar downstairs scratching and forces himself to get up and let the dog out. The staircase conspires against him and he falls the last few steps, which jars his neck. Pain shoots up over the back of his head and lodges itself with the other pains behind his eyeballs. He tries shouting ‘Fuck!’ but the noise makes it worse and he resolves to refrain from speaking until this hangover shifts. Which could be quite some time.

Kumar, excited to see him yaps and jumps but Gary is too fragile to even pet the dog. He opens the door and the dog bounds out, watering every plant in sight for several minutes while Gary tries to re-negotiate the stairs and return to bed. Food. He forgot the dog food. Bugger. Back downstairs it is, this time more carefully. God, what on earth had he been thinking of? She’ll never speak to him now. What a complete and utter wanker! But even those thoughts are too much for him and after feeding the dog he climbs back to bed to nurse himself better. The situation with Jayne will have to wait.

11.15 a.m.
The Rise

Jayne shakes as she picks up the phone. She dials Lizzie's mobile, then changes her mind and puts it down. What can she say? She doesn't want a lecture but she feels she should let Lizzie know, to put her mind at rest. Steeling herself she picks the phone up again and dials.

'Hello?'

'Lizzie, it's me. You're not in yet?'

'Not yet. Are you okay?'

There's a long pause, then Jayne continues, 'Sandy's gone.'

'When?'

'This morning.'

There's another pause, then Lizzie says, 'Good. I'm glad you've seen sense and kicked him out. Did he—'

'I didn't kick him out. He left again.'

There's a pause, then Lizzie says, 'Oh, Jayne,' her voice softening.

'I know, I know. You don't have to say it.'

'Are you okay?' asks Lizzie.

'Yes. No. I dunno.'

'You sound dreadful. Can I get you anything?'

'No, I just need to rest. I'll be fine. Really.'

'I'll come over when I get back, if you like?' offers Lizzie.

Jayne hesitates then says, 'No, I want to be alone for a bit. Till Adam gets in from school.'

'Okay, but ring me. Promise?'

'I promise. 'Bye. And good luck with the interview.' Jayne puts the phone down and the tears come again, wetting her cheeks, dripping off her chin but she is oblivious to them. She heads for the settee and lies down.

1.17 p.m.
South Row, Nenthead
As soon as Lizzie gets home she looks up Gary's number and calls him. His answer machine is on so she leaves a message telling him the good news. Lizzie doesn't usually like interfering, but taking a few liberties now and again in Jayne's best interests isn't very bad. After all, Gary's perfect for Jayne, she just doesn't know it yet.

1.44 p.m.
Gary's head still hurts. He looks at the phone rather sheepishly and wonders what to say. The answer machine is flashing and he hesitates, hoping it's not from Jayne. If only he can apologize, sort things out with her, tell her how much she means to him…

1.50 p.m.
Crofter's Wood
There is a light showering of rain in the air, the kind you can almost breathe and it has its own special way of soaking after a while. Everything is covered in wisps of moisture and above, the sky is dramatic, with grey and black clouds worrying the hilltops; the trees, tall and dark, almost blend into them. The previous night squalls of wind battered through the squares of plantation and now several trees on the perimeter have cracked and fallen, producing a domino effect on some of the others.

Johnny has come equipped with rope and saw. Ignoring the newly felled trees—they take too long to dry and the green wood produces too much smoke—he carefully selects an old one, quickly removing extraneous branches. He then secures one end of the rope round the tree and the other he loops diagonally round his chest, under an armpit. He strains forward, testing the strength of the rope and the weight of the tree, then puts his head down and concentrates on moving forward, dragging the trunk behind him. It takes him over half an hour to reach his destination.

Arriving at his cottage Johnny wipes his brow, unties the trunk and turns to go back for another. He is running low on logs and these are just what he needs to keep him going for a while. Theoretically he's stealing, but he only takes the old ones the Major has no use for. Johnny feels good at the prospect of hard work and the rewards at the end of it. It will take him the rest of the day to cover his tracks, chop both trees into logs and stack them to dry out. If only every day could be like this, a sweet-sky sort of day, when the burden of loneliness is lifted and the brackish presence of his past is forgotten, if only for a little while. Then the dark thoughts and memories would be kept at bay just that bit longer.

2.06 p.m.
Coglin Mews

Sue puts her cup of coffee down on the coaster and opens the first page of the album. Curled up on the settee, dressed in a grey tracksuit and white tee-shirt, she is enjoying her day off. Every once in a while she likes to have a 'duvet day', where she doesn't both to get dressed or put on any make-up. This is one such day.

Something someone said yesterday got her thinking about who she looked like, her mam or her dad. She never really noticed a resemblance to either, nor did it bother her, but today, for some reason, she needs to see herself in one of them. To belong again. It also has to do with the situation with Grace, lying there, no one visiting; even her own daughter doesn't want her. It is probably coincidence, but since Grace arrived on the ward Sue has suddenly found herself experiencing emotions she has managed to control for years. It disturbs her, but for once she is going with it and not running away. Hence the photo album.

She was thirteen when it happened. It was the start of the summer holidays, each day of the six weeks ahead felt like unopened birthday presents. The car was hot and stuffy so the window was down because Sam, her ten-year-old brother, was feeling carsick. They were driving to the airport to catch a plane to Cyprus where her parents, both doctors, had hired a villa. What happened next came back to her in pieces over the years but there are still parts missing. She remembers her mother turning round in the seat yelling at them to get their heads down, her father struggling to control the car, Sam looking at her, his new sunglasses slightly askew as Sue tried to pull his head down onto his lap, then loud bangs, tearing metal, explosions, screaming and blackness. A lorry had jack-knifed ahead of them and they ended up in a pile-up of fourteen vehicles. Sue was the only survivor in their car.

The photos on the first page in the album show her as a baby in various poses with her parents. As she turns the pages she sees her life developing, her body changing. Enter Sam. His sweet baby face, the smell of his head, the softness of his skin; she thinks she remembers them but can't be sure she hasn't appropriated these memories from holding other people's babies. She so desperately needed to have something to hold onto in those first few years after the accident, yet the professional she is knows she may have created her own memories to fill the gaps. It is why she went in for mental health rather than mainstream nursing; the brain and its ability to heal and protect always fascinated her. But a bit of knowledge can be a mixed blessing. She knows the reason she's afraid to let people get close, close enough to be missed or to hurt her, but knowing why she's afraid doesn't stop the fear. *"There's no way through it, other than through it",* so they say, and she has not been prepared to go on that journey. At least, not yet.

She returns her thoughts to the album resting on her knee and continues searching for any facial similarities between herself, her parents and her brother.

2.30 p.m.
The Rise
Jayne picks up the phone to call Lizzie and hears the tone that indicates she's got messages. She dials 151 and hearing Gary's voice, deletes the message without listening to what he has to say. She slumps into a chair. She'll ask Lizzie about the interview later.

It's almost 3 o'clock and I still haven't done much except sit here by the window looking out into the garden. Adam will be home soon and the bed's still to strip. The dishes can wait. They've waited days already, another won't harm. There aren't many anyway—there's only the two of us now...Liz offers to help, but I should be able to do it myself....

4.03 p.m.
Adam runs in from school, banging the door shut behind him. Jayne hears his feet thumping upstairs, then

there's another slam and his bedroom door rocks in its frame.

'Adam? What's wrong, baby?' she asks, shouting up to him from the bottom of the stairs. She removes the rubber gloves from her hands and starts to climb the stairs. She has been cleaning the kitchen worktops and was feeling a small sense of achievement. Now this!

Pushing open the door Jayne sees his small body face down on the bed, his hands in fists.

'What's wrong, Adam?' she asks again.

'Go away!' is his response.

'I'm not going anywhere, honey. Now tell me what's wrong.'

'Nothing!'

'Well it doesn't look like nothing. Who's upset you?'

Adam turns over and faces her. 'I'm not going to school next week,' he asserts.

'Do I get to know why?' asks Jayne.

'John's an idiot! I'm supposed to be his partner for the week, so I'm not going.'

Jayne sits on the bed and draws him towards her, maintaining eye contact. 'Why've you fallen out with him?'

Adam looks scornfully at her. 'He winds me up all the time. Then I get into trouble. It's not fair! She never sees what he does, just me. I hate him!'

Pulling her son into her arms, Jayne rocks him quietly. 'It'll be all right,' she promises, holding him tight.

5.10 p.m.

Adam drags his bag across the kitchen floor before plonking it on one of the chairs and taking out his PE kit for Jayne to wash. His face is pale and drawn and there is the slightest shadow of dark circles around his eyes.

'Are you okay, Mam?' Looking at her tears he asks, 'Where is he this time?'

'He's gone, sweetheart,' Jayne replies. Sitting back in the chair she wipes the tears away and asks, 'Now what do you want—fish fingers or beef burgers?'

'I'm not hungry.'

'You have to eat, Adam.' She turns to face him, to look into his eyes, but he avoids her gaze.

'You don't.'

'I will. Later.' It is her turn to avoid eye contact, looking down instead at the kettle, coffee and cigarettes. She has started smoking again.

'Me too.'

'This isn't helping, Adam.' She looks at his young face, its skin slack, hanging there. Silence ticks away between them as they avoid each other's eyes.

'I'm going to my room.'

'I'll call when it's ready. Are fish fingers okay? And I'll try some too. All right?'

'All right.'

He drags his bag off the seat and up the stairs to his room. The bumping noise it makes is comforting, breaking the silence of the house.

7.13 p.m.
The Rise

Adam is having a bath and Jayne is on the toilet when Adam asks, 'Mam, what happens when you die?'

'Adam…I… you go to heaven.'

'John says there is no heaven. That when you die you're worm food.'

'You shouldn't listen to John.'

'But is it true? What really happens when you die?'

‘Adam, I really can’t talk about this right now.’ Her voice has started wobbling again. She has to get away, so she wipes herself and leaves the bathroom, throwing herself onto the bed to suffocate the sobs.

It takes her a few minutes to regain control, then she notices it. It’s too quiet. There are no bath sounds, no splashing. Hurrying back into the bathroom she finds Adam lying on his back under the water. Her breath turns to icicles as she yanks him upwards onto his feet and shakes him.

‘Don’t do that! Don’t ever do that again!’ she screams, crushing him to her chest, suffocating him with her fear. She can feel her ribs sticking into the side of his face as she holds him there. He struggles to free himself, gasping for air. She releases him a little but still holds him, forcing him to face her.

‘Don’t you ever, ever do that again! What on earth were you thinking of?’ Feeling the rage rise within her she turns him round, smacking him hard on his bottom, leaving red fingerprints there, like bloodstains on his soft white skin. He is red-faced but doesn’t cry. He just looks at her, spearing her with his glare.

Jayne is shocked at her actions. ‘Oh, Adam, I’m sorry. I’m really, really sorry. But what were you doing?’

There is silence for a few seconds, then he whispers, ‘You’re always crying. It’s quiet under there.’

More gently now, she holds him close and hugs him, but he is as stiff as a toy soldier.

7.19 p.m.
Fletcher Ward

The wind sighs softly, waking Grace from her dream. She has been fighting it, tears silvering her cheeks, but now she surrenders to the memories…

You're nine years old and on a swing in the garden. Your long hair is tied back into plaits that are too tight at the temples, giving your face a stretched, surprised look. Mother is pushing you on the swing, higher and higher, and you scrunch your eyes up in fear, unable to look at the see-sawing ground beneath you. Dad is reading a newspaper at the table Mother has set up on the lawn and occasionally glances over at you both.
'I think I'll get some water. It's a hot one today, right enough,' he comments, rising from the chair. He makes his way into the kitchen, then it happens.

Suddenly you are catapulted out of the swing and into the air. Your body arcs momentarily and in that time, before you hit the ground, you see Mother's face, smiling. As you connect with the ground and the lawnmower you hear something snap and feel tremendous pain in both legs and the right side of your head and face. You scream, then pass out.

In the hospital the nurses are very kind. They give you boiled sweets from their pockets and extra helpings of ice cream when it's on the menu. You're quite well known here, being a 'clumsy' child, and enjoy the attention and sympathy they give you. If only you could stay here till the legs heal! You've been here for two days' observation, in case of concussion, but now it's time to go home. Dad has come to pick you up and is in with the doctor. You hear raised voices coming from the doctor's room, then Dad bursts out, his face red with controlled anger.

'Are these all your things?' he asks, indicating the tartan bag on the bed.

You nod, he scoops the bag up and attaches it by its handle to the wheelchair and pushes you out of the ward, towards the main entrance where the car is parked.

Once he has got you settled in the car he turns to you and asks, 'Grace, you'd tell me if there was anything... wouldn't you?'

Your heart races. He knows! But you can't tell, so you nod, sheepishly, praying he'll not believe you. Hoping he'll see through the charade. Once again, you're disappointed.

'That's what I thought. Bloody man doesn't know what the hell he's talking about. But you have to be more careful, my darling. You're just far too accident-prone. One day it could be very serious. You could hurt yourself badly, and we don't want that now, do we?'

'No, Dad.' Your voice is flat, devoid of any emotion.

'That's my girl. Here's Mam. She's bought a lovely new skirt to cheer you up.'

You watch Mother approach and feel the rays of malevolence radiate from her.

Saturday 17 May

8.22 a.m.
The Rise

Jayne can hear Adam moving in his room. Normally on Saturdays he would be running round the house chasing Claire, or watching cartoons with her. He always got up with Claire to let Jayne lie in bed a bit longer and was good at setting the table for breakfast at nine. They breakfasted together—waffles or pancakes—while planning their weekend, which usually involved football at some point, either watching or playing.

There are times when Jayne thinks she can't bear the loss, not just of her daughter but of her son too. He is not the same little boy hell-bent on packing fun and games into every minute—he's serious and solemn and she doesn't know how to cope with this, let alone the overwhelming emptiness without Claire.

Forcing herself up Jayne calls to him and he appears in the doorway.

'What do you want to do today?'

'I dunno. Nothing. I don't care.'

This is hard. 'How about we go to John's? He's got some new games for his computer.'

'No. I don't want to.'

'Well, what do you want to do? Go for a walk? Play in the garden?'

'No. I don't want to go out. It's not the same,' and he turns and runs into his room, slamming the door.

8.31 a.m.
Disused Shaft near Crofter's Hush

Johnny is making his way along the tunnel to the disused shaft, taking care not to fall through the floor. There are all sorts of false floors and he can't be too careful; deep water is often backed up behind falls of shale. The original timbers are rotted in places so ladders are also hazardous. In the 1950s, when there was a decline in workings, many shafts and levels were closed. When they were re-opened they were found to be flooded and further decline was created by local people robbing wood and stones causing tunnels to collapse.

Johnny doesn't want to be seen—other farmers aren't as understanding as the Major—so he uses this route rather than over the fells. Accessing the shafts and horse levels is easier in places that have been excavated or renovated, but he tries to avoid these as he never knows when he'll come into contact with cavers or day trippers. Most of the horse levels were originally interlinked but now cross-valley links are no longer traversable because of cave-ins and flooding. However, it is possible, though very strenuous, to make a through trip of the Nent Valley via various sumps and rises from Capelcleugh Mine to Nentsberry Haggs Level. He's become familiar with them all over the years, especially the disused and inaccessible, and has devised several detailed escape plans and contingencies should the need arise.

The light from his carbide lamp shines on wet walls, revealing all its underground beauty; turquoise-blue brain-like mineral deposits from copper, yellowy-orange from lichen, and further along the walls are white and cream from quartz and calcite. He loves the sheer awesomeness of nature, of her power, her transience, her ability to heal and her breath-taking beauty.

Bringing his attention back to the present he moves forward. His haul today is a bit meagre—only three crows and a hedgehog—but it's better than nothing. The rucksack is light on his back but it still snags occasionally on the roof of the tunnel. He makes a mental note to collect plenty of water to boil the crows—all carrion need to be boiled to get rid of parasites—and clay to roast the hedgehog because the spines come off in the clay when cooked. It is not a great feast, but he still has plenty of dried meat in his store. He always tries to make sure he consumes enough calories and vitamins because he finds being underground uses up a lot more than on the surface. He can't always guarantee he will have enough to eat so he started planting potatoes and different dark green vegetables—broccoli, cabbage, sprouts—years ago. He has added a few more items to his repertoire at different times—peas, onions and lettuce—but the amount of water needed throughout the summer, which has to be hauled out of the river and carried, makes it too time consuming, so he sticks to potatoes and alternates the green vegetables each year. He can supplement his diet from the fields and hedgerows. After all, he is a hunter, not a farmer. Now just this bit to watch and he's nearly there.

9.08 a.m.
Path through woods near Merry Farm

Kumar yaps happily as she retrieves the stick. Her tail wags as she drops the stick at Gary's feet and watches it greedily. Gary doesn't pick it up straight away so the dog looks up at him. Despite himself and the depression that's settling on him like soot, he smiles. The dog looks at him expectantly so he reaches down for the stick only to have it snatched away by Kumar.

'Drop it, you daft bugger. I can't throw it if you don't drop it.'

The dog dances round him, then drops the stick again. This time Gary is swift to grab it and with all his strength he hurls it into the wood. As he watches the dog bounce after it and dive through the undergrowth, his mood lifts. Within seconds Kumar is back and the ballet with the stick takes place again and again, until they reach the end of the path and home. The particles of depression shift again and settle on Gary's shoulders. He's really fucked up big time. If only…

6.45 p.m.
Coglin Mews

It is Sue's birthday party and it has taken an age to get ready. However, it's been worth it and she looks great, even if she does say so herself. Her outfit consists of a strappy black top over black stretch crepe trousers. The top is almost see-through and has silver threads and a sprinkling of rhinestones embroidered across the front, catching the light. A necklace of several fine silver strands tied together by a single strand caresses her throat, before dangling down delicately into her cleavage. On her wrist is a matching silver bracelet and her ears contain rhinestone studs. She feels like the wicked stepmother in *Snow White* standing before her mirror, hoping she's the fairest of them all tonight. And wicked she will be, if she gets the chance!

Turning away from the mirror she consults her list. There are only the mints to check off and put into the box and then she can leave, but she stands there, shaking. Another drink, that's what she needs. She picks up the glass she is using from the bedside table and takes it into the kitchen where she refills it with vodka. She has run out of cranberry juice, so orange will have to do. Is this a sign of things going wrong? Of course not. She swallows the drink far too quickly and returns to the mirror. You're beautiful, girl, that's what you are, so get out there and get your man. Yeah, right.

7.33 p.m.

Lounge, the Duke of Northumberland

The guests have started to arrive. Sue greets them all enthusiastically, hugging and kissing them, French-style, on both cheeks. Overbalancing a little in her high heels she tells herself to slow down with the booze, but another arrives to join the three she already has waiting on the table.

-Pace yourself and you'll be fine. Just don't disgrace yourself. Not tonight. You need all your wits about you if you're going to get off with Darren.-

Lisa told Sue that she's meeting him for a drink before the party because she doesn't want to walk in by herself—since when did that bother her?—so Sue is feeling a bit anxious about it all. But then Lisa is her best friend. She wouldn't do anything.

8.45 p.m.

The party is in full swing when Darren and Lisa arrive. Sue rushes over to meet them and there are hugs all round. Sue admires Darren's beige cargo pants and sunburst-orange short-sleeved shirt, and Lisa's short, almost see-through, dress in a black and white geometric pattern, then adds, 'I thought you two had got lost.'

'Sorry. We were talking and lost track of time.' Lisa giggles.

'Well you're here now, and that's the main thing,' Sue says as she hugs Lisa who is surveying the scene.

Lisa is impressed. 'Hey, this is great. Loads more people have turned up; much more than I'd have thought.'

Sue surveys the party and agrees, 'Yeah, it's not bad. And the music's really good too. Come on, get yourselves a drink. The food won't be long. They're serving in about ten minutes.' She turns to Darren. 'You're quiet, Darren. Lost your tongue?'

'I can't get a word in with you two. You look great by the way, doesn't she, Lisa?' His eyes are staring at Sue's breasts. Under his gaze the nipples tingle and harden.

'Yeah, great. Come on, Darren, let's get that drink.' Lisa grabs his hand and moves to take him towards the bar. 'Do you want one, Sue?'

'No, thanks, I've had enough to sink a battleship. Maybe later, when this lot's been pissed out.'

'You've such a lovely turn of phrase,' Darren comments, wrinkling his nose at her. He disengages his hand from Lisa's and tells her, 'You get the drinks in, Lisa, it's your turn. I want to dance with the birthday girl.'

'Fine. Whatever.' Lisa turns, rather disgruntled, and walks to the bar alone. Her hips sway exaggeratedly, the line of her thong clearly visible through the fine material of her dress. Darren's eyes never leave Lisa's retreating figure until she's obscured by Ben, one of Sue's neighbours, who follows Lisa to the bar.

'Come on then, Birthday Girl,' Darren says as he turns back to face Sue and offers her his hand. He leads her out onto the dance floor amongst all the other dancers crowding the small wooden area at the bow end. 'So, what's it like to be thirty?' he breathes into her ear.

'You should know; you're thirty-two.'

'Thirty-two isn't thirty, is it?'

'No, but unless you've got some sort of dementia you should remember what it was like two years ago.'

'Aha, but two years ago isn't now. What's it like to be thirty, now?'

‘Compared to what? Twenty-nine? Ten? Or sweet sixteen?’

‘Oh, shut up and dance. This is getting far too deep for me.’ He pulls her into him so that she has to put her legs inside his to move. Her hip brushes his groin and his right leg moves seductively against hers. She could dance like this all night, but unfortunately the disc jockey announces that the food is served. The music changes to background sounds as the lights are turned up. Sue puts her hands to her face in mock horror and says,

‘Oh no, not the light, not the light! I burn, I burn!’ and pretends to crumple up and shrivel, much to Darren’s amusement. She turns as she straightens up and in her peripheral vision sees Lisa standing behind her with a drink in each hand just as Ben is somehow pushed backwards into Lisa. The contents of the drinks fly out of Lisa’s hands, one of the glasses smashing on the wooden floor. Sue is hit full in the face with a pint of lager, drenching her hair and top, splattering her trousers. She is speechless for a few seconds, but as Darren and Lisa laugh hysterically she turns and runs away, taking refuge in the toilets.

Looking in the mirror she sees the extent of the damage, and it’s not good. Her hair is sticky and flat against her head, her makeup is smudged and the top has become transparent in places. What is worse is that she smells like a brewery. It’s all she can do not to cry in front of the two other girls in there. They are not from her party but offer to go and get someone for her. She thanks them and tells them she’s fine, but when they leave she locks herself in a cubicle and breaks down. She was getting on so well, why did this have to happen? And where’s Lisa? Some friend she turned out to be.

As if on cue she hears Lisa come into the toilet and call her name.

'Sue? Are you okay?' Lisa giggles.

Sue sobs from behind the toilet door. 'Of course I'm not bloody okay. What a stupid bloody question.'

'What're you going to do?' asks Lisa, applying more lip gloss and checking her mascara in the mirror.

'Huh, a lot you care. You seem to think it's hilarious,' Sue sobs.

'I'm sorry. It's not funny.' Lisa starts to giggle again, but manages to suppress it enough to justify her actions. 'I couldn't help it, it was just the way it looked. You'd have laughed if it happened to me.'

'Well it didn't. I can't go out like this, I'm a mess.'

'I'm sure it's not as bad as all that. Come on out and let's look.'

Reluctantly Sue opens the door and Lisa giggles again at the sight of her. 'I'm sorry, I'm sorry, but you look awful,' and she collapses into a fit of the giggles.

'Great. I'm glad you find it so funny. At least I've made your night,' Sue manages, sarcastically.

'I'm sorry, I can't help it,' Lisa apologises, unsuccessfully trying to stifle her laughter. 'Look on the bright side, you can always get Darren to take you home,' she manages to say between laughter and crossing her legs. 'I must have a pee, move over.' Then from inside the cubicle, 'Look, I'll go outside and ask Darren to take you home to get changed and then it's up to you after that. Okay?'

'No. It's not okay. I don't want him seeing me like this. I look dreadful.'

'Stop whingeing and let's tidy you up. He's had a good drink so he'll not notice what you look like,' offers Lisa.

'Sure he won't,' she responds sarcastically.

‘Stop worrying and get your head under that tap,’ orders Lisa.

Obediently Sue does as she is told and Lisa runs the water and tries to get the majority of lager out of Sue’s hair. That done, she uses the hand drier to blow it dry whilst Sue uses a compact mirror to touch up her makeup.

Lisa nods approvingly. ‘There you go, that’s not bad at all. Now will I ask Darren or not?’

‘What d’you think he’ll say?’ Sue is nervous again.

‘I don’t know till I ask. So, d’you want me to ask?’

‘Oh God. What if he says no?’

‘Then he says no.’

‘What if he says yes?’

‘Then it’s up to you.’ Lisa winks at her friend.

‘All right, but I’m coming with you. And be subtle, will you?’

‘As always.’

9.20 p.m.

The two leave the toilet and make their way back into the disco lounge where everyone is standing around tables devouring the food. Darren is chatting to a slim blonde who looks joined at the hip to her boyfriend Carl, who has a proprietary arm clasped tightly around her waist. Lisa calls Darren over.

‘Glad to see you’re all right,’ he says to Sue.

‘She’s not though, is she? I mean, she needs to go home and get changed. Her clothes are ruined and she needs to get something dry on. It’s her birthday and she can’t spend the rest of the night looking like a beer mat, can she?’

‘I suppose not.’ He turns to Sue. ‘But you look fine to me.’

Lisa interrupts. 'Darren, she can't walk home by herself. Why don't you take her and bring her back when she's ready?'

'Why don't you?' he asks Lisa.

'Don't worry, Darren, I'll be fine,' Sue says huffily over her shoulder as she turns and leaves.

'Now look what you've done,' says Lisa as she chases after Sue.

Rolling his eyes heavenwards, Darren follows the pair out and catches up with them on the gangplank.

Sunday 18 May

11.08 a.m.
Coglin Mews

Sue opens her eyes and shuts them again as the sun streaming in through the window feels like it is slicing the top of her head off. Her eyeballs hurt and she is afraid that if she moves her head the pain will kill her. The hangover is bad enough, but then she remembers the previous evening and shudders with shame. What on earth was she thinking of?

It had started innocently enough, just a bit of fun. She was getting undressed in the bedroom and could hear muffled giggles and slurping sounds, so in anger charged out of the bedroom in only her underwear. The underwear she'd wanted Darren to see after she seduced him. He lurched towards her and started snogging her, but then things kind of got out of hand and Lisa's tongue was in her mouth, Darren's hands on her breasts and inside her thong, and now she doesn't know what to do or say to either of them. Her face burns with shame.

-Oh God, oh God. How can I face them? They're workmates, for God's sake.-

Her skin crawls and she feels vulnerable and exposed. Turning towards the wall she cries softly into her pillow, remembering all the guests she just left at the party without a word, and all the explaining she needs to do.

11.20 a.m.
Crofter's Wood

There's a dark mist blowing in from the hills, dirtying the clouds. The weather is changing and Johnny feels unsettled. He has been having lots of nightmares again and is tired and jittery. What he wouldn't do for a good drink to knock him out for a day or two! He has not had a drink for years but still craves it. The sight, the smell, the glug of it filling the glass. Even the hiss of gas from opening a ring-pull. What he's knocked back in the army and afterwards…well…he's had enough to last him several lifetimes. But he still misses its seductive power.

A twig snaps and he is on the alert. That shouldn't have happened. He is better trained than that. Losing concentration costs lives so he quickly shrugs off reminiscences about booze and returns his attention to the job in hand. He has already been out trapping but he needs something to help him sleep and he knows just the place to get it.

1.46 p.m.
The Rise

Jayne has made a big effort today. She has been up and dressed since ten and prepared a simple version of Sunday lunch. Normally she cooks everything from scratch but she asked Lizzie to get Auntie Bessie's roast potatoes and Yorkshire puddings, a tin of peas (Adam's favourite) and some chicken breast. The gravy has not gone lumpy and all in all it is quite a successful meal. The problem is, neither she nor Adam feel like eating. Lunch lies cold, pushed around on their plates.

'Don't you like it?' Jayne asks.

'I'm not hungry, Mam,' he replies.

'Me neither. What would you like to do this afternoon?'

He sighs, his pale forehead creased in a frown.

'Nothing.'

'Don't you want to play with John?'

'I dunno. Later.' He rises from the table and slowly makes his way upstairs, like an old man dragging sacks of coal behind him. Jayne separates the food and scrapes the vegetables into the compost carrier, the meat into the bin, then cries when she remembers telling Claire about compost and wormeries. Oh God. Why Claire? No answer comes.

3.30 p.m.
Lounge, Fletcher Ward
Grace is having a fairly good day. She has been well enough to get to the dining room for meals, has engaged in a short conversation with Harvey and Muriel, and been to see the craft workshop. The art therapist, Jasmijn Marcusse, a pretty, fresh-faced young woman from The Netherlands, doesn't work weekends but Grace has been assured that tomorrow she can use the workshop and paint if she feels up to it. At the moment she is listening to Harvey's music, a book resting, unread, on her lap. She is participating in everything asked of her, keeping staff unaware of the landscape she visits inside her head.

7.09 p.m.
Merry Farm
The whisky bottle is nearly empty on the coffee table and Gary is trying to watch television but his eyes cannot focus properly. This is ridiculous! He hates whisky. And it's not helping at all, it's only making him more maudlin. Another bout of self-pity washes over him, filling his eyes with tears. He lets them dribble down his cheeks and onto his tee-shirt, which by this time is getting quite wet. He looks at the phone, but then logic kicks in and he realises he will only make matters worse by phoning her in this state. So he pours another drink and lights a cigarette. Maybe if he smokes

and drinks himself to death…but no. She wouldn’t care then either.

Mon 19 May

10.20 a.m.
Merry Farm

Gary has slept in. Another hangover rages and the ringing of the telephone isn't helping. Shit! It's probably Scottie. He was meant to pick him up to go to Carlisle for timber. This has got to stop. He can't keep this up and still run his business. He has to get a grip. She'll come round eventually. She has to. Right now his priority is getting ready and out, but first he has to answer this bloody telephone. Then he remembers the dog hasn't been fed or taken out. Dear God…

11.50 a.m.
St Julian's Hospital

So far Sue has managed to avoid Darren and Lisa but as lunchtime approaches she knows she cannot avoid them any longer. Taking a deep breath she opens the staffroom door and breezes in.

'Hiya. All right?' asks Lisa.

'Yeah. You?' Sue responds. This is awkward.

'Want some?' Lisa holds out a packet of Maltesers.

'No, thanks. I've got a salad with me. Where's Darren?'

'He's not in today. He's on that course in Manchester, remember?'

'Oh, right.' There's a long silence until Lisa pipes up, 'Look, about Saturday...I—'

'We all had far too much to drink. It's no big deal.' Sue is desperate to drop the subject.

'But it is. I really enjoyed it. Didn't you?'

Sue feels nausea rising. 'I'd rather have my fun with him on my own, thanks.'

'Ooh, you greedy cow! Share and share alike, that's my motto.' Lisa laughs, but her eyes aren't smiling.

‘You know how much I like Darren. It’s not right.’

Again Lisa laughs. ‘I never took you for a prude. Look, it’s only sex. You put it about a bit. It’s not like it’s with strangers, is it? I mean, look at all the risks you take picking up blokes in bars.’

Sue’s indignant. ‘That’s different. And anyway, I like Darren more than that.’

‘If you want the “forever after” thing then think again. Darren’s the biggest commitment-phobe I’ve ever met.’

Sue struggles with rising emotions. ‘Maybe he’s not met the right person, that’s all,’ she insists, but she knows the words are hollow and clichéd.

‘Will you listen to yourself! How long have you known Darren? How many girls have lasted longer than a month? Get real, Sue.’

‘Well, I’ll never find out how he feels about me with you sticking your oar in, will I?’

Lisa flounces up out of the chair. ‘Whatever. Forget I mentioned it. But don’t say I didn’t warn you.’

1.10 p.m.

Back on the ward Sue is distracted. Entering Grace’s room it takes a couple of seconds to realise that Grace isn’t staring at the wall or out of the window. As she moves closer Grace smiles and says, ‘Your aura’s changed. It’s gone grey. You’re upset. Be careful who you trust.’

‘Excuse me?’

‘Your aura. It tells me a lot. You’re not happy. You’re out of balance. You have conflicting emotions.’

‘I don’t understand. How—?’

‘Can I use the phone please?’ Grace is agitated, moving from one foot to the other.

‘Grace, what are—’

'Can I use the phone please?' Her voice is getting shrill so Sue tries to placate her.

'Of course you can. Who would you like to speak to?'

'My daughter. I need to speak to her.'

'That's fine, Grace, but I should to warn you that she may not want to speak to you. I've tried contacting her on your behalf but she wouldn't talk to me.'

'I need to speak to her. I need to tell her…'

'I know. But we have to think about your treatment and how we can help you cope in the event she won't speak to you.' Sue hesitates then asks, 'We haven't been able to find any of your previous records. We think you may have had this problem before and it would help us to look at any previous treatments or diagnoses you might have had. Have you been in hospital before?'

'I need to phone Jayne.'

'And I need to know—'

'After I've phoned. All right?'

'I can't stop you phoning her but I would recommend you speak to Dr Norman first.'

'I need to speak to Jaynie.' Grace is getting really agitated now. Sue tries to calm her down but isn't successful.

'I haven't any money. Where's my money?' Grace asks.

'Let's talk to Dr. Norman,' Sue says as she gently invites Grace to accompany her to the doctor's office.

8.20 p.m.

At last they have given you money. It is dark in the corridor so you turn on the light to see the numbers on the payphone.

-There must be a storm brewing. It's no wonder with all this heat lately.-

Your heart is pounding and breath exits your body in rags as you pick up the handset and dial. Your mouth is dry and your tongue in danger of sticking permanently to the roof of your mouth.

-It's ringing. Perhaps she's not in. Perhaps she doesn't answer after a certain time of night. Put it down, call another—

'Hello?' She answered. Just to hear her voice is wonderful.

'Jaynie, it's me.'

'Why do you do that?'

'What?'

'Call me that stupid baby name. Jayne. My name's Jayne.'

'I'm sor—' You try to explain but she won't let you.

'I've said I don't want to talk to you.'

'Please, Jaynie. Please. Don't put the phone down.'

The dialling tone clicks and it's too much. You can't keep fighting any more if she won't talk to you. You feel your strength ebbing away as you fall to the floor. Energy seeps out of your pores, dripping onto the carpet as you spread like a puddle of warm water. Mother's laughing again. She goads you but you've no strength left. She screams at you to get up but her voice is receding as you're absorbed by the carpet.

Hands under your armpits raise and transport you to a soft resting place. Warm breath gently smudges the hairs covering your arms, legs and knees. Your brow is stroked and strands of hair coaxed from your eyes. You're tired. So, so tired. If they'll just go away and let you sleep… But the light won't go out. You want the blackness, but it doesn't come. You scrunch up your eyes to keep out the dazzling brightness.

8.27 p.m.
The Rise

Jayne runs to the toilet to be sick. Lizzie follows her and rubs her back until she's finished.

'Who was that?' she asks.

'Just my bloody mother, that's all,' Jayne replies.

'How is she?' enquires Lizzie, still rubbing Jayne's back, aware of a stiffening in the back muscles.'

'How the hell should I know?' Jayne shrugs Lizzie away and goes back into the living room, Lizzie following her.

'Jayne, she's your mother.'

Jayne plonks down on the settee. 'Not anymore.'

'Look, I know you don't want to hear this—'

'Then why say it?'

'Because I'm your best friend and I care about you. She didn't do it on purpose, you know.'

'How the hell do you know that?' Jayne's up and pacing, trying to find her cigarettes.

'Come on, Jayne. You don't honestly think she wanted that to happen, do you?'

Jayne stops what she's doing and stares at Lizzie. 'Look, Lizzie, I know you mean well but you have no idea what my mother's capable of. She's totally irresponsible and has been for years. She abandoned me when I was four. I had to live in a convent for two years.'

'You never told me this. Why did she abandon you?'

Jayne's off again, pacing. She finds her cigarettes and starts looking for her lighter.

'She said it was severe depression but she'd always been loopy. You've no idea the bullying I had to put up with because of her, always talking to herself. And then there were the visions. Premonitions. That sort of thing.'

'How does that make you think she deliberately…'

Angry now, Jayne flashes at Lizzie. 'She's just like her mother. She was loopy too.'

Lizzie reasons with her, trying to calm her down. 'You said you never met her mother, so how do you know that?' There is no answer from Jayne so she continues, 'Oh, come on. Don't you think it's about time you started talking to her. Let her explain what happened with Claire—'

'I know what happened! Adam told me! The police told me!' Jayne's voice is shrill and angry. Pushing Lizzie aside she moves towards the kitchen where she fills the kettle and starts breathing deeply in an effort to calm down. She looks at Lizzie and confides, 'Someone from the hospital rang just after Claire's funeral. She said she wanted to talk about Mam. Mam wasn't getting better and I told her I don't care. I really don't. She may be my mother but I can't forgive her.'

Lizzie tries to embrace Jayne but is pushed away, so she offers, 'I've read somewhere that there's no healing without forgiveness—'

'Oh, please. Not that crap! Look, just butt out and mind your own business, will you, and leave me alone!'

Lizzie walks out the house and slams the front door. Jayne still hasn't asked how the interview went.

Tuesday 20 May

8.15 a.m.

South Row, Nenthead

Next morning, after tossing and turning all night, Lizzie comes to a decision. She discussed it with her husband, Derek, who warned her repeatedly not to interfere, but she feels duty bound to do something. After all, she and Jayne have been best friends for years, even if sometimes it has seemed a one-way street. Like now.

Not particularly handsome by other people's standards, Derek's ear lobes, eyelashes and sausage fingers do it for Lizzie every time. He is hard working, giving his job his full attention when there, filling his days but not his heart. He is ambitious for the quality of life, not for attainment or possessions. He is intelligent, attentive and hasn't a jealous bone in his body. And, more importantly, he loves Lizzie unconditionally. He always encourages her to do whatever she wants, never interferes or tells her what to do. Until now. Which is why she's agonising so much about what to do about Jayne. Still, it's her friend, her problem.

Picking up the phone she dials the hospital.

8.20 a.m.

Fletcher Ward

Sue is at her desk in the office when the call comes through.

'Hello, Fletcher Ward. Can I help you?'

'I hope so. It's about Grace Watson,' offers Lizzie.

'Are you a relative?' asks Sue, hopeful of some sort of breakthrough with the family.

'No, but—'

Sue's disappointed. 'I'm sorry, but I can't discuss a patient's case.'

'No, you don't understand—I'm ringing to give you some information.'

'Can I ask who's speaking please?' asks Sue, opening Grace's file.

'My name is Lizzie Waites and I'm a friend of Jayne Freeman, Grace's daughter.'

'I see.' Sue pauses, crossing her fingers. 'Does Mrs Freeman know you're calling?'

'Not really. No.'

Sue uncrosses her fingers. It was a bit too much to hope for.

Lizzie continues. 'The thing is, she told me you'd rung and needed information about Grace, background stuff, that kind of thing, to help her get well.'

'Go on.' Sue's pen is poised, ready to make notes.

'Well, I know she was in hospital in Co. Kerry for two years after some sort of breakdown or accident. That would be way back in about, let's see...nineteen-eighty or 'eighty-one. Before that she was in some sort of Catholic home for unmarried mothers near there; that's where she was sent to have Jayne. Grace wouldn't give Jayne up, so one of the priests arranged for her to live on a farm nearby.'

Sue scribbles throughout Lizzie's speech. She asks, 'Any other medical establishment she may have been in?'

'Not that I know of. She's very…oh, what can I say? Private. She's very nice but always keeps people at a distance. And she loves to paint. She's an artist, you know. Quite successful too. I think Jayne told me she picked it up in hospital—some sort of therapy thing that she found she was good at.'

'Thanks, Mrs Waites, that's been very useful. How is Mrs Freeman?' Sue puts the pen down and listens carefully.

‘Oh, you know. “As well as can be expected”. Actually, I’m sick to death of that phrase but I can’t think of a better one.’

‘Well, thanks for phoning. And if you could get Mrs Freeman to speak to Grace, it would be a great help.’

Lizzie pauses. ‘I’ll try but I’m not holding my breath.’

‘Thanks for calling.’

‘Bye.’

Closing the file on the desk Sue opens the filing cabinet and pulls out a directory. This is going to take a lot of tracking down…

2.00 p.m.
Meadow nr Merry Farm

Gary strides across the fell, then down through the meadow. Kumar jumps up at him, yapping happily. The exercise feels good and Gary’s head starts to clear. He has to do something to get Jayne’s attention, to show her that he’s reliable and nothing like Sandy. He starts to fantasize about different ways of being a hero and rescuing her, but eventually Kumar wins and he turns his full attention on her,

‘Daft bloody dog,’ he asserts affectionately.

2.23 p.m.
Nenthead School

Anna Hart has been at the school since September, completing her probationary year. Young and vibrant, she has lots of new ideas and approaches, which the school has welcomed. Popular with the children she enjoys teaching mixed-year groups and is busy helping Sonny with his collage when a disturbance breaks out.

‘Adam! Leave him alone! Adam!’ Miss Hart pulls the two boys apart. John is screaming and Adam has a pair of scissors in his hand. She checks John for any damage, then marches outside with Adam, holding his hand tightly. Swinging him round to face her she asks, 'What was all that about?'

Silence.

'Adam, I'm asking you a question. What happened in there?'

Still nothing. Adam is staring at his feet, refusing to meet her eyes. She hunkers down and leans her body in towards him to try to make eye contact but he steps back a little. She waits, but there is still no response from him. She sighs and speaks softly to him.

'I know you're having a hard time—'

'I'm not!'

His yell takes her by surprise and she rocks backwards a little on her heels.

'Adam, it's me you're talking to—'

'Don't care.'

'Come on, let's not make this worse than it already is. Do you want me to send you to Mrs Graham?'

'Don't care.' Adam is defiant, but still looking at his shoes.

'I know that's not true. Can't you tell me what's wrong? Why did you attack John?'

Again, silence.

'Look, Adam, you're not leaving me any choice. If you don't tell me what happened then I'm afraid I'll have to send you to Mrs Graham. She'll have to contact your mam again. You don't want that, do you?'

'I don't care.'

'What will your mam think?' she ventures. That does the trick. He looks up, so she continues, 'You should be helping her at a time—'

Suddenly he pushes her; she overbalances, then falls to the ground as he races past her and tries to get out the front door but isn't quite tall enough to undo the security lock. Panic on his face, he bolts through the hall where Year 3 are having PE with Mrs Bolton, then on through the art rooms and finally escapes outside after barging past Mr Harrison, a bald-headed, sandal-wearing peripatetic music teacher, as he backs into the building carrying a huge pile of books. The books fly upwards and despite a valiant attempt by Mr Harrison to catch them, most end up on the floor.

'What the hell—!'

'Stop him!' yells Miss Hart, but it's too late. She watches Adam disappear through the school gates.

2.27 p.m.
Overwater

Outside the yard he tugs at his tie, managing to free his neck from its grip. He throws it down onto the ground, along with two buttons from his shirt, which have been ripped off in the process. He runs without a backward glance, past Nenthead Mining Heritage Centre, past the pond and up through the old riverbed of Dowgang Hush, named after the process called hushing.

Hushing is a way of extracting lead from just under the surface. A dam was created at the top of the hill forming a reservoir and when it was full it was broken and the water rushed through the valley washing off all the topsoil and exposing the ore. Once the site had been hushed then the veins of ore were mined by access through the shaft levels. Cobbles were then laid on the riverbed to prevent further leakage.

Adam runs, not really aware of his direction or surroundings, his body just keeps going; the steep incline doesn't even slow him down.

3.03 p.m.
Alston Police Station
PC Joe Dickinson replaces the receiver and curses. He is in his mid-thirties and is the officer in charge of Alston station. It's nearing the end of his shift and he did have plans to play squash before heading off home to his cottage outside Allendale. The call was from Nora Graham, head of Nenthead School. Joe checks his watch and finishes filling in the online form sending the information to SLEUTH, the police computer intelligence system. That done, he makes sure all the Actions sent to him that morning have been dealt with, then grabs his hat and drives over to the school. It's probably nothing, but something tells him it's going to be a long night.

5.41 p.m.
Garrick's Fell
Adam is hot and his chest feels tight as he runs and runs, putting a lot of distance between himself and the school. It's much cooler now that the sun has gone down, but running uphill has made him hot and sweaty. However, the wind makes the sweat feel freezing on his skin and Adam shivers. A whistling kind of noise catches his attention. It reminds him of telephone wires singing in the wind and he remembers something. It was before Claire was born, so he must have only been about four or five, when Grace urgently picked him up and shielded him with her body as she ran away from some overhead cables. He had felt safe and protected, but his mother had laughed at Grace, until the lorry careered out of control round the corner. He remembers the lavender smell of her silk blouse and the softness of her body. His mother never held him like that, never felt soft and warm like Grace. She loved and cuddled

him, but his grandma had a way of holding him that made him feel both safe and special at the same time. He wonders where she is now. What have they done to her? It wasn't her fault. He was the one who…

He kicks at some stones then picks up a stick and starts whacking nettles and grass. Following the track he makes his way towards a gate. There are animal prints in the mud and he can't quite undo the gate, so he leans forward and wriggles his body through. The track is muddy and he trips occasionally over outcrops of half-hidden stones. The drystone wall to his left is covered in moss and lichen and is broken in places where several stones have toppled over and lie on the ground waiting to be put back in. He presses on towards another wall with a wooden stile over it. He can see a yellow arrow pointing the way over the stile but he hesitates. He is suddenly much more aware of his surroundings. The rows of familiar houses are gone and the countryside looks a bit like Grandma's, with its dipping hawthorn hedges and stone walls. He climbs to the top of the stile and does a complete swivel but doesn't recognize anything. There are no farms or any buildings and it's getting dark. The sky has turned grey as clouds roll in and the light fades. Only now does he feel the needles of cold in his bones. He is also hungry.

Searching in his trouser pockets he finds the crumpled-up business card Gary gave to him. He also finds some chewing gum, the gob stopper he started sucking at lunch, which has quite a few pieces of fluff attached, and an elastic band. This last object was what had caused all the trouble with John. He'd been playing with it, trying to use it to catapult paper balls at Janine when John had snatched at it, trying to take it off him. There had been a scuffle and somehow the scissors had got into his hands.

Adam puts the gobstopper in his mouth, stuffing the rest of the items back into his pockets. As he crosses over the stile he decides to follow the arrows. Back down the lane there is a wooden signpost pointing in this direction. He couldn't read where it was pointing to because the weather had worn it away, but he thinks it said 2½ miles. Last year's field trip was further than that; he knows that he will arrive somewhere soon. But he has to be careful; he doesn't want anyone to find him just yet, even if it means staying out all night. He remembers the business card and decides—he needs to get to a phone. His anger is replaced by a sense of adventure. He's going to phone Gary. Right now, though, he has to find somewhere to hide and shelter from the cold. But it's going to be all right.

6.00 p.m.
Merry Farm

The call comes while Gar is still at work, checking out the timber and tools for an elaborate kitchen conservatory he's starting work on tomorrow. Jayne is hysterical and he can't make any sense of what she's saying, then she passes the phone to someone.

'Mr Hindmarsh? It's PC Joe Dickinson here. I'm with Mrs Freeman. Her son, Adam, ran away from school this morning and we're having difficulty finding him. I wondered if you've seen or heard from him?'

'My God! Sorry, no. I've been at work all day.'

'Can you search your premises, sir? Any place where he may be hiding.'

'Certainly.' Gary is trembling, his voice unsteady as he asks, 'What happened?'

'We won't really know till we find him. At the moment we're contacting family and friends to see if they know where he might be.'

Gary is stunned. Not this, on top of everything else. 'How's Jayne—Mrs Freeman?'

'She has a friend staying at the moment. Be sure to call us if you see or hear from him.'

'Yes. Yes, of course. If there's anything, anything at all—'

'Just let us know if you see him.'

'About Jayne—' but the line goes dead.

Fucking hell. He'd given Adam the bloody business card but he hadn't meant for him to run away. If he's here there'll be no making up with Jayne now. He tries the warehouse first. Scottie is still in there.

'Hey, Scottie!' he calls. 'I don't suppose you've seen Adam, Jayne's lad, hanging round today have you?'

'No. Why?'

'Adam ran away from school this morning. Can you look around in here in case he's hiding anywhere while I check out back?'

'Sure thing. What do I do if I find him? D'you want me to hang onto him?'

'Just give a shout. I'll try to talk to him. If he runs away, catch him. Don't hurt him though.'

'As if.'

They both check the place thoroughly but Adam is not there.

'Thanks, Scottie. See you in the morning.'

'Aye.'Night.' He leaves Gary in the car park.

Gary agonises over whether to go round or not. Jayne has made it very plain she wants nothing to do with him and he doesn't want her to feel he's stalking her or anything, but he can't stay away. He can't just sit and do nothing. He picks up his car keys and decides to risk it.

The school rang to let me know Adam had run away after some sort of 'incident' with a pair of scissors. I don't quite remember the full story, I just remember feeling numb and thinking that this couldn't be happening. I promised to phone and let them know if he came home, but he didn't. He hasn't even got his coat. By teatime I was frantic and Lizzie phoned the police but they already knew. The school had phoned. Apparently they have to do that for some reason, if they think the child is in danger.

Lizzie's already questioned her John to see if he knew where Adam might have gone but he said he had no idea. The policeman was nice and said not to worry, that children do this sometimes, but he needed to take down details and a description, just in case. He wanted a photo of Adam so I gave him one of the latest, when Adam was playing with Claire in the garden. Someone must've seen something, surely. I remember when Jamie Bulger went missing and thinking How on earth can you lose a toddler and no-one notice? *But it wasn't difficult. Oh Adam. Please be safe.*

I called Gary because the policeman suggested it, but I couldn't speak to him. The policeman had to explain what had happened.

I feel sick. I haven't been able to eat anything but all people seem to do is try to push food at me, or make endless cups of tea.

The policeman searched Adam's room for clues to see whether his disappearance was premeditated, whether he's being bullied or something like that, but I told him Adam's never said anything. I keep trying to think of anywhere Adam might be hiding but can't. Before Claire's accident, he was always out playing; since then he's never been anywhere but school. But then, can I be sure about that? How would I know? I've never really taken much notice these days, have I? Oh, Adam, this is so unlike you. What's happened?

7.50 p.m.
Garrick's Fell

The light is staring to fade when Adam sees them. The small clearing in the middle of the pines looks as if it has been used as a campsite, with logs drawn around a central area where the charred remains of a bonfire sit. Rusty-brown caps protrude from the grass nearby and Adam is excited. Last year his grandma took him on a morel hunt and they found lots and lots of them. She cooked them in butter, onion and nutmeg for lunch and they were delicious. He remembers the honeycomb appearance of the cap and wonders about this brain-like one, but decides it's just another variety. He is really hungry by now and Grandma's advice about never eating anything unless an adult checks it first doesn't seem relevant. Tentatively snapping off a small piece of the raw mushroom, he sniffs it. It smells very faintly of chocolate, nothing like Grandma's mushrooms, but he chews and swallows anyway, then he decides to do without. Maybe he'll find something else to eat further on.

8.07 p.m.
The Rise

Gary pulls up outside. He has been home, showered, shaved and put on the aftershave she likes. Dressed casually in jeans and tee-shirt, his tattoo on display, he hopes he looks okay. Taking a deep breath he gets out of the car, walks up to the front door and rings the bell. Lizzie opens the door, but stands there, blocking his entry.

‘She’s in bed,’ Lizzie offers, but doesn’t meet his eyes. He knows she’s lying.

‘I don’t believe that. Not while she’s waiting for news. I need to see her.’

Jayne calls from inside, ‘Let him in.’

Lizzie moves to the side and he enters.

He finds her in the lounge, by the telephone. ‘I didn’t ring, didn’t want to tie up the line… How’re you doing?’

‘Just great,’ she says, sarcastically. ‘How do you think I’m fucking doing? Going out of my head with worry—’

‘Try to keep calm, Jayne,’ Lizzie interrupts, gently.

Jayne deflates and shakes her head. ‘What are you doing here, Gary?’

‘I wanted to see how you are. I wanted to help, to see if I could—’

‘Could what? There’s nothing you could ever do, Gary. Not now, now ever.’

‘Don’t be like this, Jayne. Look, I care about you, about the kids—’

Jayne glares at him.

‘Please, Jayne, let me help.’

Her voice is small when she replies. ‘You can’t. Just go away. Leave me alone.’ She brushes past him, runs upstairs and throws herself onto the bed; her sobs are heard downstairs. Gary looks to Lizzie for support but she shrugs and shows him the door.

8.33 p.m.

PC Joe Dickinson knocks at the door. He has come back for Jayne to identify a tie and a couple of shirt buttons that were found on grass near the school. He explains this to Jayne and that he also wants more photos of Adam and his other school sweatshirt, so they can circulate descriptions of what he's wearing. He has a bad feeling about this so, to be on the safe side and to save time later, he suggests he takes Adam's toothbrush for fingerprints and DNA samples. Jayne is horrified, but he assures her it is just a precaution. He explains that they have search parties organised for the immediate area through Farmers Watch, a sort of pyramid system of volunteers who each have contacts of two other people, but not much can be done further afield till daylight.

After he leaves Joe reasons he has done as much as he can here; it's being passed to HQ at Penrith who will set up an Incident Room. Joe has organised a mobile unit to be set up in the car park at Nenthead Mining Heritage Centre in the morning so he is off home now for a few hours to try to unwind. It's much more difficult when it's a child—he has three himself. The fells are extremely cold and unpredictable; Joe hopes the boy has found shelter if he's up there.

8.54 p.m.

PC Dickinson has gone now and Jayne sits, her stomach in knots. He tried to reassure her, but Jayne sees things in his green eyes, in the way he avoided looking at her. Things she doesn't want to see because they're her worst fears too.

10.12 p.m.
Garrick's Fell

It is dark as Adam reaches the old barn. Rotting timbers flake in his hand as he grasps the lintel to steady himself whilst he puts his right foot over the threshold. Suddenly there is a squawk and a beating of wings from the rafters and he screams as he falls backwards, using his arms to shield his head. His sweatshirt snags on something and as he pulls it clear he feels a rip at his elbow. He'll be in trouble now—it was new at Easter. The flapping eventually stops, the bird settles back onto its perch, but Adam still crouches over, trembling.

Straightening, he turns round and looks back the way he came. The sky is clear but the quarter moon only casts a watery glow over the landscape, not enough to show the way properly. He is really, really scared now. He lifts his head and sees through the gaps in the roof a scattering of stars. It's quiet and still, but he continues to tremble. He looks at his hands but the shaking is inside his body, loosening him. He sits down suddenly, exhausted. He is so cold and tired his toes have gone numb. He stuffs his hands inside his armpits for warmth and starts to rock back and forth, ignoring his wet face and runny nose. The air has a bite to it; he can't stay here. He must keep moving and find somewhere else. His legs are cut and he knocks off some dried blood from numerous bramble scratches as he stands up and makes a hurried exit from the barn, before the bird is disturbed again.

Looking round he can't see very far, but notices at the back of the barn there is a lean-to. The door has to be lifted upwards, like the one in *The Wizard of Oz* when the twister is coming and all the family, except Dorothy, hide inside for shelter. It is cramped in there because it's filled with wood but it is dry and looks safer than the barn. He kicks the wood aside as best he can and climbs in, closing the door hatch on top of himself. He is asleep in minutes.

11.50 p.m.

The sounds of scuttling wake him. In his panic he doesn't know where he is and tries to stand up, cracking his head against the hatch. A little dazed, he falls back onto his haunches and cries, wishing he was safe at Grandma's. Rocking himself he remembers the preparations of that day, and Gary driving them there. It hurts to remember, so he screws up his eyes and starts counting. Every time he misses a number, he goes back to the beginning. It's something Grandma taught him for getting off to sleep. His mam had told him to count sheep, but Grandma told him the sheep don't matter, it is the concentration on numbers that does the trick. He is asleep before he reaches forty.

Lizzie's staying with me so I put her in my room; I'm in Adam's. I can smell him on the pillows, see him lying twisted in the sheets, his left leg out of the covers and I want him back. He's all I've got left. How can I lose him as well? Lizzie thinks I should let my mother know but I can't do that. If it wasn't for her this wouldn't have happened!

Oh, Adam, where are you? Come home, sweetheart, you're not in trouble. Just come home. But what if he can't? What if someone is holding him? Or worse? Please God, no. I'll do anything, anything, just bring me my boy back safe and sound. Please! Please! Please! I'll be a proper mother this time, I promise. I'll even make it up with Mam if you'll just keep him safe and bring him home.

After Claire, I thought I'd given up God—who can believe in Him after that? But here I am bargaining again. It's a bit like when I had to stay with the Sisters when Mam was ill. They told me she'd tried to kill herself. She'd lost a baby, but I didn't know that till I was a lot older. She nearly died herself from the loss of blood, but all I knew was that she wanted to die, she wanted to leave me on my own just because she'd lost that baby. I remember praying and praying, promising all sorts if God would only make her take me home and love me again. But when she did, things weren't ever right between us because *I couldn't forgive her for.*

Strangely enough, now I understand a bit more about how she must have felt, but I still can't forgive her. When I saw Claire's little body, so cold and lifeless, I wanted to die. I didn't think about Adam at all—I was way beyond thinking—because my whole body was just an organism of acute pain that I wanted to shut down. But now ...

I can't bear to think of losing Adam as well. There's so much we haven't done yet, so much I haven't told him, so much he has to look forward to. He must be all right. He must.

Wednesday 21 May

7.04 a.m.
Garrick's Fell

The light is grey as Adam retches. He has had stomach cramps all night, his neck is stiff and his head throbs, but it feels good to have survived. Hungry, thirsty and a little frightened, he decided to wait until daylight before trying to leave the safety and warmth of the lean-to. Grandma told him, when you're frightened, it helps to think of something nice, something that makes you happy, to chase the fear away. He tried to think of nice, happy things, but they all had Claire in them, and that make him sad and want to cry.

He lifts the cover of the lean-to and looks out. The barn looks very different in daylight, much less threatening. Rummaging around in his pockets for something to do, he feels the business card Gary gave him. It is creased and some of the print has rubbed off but he can still see the phone numbers. He smoothes it out as best he can before returning it to his pocket. He is excited now. Maybe Gary can help him get to Grandma's! He'll know where she is and how to get in touch. Adam overheard his mam talking to Liz and knew Grandma was in hospital, but he doesn't know how to contact her. It seemed so easy yesterday afternoon, but the enormity of what he has done is dawning on him. He doesn't want his mam, she'll be too angry and upset. No, he wants Grandma. She'll make everything all right. She always does. But to get to her he needs Gary, and that means finding a phone. Maybe following telephone wires will lead him to a house or something?

Feeling purposeful he looks around but there doesn't appear to be any telephone wires to follow and he has no idea which way to go. He is cold and thirsty but knows he will warm up once he gets going, so he chooses the flattest way forward and begins to walk.

8.00 a.m.
Police HQ, Penrith

The shift have gathered for the morning's briefing. There is a large map dominating one wall and several photographs of the school and Adam's house are pinned underneath it. Alongside is a recent photo of Adam in his school uniform as well as crime scene photos of the tie and buttons found at the school gates. DS Harry Thompson removes his grey jacket and addresses the team.

'Right, everyone. The immediate area and wasteland around the school have been searched, as well as near the boy's home. Friends and neighbours have been contacted for information and also asked to search their gardens and outhouses but so far nothing's turned up. There's been a house-to-house—how's that going? Have we got the list of those not in last night?'

A young officer moves forward and hands it to him.

'Yes, sir. We've twenty-three repeats to do.'

'Right. Who's contacting the ex-husband?'

'Me, sir. I rang the last known address we have for him but he's moved. I was given the phone number of his girlfriend, but so far haven't been able to speak to her.'

'Keep on it. What about other family members?'

'On Mrs Freeman's side there aren't any known, other than her mother, who's in a psychiatric hospital. We'll know more about Freeman's side when we get hold of him. Mrs Freeman thinks his father may still alive, but she never had any contact with him even before they divorced. We've also established that Freeman is the kid's step-father.'

Thompson absently strokes his chin, which is in need of a closer shave. He makes a mental note to get new heads for his razor, then says, 'The father's—sorry, stepfather's—just done a runner again so we need to take this into the equation. Social Services—have they been contacted yet?'

Another member of the team pipes up, 'Yes, sir. Neither of the children have been on the "At Risk" register.'

'What's happening at Missing Persons?' Thomson asks.

A greying DC consults his notes and replies, 'His physical description, details of his clothing and the circumstances have been circulated on the PNC, PNMPB and NMPB and we've checked that he's never absconded before.'

'Good work, people,' he tells the room then asks Carter, 'Any luck at the school?'

Carter clears his throat. He's young, ambitious and aware of his dark, sultry good looks. 'His teacher, Miss Angela Hart, is very worried about him. Normally he's a very outgoing little boy but since his sister's death he's become more withdrawn and angry. She's not aware of any bullying, but that doesn't mean it hasn't happened. She's not been able to get through to him and hasn't been able to speak to his mother about her concerns. Every time she's tried to get the mother into school Mrs Freeman's cancelled the appointment and refuses to speak about it over the phone. She gave Joe Dickinson a list of his friends, which more or less matches Mrs Freeman's list, and Kelly's been checking them.'

'Found anything, Kelly?'

Kelly Reid is the youngest member of the team. 'No, sir. His best friend's John Waites and he was the boy

Adam attacked before running away. John doesn't know of any special place he likes to go to or anyone he might be staying with. He also said there hadn't been any bullying.'

DS Thomson scratches his head and looks absent-mindedly out of the window. This is looking more dodgy by the minute.

A female voice pipes up, 'It may be nothing, sir, but…'

'What is it, Caroline? Out with it.'

Caroline Sanderson joined the team two years ago. 'It's just… there's a boyfriend, an ex really.'

'And?'

'Well, I just wondered… he's twenty-four, she's thirty-three—'

'Jammy bugger!' Carter offers and she glares at him.

'Go on,' encourages Thomson.

'Mrs Freeman phoned him to ask if he knew where Adam was but she broke down and couldn't speak to him. Joe Dickinson took over and told him about Adam, asked him if he'd seen him or knew where he might be and he seemed...'

'What?'

She consults the faxed report. 'Joe's written that Hindmarsh seemed "emotional and cut up about it".'

'And you think that's suspicious, do you?' presses the DS.

'Not in itself, but then he's only been going out with Mrs Freeman for a couple of months. It's not as if he's living there, or a stepfather or anything. It just seems…odd.'

'Odd?'

'Look, I just think we should keep an eye on him or something. I have a feeling about him, that's all.'

‘We all know about your feelings, Caroline,’ Carter quips, and bawdy laughter breaks out.

‘This isn’t getting us anywhere nearer finding that little boy, so let’s concentrate on the job in hand and save the banter for the pub. Okay?’ DS Thomson glares at them.

‘Yes, sir,’ several voices affirm.

‘And Caroline…’

‘Yes, sir?’

‘Go with it. Have a word with the boyfriend at home. See what you can find out about him. We need to keep an open mind to all possibilities. I’ll liaise with Joe and his team in Nenthead. This is high risk now, and with the discovery of the tie and buttons it may turn out to be an abduction. So make sure all your paperwork’s up to scratch.’

‘Yes, sir.’

‘They’re running the press release today to see if anyone remembers seeing him and we’ve got groups of army volunteers and mountain rescue ready to start searching. Any questions?’

Silence.

‘Fine, get on it then report to the Mining Heritage Centre car park. They’re organising the search of the fells from there. We’re covering this quadrant first, including the river and the caravan park,’ he indicates on the map, ‘then if that doesn’t turn anything up we’ll fan out and cover this area here…’

9.12 a.m.
Merry Farm

Flicking through his diary Gary checks his appointments for the next couple of days, just in case he has to re-schedule. This morning’s is clear—all he has to do is check that the delivery of a new kitchen has arrived for Mrs Benson. If it has he'll pop round and make sure all the bits are there, then work can start bright and early tomorrow. This afternoon he had planned to do paperwork, something he hates and easily puts off, especially when the sun's shining, like today. He would much rather be outside in the fresh air, playing with Kuma.

Thoughts of Kumar bring him back to the fact that Adam still doesn't know about her, and the likelihood of them all becoming a family is not looking good at all. He keeps hoping things will change and he will get back with Jayne eventually, when she has had time to grieve. But now this, on top of everything else…

Picking up the phone he dials her number. It is answered almost immediately.

'Jayne, it's me. Any news?'

'Get off the line, Gary. I thought you were… just get off the line!'

The phone goes dead.

'C'mon Kuma, let's go for a walk. I need some fresh air.'

10.05 a.m.
Garrick's Fell

The sun is quite strong now. Adam has been travelling for a while, vaguely following a river, but still there are no buildings or houses anywhere, other than disused sheep pens. He had a drink of water about an hour ago but it tasted a bit funny so he didn't drink much. Maybe he should try here? The ground is uneven and bumpy so he watches where he puts his feet. Heather and bracken make walking difficult and Adam tires easily. There is a wood ahead on the other side of the river and he thinks about turning back. It doesn't feel right. He remembers the stories of *Hansel and Gretel* and *Little Red Riding*

Hood and starts to falter, but also remembers that they were saved and had happy endings, so he has a quick drink and presses on.

10.20 a.m.
Crofter's Wood

Just a few metres inside, the sunlight is shut out. The trees on one side of the track are in perfect rows but on the other are a bit more untidy. He can see large red crosses on some and remembers Grandma told him they're for the woodcutters to know which ones to cut down. He feels safe knowing there are woodcutters around. After all, one of them did save Little Red Riding Hood. Adam knows it's only a story, but Grandma always says that stories tell the truths of life and that comforts him.

On the neat side of the track there are gaps in the trees. Gary told him these are firebreaks and he can see quite a way through them, making out tyre tracks and the odd footprint. He should reach a house or something soon. Maybe they'll have food and a phone so he can call Gary to come and get him.

Squirrels scamper up pines, out of his way, and he stops to watch them. They're grey with fluffy tails and he thinks Grandma will be so pleased when he tells her he spotted them. She used to tell him off for making so much noise teasing Claire that they frightened the birds and animals away. She'll be pleased with him now. And he remembers that they're… What did she call them? Vermin. That's it. Vermin. The greys kill off red squirrels, which are extinct in lots of places now. Pleased with himself he presses on, the way easier now. He walks for ten minutes then leaves the wood and returns to moorland.

10.38 a.m.
Nr Merry farm

The air is still crisp as the day expands, the sky becoming a dazzling blue. Sunshine has dried up patches of dew on the grass as Gary makes his way towards the river. Kuma, off the lead now, bounds playfully around him then scampers off to investigate bushes on the bankside. Catching a scent she races, yapping happily, in and out of the foliage, catching burrs and twigs on her fur in the process and Gary smiles at her, until he remembers why he bought her in the first place.

-I'm not sure how much more of this I can put up with. Why take it out on me; I've not done anything wrong? Why the hell does she keep punishing me like this? If I was a shit like Sandy there'd be no problem. What the hell's wrong with women? Why do they always go for the shits of the world and people like me never get a look in?'-

Venting his own frustrations he kicks at the grass and a battered can of Irn Bru is dislodged from its resting place. He kicks it again, imagining it to be Sandy's head and feels the satisfaction as it's dented and twisted by his kicks. Kuma, not to be left out, bounds up and the pair play football with the can, until a powerful kick from Gary sends it arcing into the air. It lands in the river several feet away and Kuma launches into the water to retrieve it, dropping it on the bank and shaking herself.

'Drop, Kuma. Drop it!' he yells as the dog starts to bite at the can. 'You'll cut your mouth, you stupid dog. Drop it!'

Kuma obeys, dropping the can at her feet, then shakes the water off again and trots towards Gary who rewards her with a lot of patting.

'Good girl. That's a good girl.' Then for no apparent reason he can think of, he starts sobbing.

11.02 a.m.
Martyn's Copse, Marshalldale

After half an hour his stomach starts churning again and Adam has to drop his pants quickly, wrinkling his nose at the smell as the watery contents squirt out. The griping pains continue for a couple of minutes, then subside as quickly as they came. He has no paper to wipe himself and doesn't want to pull his pants up until he is clean, so he looks round for anything appropriate he might be able to use but there is nothing but grass, bracken and heather. He doesn't want to use any of them in case he touches himself and there's nowhere to wash afterwards. He is angry and upset but finds a lump of moss which he uses gingerly, then throws it far away, wiping his hands in the dew on the grass. He retches a few times, pulls his pants back up and gets away from the smell, running and stumbling in his haste, failing to notice the business card, which has fallen on the grass.

12.40 p.m.
The Rise

It takes a few minutes before Lizzie opens the door and steps back to let him in. Jayne is in the sitting room, staring out of the window. She turns as he enters and he is shocked to see her white face, devoid of make-up, black circles around her puffy eyes. She says nothing, just stares at him.

'I had to come back.'

She nods, then turns back to the window.

'Has there been any further news?'

Lizzie breaks the silence. 'Not yet. They checked all the gardens and sheds around the school then moved into a wider circle last night before they had to call it off. This morning they've been checking the wasteland near the old tip.' She looks at Jayne, then says, 'Last night someone handed in his school tie so they've started to check the river and caravan park.'

Jayne looks up, but says nothing, a hollow silence settling between them.

Lizzie continues, 'I'm sure they'll find him soon.'

'How're you keeping it together, Jayne?' Gary asks, making a move towards her, but is halted by a warning look from Lizzie.

'She's doing well, aren't you, Jayne?' Lizzie answers for her, 'given the circumstances. We've got a few friends to keep her company and the police liaison officer keeps us updated. It's just the waiting… She'll be fine, I promise. You don't need to worry about her.'

'Don't need to worry! That's all I have been doing.' He turns to Jayne and pleads, 'Don't shut me out, please. I can't bear it. I want to help. I want to help you, to share…'

Suddenly Jayne is on her feet.

'To share what, exactly? My guilt? Well that's appropriate, isn't it? You were there. You were fucking me while my baby was drowning. I told you something was wrong but you wouldn't believe me. You said nothing could happen… Ha! Well, you were wrong, weren't you?... Weren't you?' She's bordering on hysteria so Lizzie steps forward.

'Calm down, Jayne, please. Gary, I think you'd better go.'

'No, I'm not going anywhere until we talk this through. You owe me that much.'

'I don't owe you anything! Just get out of here!'

Jayne rushes towards him and attempts to hit him but Gary holds her wrists and grapples with her until her strength subsides and she crumples, sobbing. He lets her sink to the floor and kneels beside her, still holding her wrists. Gently he releases them and tentatively puts his arms around her, pulling her into his chest. He rocks and shushes her until the crying stops.

Lizzie watches, then says, 'I still think you'd better leave, Gary. She doesn't need complications right now.'

'How would you know what she needs?' he asks nastily.

'Look, Gary, I don't want to argue with you, but your being here complicates things. She'll let you know when she's ready, okay? It's not about you, what you feel, what you need. It's about Jayne and Adam and your being here isn't helping. So please leave.'

'Is that what you want Jayne?' he asks.

He lifts her face level to his. Jayne nods. Gary drops her arms, stands up and walks towards the door. His hand on the handle, he turns and says, 'You know the number,' then he is gone.

12.58 p.m.
Nr Martyn's Copse, Marshalldale

Adam's stomach hasn't cramped for at least half an hour and despite feeling thirsty and weak with hunger, he has starting to feel better. Ahead he can see and hear running water making its way over stones down the hill. He reaches the stream and scoops up some water in his hands, feeling the cold liquid trickle down his throat. It tastes funny and he spits it out, but then thirst gets the better of him and he drinks greedily, feeling his stomach swelling with the fluid. He leans back against a rock and looks around. Something dark on the horizon catches his attention. Maybe it's a house or something?

Maybe they've got a phone?

Standing up quickly, he starts to run, then trips, twisting his ankle, spraining it quite badly. He yelps with the pain and sits down heavily, tears streaming down his cheeks. He just wants to go home now. He wants someone, anyone, to find him and take him home. That's how he felt after the accident.

The fabric of the present is tearing, falling into where the past waits. His memories of that day, of how the nightmare began, he has polished like a shiny marble, which he takes out to look at as he sits there in the sun—the sand, the bike ride, the fish and chips.

He's tired and his ankle hurts. If only he had his bike. He's hungry too. He hasn't felt hungry for so long now that this surprises him. He thinks about hot dogs and burgers, fish fingers, his favourite, and fish cakes. He hasn't thought about fish for ages. Not since that day.

Sitting here in the sunlight those events seem a lifetime away, a dream maybe, but the feeling of lead dragging him down is real enough. He must get up and get going again if he is to find a phone. A fresh wave of cramps hits him but he is not quick enough to get his trousers down in time and he soils himself. This seems the last straw and he throws himself down on the wet grass and bracken and howls. For his sister, for his grandma, for his mother, for Gary. But most of all, for himself.

1.22 p.m.

When he has cried himself out he wipes the snots from his face, undoes his trousers and takes off his soiled underpants, hurling them away in disgust. He cleans himself as best he can, then determines to keep going. He has no idea of time, but knows that when it gets dark the chances of his finding help are greatly reduced. He doesn't want to spend another night in the cold and starts crying again for his lovely warm bed, his toys and TV. He could even bear his mam's crying now and the emptiness of the house without Claire, if only he can get out of this place. And if only his ankle didn't hurt so much. He remembers his grandma telling him how brave he was the time he had stitches in his foot after coming off his bike and he knows he can do this. Gingerly he gets to his feet and starts walking towards the dark shape on the horizon.

2.16 p.m.
Merry Farm

WDC Sanderson is making copious notes.

'So, Mr Hindmarsh, can I just check I've got this right?' She looks at her notes and starts to read. 'You met Mrs Freeman two months ago in a restaurant. She told you that she had a family and this didn't bother you.'

'Why should it?'

She continues to read from her notes, pushing stray light brown curls behind her ears. 'You first met the children—both children—the following week when you took them all out for a pub lunch. Since then you've been a regular visitor to the house, have stayed over but always left before the children woke up,' she glances up at him and he nods, 'and have looked after the children on your own on two occasions to enable Mrs Freeman to go out with people from work.'

'Yes.'

'So would you say you had a close relationship with the children?' She looks directly at him, maintaining eye contact until he looks away.

'Yes, I'd like to think so.'

'How close?'

'What do you mean?' Gary stiffens, engaging in eye contact again.

'Close enough to know where Adam might go if he wanted to run away, or hide for a while?'

Gary relaxes a little and replies, 'Not really. He talked to me about his stepdad, Sandy, and John, his best friend but—'

'What did he say about his stepdad?'

'Just that he was glad he left because his mam was always crying. Sandy left Jayne when Claire, his daughter, was only a few weeks old. From what I can gather he was a bit of a ladies' man and not too good with money. He left her in loads of debt, that kind of thing.'

'Adam told you this?'

'No, I got that from Jayne.'

'Mr Freeman came back for the funeral?'

'Yes.'

'But you took Adam home from the funeral?'

Gary nods.

Sanderson continues, 'According to a neighbour, you turned up at the funeral and took Adam off in your car without Mrs Freeman's knowledge.'

'Jayne was out of it. She didn't really know what was going on, so I took him home. It wasn't good for the lad to see his mam in that state. I told Lizzie. You make it sound like I abducted him or something,' Gary replies.

'Then a couple of days later you were trying to beat the door down to get in. Apparently you caused quite a disturbance before you finally left.'

'That was because that prat—'

'You mean Sandy?' asks Sanderson.

‘Yes. He wouldn’t let me see Jayne.’ Gary is angry now, but manages to keep himself under control. ‘I just wanted to see her, to make sure she was okay. But he wouldn’t let me speak to her when I phoned, so I went round. I didn’t get in, so I left.’

‘I see.’ She continues to write in her notebook. ‘Now, about Adam. You say he confided in you.’

‘I wouldn’t put it as strongly as that. He sometimes told me things, but—’

‘What things?’ She looks at him intently and he looks down at his feet.

‘I dunno. Just…things. Like which football team he supports… er, what happened in school—those kind of things.’

‘Did Adam tell you anything else?’

‘I can’t remember.’ He considers, then continues, ‘He likes Spiderman and the Hulk. He loved his sister.’ His voice catches.

‘And Claire. What can you tell me about her?’

‘She’s dead. Look, is this relevant?’ His voice is hard and brittle.

Sanderson continues, ‘How did you get on with Claire? As well as you did with Adam?’

Gary sighs, releasing his anger. ‘No, she’s just—was—a baby. A sweet little thing, such a lot of life in her…but…no, I got on better with Adam. He’s older. A boy. I could identify more with him and *Spiderman*, than *Dora the Explorer*.’

‘So you’re saying you have a special sort of relationship with Adam, boys together, that sort of thing?’

‘I suppose... Has there been any news?’

‘I think that’s all for now. I’ve got all your phone numbers so we’ll be in touch if there’s anything else you can help us with. That's a nice dog you've got. What blue eyes.'

'I got her as a surprise for Adam. He wanted a dog, but Jayne wasn't keen on the idea. I hoped she'd get used to it and change her mind.'

'She never mentioned this when I spoke to her.'

'She doesn't know. I picked Kumar up just after the funeral and…things have been difficult... I haven't really had a chance to tell her yet.'

'Just one last thing. Where were you about 2.30 p.m. on Tuesday the twentieth?'

'I was out walking the dog. I had a lot on my mind so I took a bit of time off.'

'Did you see anyone? Can anyone vouch for your whereabouts?'

'I don't think so. We went down to the woods and did the circular route that runs past the meadow. I don't think I saw anyone…'

'Thank you, Mr Hindmarsh. We'll be in touch.'

Sanderson rises to leave and Gary shows her out

4.21 p.m.
Meldon Rigg

It is dark in the tunnel. Johnny is saving his batteries and doesn't need light to find his way. He has trained himself well. He met several Gurkhas in Aldershot and had already been impressed by stories about them. Sailing to the Falklands, these tiny men, formidable in battle, were bad sailors, terrified of water. They were given the best cabins, not that they asked for or wanted any preferential treatment, but because they were so well respected. On board they were ruthless and relentless in applying themselves to any hardship or task given to them and even lived on the ship blindfolded so that they knew every inch of it and would be able to find their way off in thick smoke or in the pitch black of night. He has taken a leaf out of their book. He knows this tunnel like the back of his hand—well he should, shouldn't he? He spent months restoring the thing; clearing out rubble, repairing the roof, shoring up the walls, replacing timbers. It wasn't easy. But no one else knows about it so it's his little secret. One that could save his life.

After thirty paces he stretches his hands out in front of him until they come into contact with earth at the end of the tunnel. Bending down he feels along the ground for the stick, then scrapes away enough earth to get his fingers under the wooden board and heaves it up. He slides soundlessly into the hole, finds the torch turns it on and and pulls the board back in place. Taking matches from the corner he lights the wick inside a homemade lamp made from a can that has been punctured with patterned holes, then turns the torch off.

Batteries are getting low. Soon he'll have to 'forage' again, further afield this time (he never likes to hit the same farms twice) for batteries, kerosene and matches. His store of rendered fat is also running low, as are his magnesium strips, so he will need kerosene or some oil pretty soon, until he can build up supplies again. Although he has become adept at using a fire bow and striking stones to light the tinder, he is not a purist for the sake of it and knows that proper supplies save so much time and physical energy. The problem he has is that he just hates having to go so close to people. This is why he never claims any state benefit or his army pension.

Putting his rucksack to one side he lies on a makeshift bed. It is made from an A-frame of wooden branches secured by thin strips of wood. A tube of orange plastic bivvy bag is supported in the middle of the frame and skins thonged together with dried sinews are strewn on top of a navy-blue polyester sleeping bag. His down bag was warmer but rubbish if it got wet, so he brought the polyester one instead. Skins also cover the floor. It takes ages to painstakingly scrape the flesh off the skins, stretch and dry them out, making sure they never get wet. But it's worth the effort for the extra warmth and sense of luxury they provide down here, where the temperature remains a constant 10°C. A couple of degrees too cold to survive without lots of food and extra warmth, but it's pleasant enough to be a refuge from the heat or cold of outside. And memories of the Falklands.

On 1 June 1982 1st Battalion Welsh Guards went ashore on the Falklands Islands with the 5th Infantry Brigade at San Carlos. Those without helicopters to lift them off were sent forward to Fitzroy by sea. The lead vessel, *HMS Fearless,* deposited guardsmen who landed overnight on the 6-7 June. Bad weather delayed the *Sir Tristram* and *Sir Galahad,* which were carrying the rest of the guardsmen, and an airstrike caught them at Bluff Cove resulting in the loss of thirty-two men. Johnny was one of the 'lucky' ones who survived. But only just. He spent two years in hospital and was discharged on a full pension. However, night after night, as soon as he dropped off sleep, his friends came to visit; Dom, with the bubbling, melting tattoos, Rich, whose first baby had been born the previous day, reaching to him with dripping stumps and blackened bones, Jockstrap, the arsey Glaswegian with the biggest knob in the regiment, his face and hair engulfed in a ball of fire. All accused him, trying to grab him, to take him with them. That's when he started drinking in earnest.

Oh, fuck. His body is alert again, the end of his penis is tingling, and he knows if he doesn't do something about it he will not get to sleep. Fumbling in his trousers he takes the stiff penis out and rubs it vigorously. He groans as his hand movements become more and more frenzied. He used to think about past girlfriends and what they used to do to him, but once he had come he felt a desperate emptiness inside, so most of the time he likes to enjoy the sensations without any images attached. Like now. He spurts semen and feels his muscles relax. Wiping himself with a rag he closes his eyes; sleep comes to him, like a long lost friend, wrapping its arms around him, holding him in its embrace. But after a while he feels as if it's squeezing the life out of him and he wakes up screaming in the dark...

4.30 p.m.
Coglin Mews
Sue has been on the internet all afternoon. Rubbing her eyes, she swears. It's like finding the proverbial needle in a haystack. Okay. Let's backtrack. Grace was born 1960, and she knows the surname, Watson, but what was Grace's mother called? There are lots of genealogy sites so she should be able to find all that. But this is ridiculous—why is she doing this? She should leave it to admin to find Grace's notes. She is becoming obsessed with the woman, and that makes her feel uncomfortable. Yet she can't let it go; something is compelling her to find out.

4.39 p.m.
Stone Circle, Meldon Rigg

After crossing the river, it has taken Adam well over two hours of climbing to reach the summit. What he thought might have been a house turns out to be some huge oblong granite stones sticking out from the ground, pointing up to the sky. He can see all around from this vantage point and below him, in a clearing, there appears to be the remains of four houses, each set apart from the others on an incline.

He decides to head there for shelter as the wind has sprung up and he is cold. His ankle has turned black and swollen inside his trainer and Adam doesn't think he'll be able to get the trainer off. There is a stillness about the place that is quite menacing. There's no birdsong, and the only sound he hears now is the swishing of the grasses as he hobbles towards what seems to be the main entrance to the nearest building, and the sounds of the wind sighing through it. There is a small wood at the back and the trees sway eerily without making a sound.

For some reason the hairs on the back of his neck stand on end and he feels cold and shivery. His mouth is dry and he has an overwhelming desire to get away from there as quickly as possible. He turns to leave but his feet are rooted to the spot as a dark figure emerges from behind the building. His stomach goes into spasm, then everything goes black.

Thursday 22 May

10.18 a.m.
Garrick's Fell

Judd Hargreaves finds it. As a senior member of the Mountain Rescue Team he has been on numerous searches, usually involving holidaymakers who have got lost, having gone out unprepared for the weather, which can change quickly on the hills. He has had his fair share of climbing accidents and in the last couple of months the team has been called out to find two missing persons; one who was having a nervous breakdown and they found safe and well, the other died of a heart attack whilst canoeing and they found her body downstream.

Judd has never been called to find a lone missing child and is not looking forward to the prospect that they might not find him alive. His brother, Dom, is part of the team searching underground. Judd is thirty-seven but has never been able to overcome his fear of being buried alive, so he leaves that sort of thing to his kid brother.

The piece of fabric is just visible as they approach the barn. They are searching in formation, checking the ground for any clues, when Judd looks up and sees it. It's blue, the colour of the sweatshirt the lad had been wearing. He points it out to the team leader, PC Milligan, who takes photos and bags it.

'Is that from his sweatshirt?' asks Hargreaves.

'Looks like it but we can't be sure until Forensics have processed it.'

The area is cordoned off and Milligan rings through to base to report their find. He and a few officers wait at the scene for Forensics whilst the volunteers are instructed to walk back to the road and wait for lorries to take them back to base, where they will be given strong cups of tea and instructions for the next area to search.

12.40 p.m.
Incident Room
DS Billy Hedley takes the fax from Forensics who found what appears to be blood, skin and hair samples on the hatch to the wood store. He dials and passes the information to DCI Truman.

'We've just heard from Forensics at the scene, sir. It looks like the lad was kept in a wood store overnight, but they'll still need to check the samples against Adam's DNA to be certain. I'll get Joe Dickinson over to the house for a toothbrush or hairbrush if they haven't already been picked up and sent to Chorley.'

Tommy Truman nods. There is a pause, then Hedley continues, 'I've been thinking. We know he was picked up outside school, because of the tie and buttons. Maybe the tie was used to bind him at first, until something stronger was available, like rope or cord.'

'Possibly, but that wouldn't explain why it was discarded. It has his name on, so it's easily identifiable and would show us an approximation of where he'd been abducted. I suppose it's possible that it was going to be used but was too short, or inappropriate, or something else, and in a struggle was dropped. Forensics say it's showing signs of being wrenched off, but there doesn't appear to be much fraying. We'll just have to wait until they've done tension tests on it, to find out what sort of pressure was used to remove it.'

'Yes, sir. By the way, uniform have managed to locate the ex-husband and his girlfriend—her mother knew where they were. Apparently she doesn't approve of him so was happy to co-operate. She hasn't a clue about what her precious daughter's been up to, though. They're taking them to Carlisle for interview.'

Truman is lost in thought for a few seconds, then replies, 'Maybe he wants to get back at the wife, or maybe he wants the lad for the death of the little girl… see what they cough up and let me know.'

'Yes, sir.'

'And has anyone interviewed the grandmother yet?'

'No, sir. She's still in the secure unit under sedation.'

Truman looks at his watch. 'Ask Northumbria to send someone out to see her. It's a long shot, but if she knows anything about the husband or the boyfriend we need to know. And keep me informed.'

'Yes, sir.'

12.42 p.m.
Lounge, Fletcher Ward

You're watching the birds circling then diving down between the trees when you hear the door open and people enter. The hair on the back of your neck stands to attention and you wait, perfectly still. Your pulse picks up a more strident beat and then you feel them, hammering away in your temples, groin and neck. How did they get in here? Your movements these days are sluggish and heavy so you invoke your will to make the words come out right. That stuff they keep putting inside you doesn't help at all. You must drink more water.

A montage of images makes your head buzz and your mouth feels dry. You see white skin; candles; your bed. There's a body, Mother's face, and sounds of Father's sobbing echo as the walls breathe in and out. Closer and closer they come, threatening to suffocate you. You put your arms up to protect yourself and hear laughter.

'It's okay, Grace, only me. How are you today?'

It's China Blue.

'You look a little pale. Are you sleeping okay?'

Those piercing blue eyes scrutinize yours but you don't pull away. Darren, his aura pulsing red, is behind her, seeing to another patient.

'I've brought you your glasses.' Sue looks over at Darren and continues, conspiratorially, 'They were on the bedside table, just like you said.' She pulls a chair towards you and sits down. 'Here's your metal cashbox. It's locked, and I couldn't see the key.'

You take the items from her as she continues, 'What a fantastic house you've got! Bet you can't wait to get home, can you? It's so peaceful there. I've never been to that part of the coast before—bet it's bleak in winter though. The trees are wonderful. I've never seen so many different shades of blossom before. They must be an inspiration for your paintings. What's wrong, Grace? Cat got your tongue? Grace?'

You have to come back and answer her. 'Sorry, I was miles away. What did you say?'

'Your glasses. I brought them for you.'

'Thanks. You're a real star.'

Sue laughs. 'Where'd you get that expression from?'

'My grandson. He keeps me informed about all the changes in "cool" language.'

'I've got some time before I have to start work. D'you want to have a walk outside?'

You nod appreciatively and rise. Your legs are fine today; no wobbles. You watch her open the secure door and the smell of freedom and space hits you in the face like cold water. It's so long since you've been outside.

Leading you out of the building to the parkland area at the back, China Blue links arms with you until you arrive at the benches and sit down. China Blue sits opposite you and looks into your eyes.

'Tell me about your mother, Grace.'

'She's dead.'

'D'you miss her?'

You shake your head.

Sue continues, 'I miss mine. Whenever I was a bit down she'd sit beside me on the settee and brush my hair. I've always had it long. She'd stroke my head and brush and brush until I was nearly asleep and then she'd tell me that no one can make you feel bad about yourself without your permission.'

'She's right. But not everyone waits for permission.'

Sue throws back her head and a deep-throated laugh escapes. Her face lights up when she smiles and laughs. Even her skin shines.

'Oh, Grace, I do enjoy your company.'

She squeezes your hand and you feel a connection from her wrap around your wrist and travel up your arm.

She continues, 'But about your mother. What was she like?'

'About five foot one, brown hair—'

'No, Grace, not what she looked like. What was she like?'

Come on. You can do this. 'She wasn't a very nice person.' Go on, don't stop now. 'She was cruel. Often she was violent.' There, it's out. You heave a big sigh and look directly at Sue.

'That's good, Grace, really good.' She's hesitant for a while, then asks, 'Tell me about your grandma? The one who lived with you for a while.'

'I don't remember much.'

'I thought she looked after you?'

'Only till I was five. Mam came home so Gran was sent away.'

'Who sent her away?'

Why does she ask all this? The connection in your arm throbs so you answer, 'Dad sent her away. She told him things, about what Mam was doing. He didn't believe her.'

'Did you see much of her after she left?'

'Sundays for dinner. Till Mam pushed…'

She waits for you to finish. When you don't she asks, 'Pushed what?'

You start to feel dizzy. This is too much. Far too much.

'Okay. Let's talk about something else. What kind of mother were you when Jayne was little? How would you describe yourself?'

You can't answer, so you sit there.

'Were you happy being a mother?'

Now that's a stupid question. How could you not enjoy the softness of her head, the smell of her, the fierce grip of her tiny fingers and the clear blue eyes? Having her cost you dear but you wouldn't change that. Not then, not now.

'Of course. Who wouldn't be?'

'Quite a few people, I can tell you. So, how did you cope on your own?'

'I've managed all my life. Having Jaynie was no different.'

'But it was different, wasn't it? You had a baby to support and look after. Without a father.'

'She had a father, he just couldn't be there, that's all. He loved her, sent us money and saw us whenever he could.'

'So what happened?'

'He was sent abroad and never came back. It was his punishment. And mine.'

There's a slight pause in her rhythm. You feel her tense, ever so slightly, then she asks, 'What for?'

'Being in love. Having children.'

You can see her puzzlement. She's not good at hiding her feelings from you.

'Those things are part of life. Why would he be punished for that?' she asks.

You can't say anything, can't tell her.

She shuffles on the seat then looks straight at you and says, 'Grace, you're so frustrating at times. Did you know that? You said "children". I thought Jayne was an only one.'

'She is. I had … a miscarriage.' She's waiting for more. 'After Jayne.'

'How did that make you feel?'

Another stupid question.

'How do you think?' You're losing patience now. Be careful.

'I don't know. That's why I'm asking.'

Don't answer her. Let her work it out for herself. She's quiet for a while and looks back at the hospital.

'The other day, Grace. You said something about my aura.'

You turn to look at her.

'You said something about—'

It's now or never. You don't want to tell her, but she's a nice woman.

'He's writing his notice. He doesn't care about you. He's only interested in one thing.' She's staring at you. 'You don't believe me but he's going to betray you soon. Then you'll understand.'

Sue shifts awkwardly on the seat. 'Tell me something, Grace. Are you aware of your condition?'

You nod, but it's complicated. Jaynie was only three when the voices changed. They made you dizzy and said strange things. There'd been the possibility of another baby then, but it hadn't wanted to stay, not without Brendan. But you had to, for Jaynie's sake.

The strain of keeping focussed, of appearing 'normal' is taking its toll. You try not to think about Jaynie but the memories keep getting dredged up. They flash in quick succession, superimposing on each other, breaking over you in waves. But then they change, like petrol spills on the surface of puddles, eddying outwards, defying definition. Jaynie blurs, her face becoming yours. You hear her voice in a cacophony of sounds intermingled with Mother's and your eardrums ooze. If only you could avoid the poisons they give you here.

'Grace… Are you all right? Perhaps we'd best go back inside?'

'No! Not yet. Please?'

'I think that's enough for one day. If the weather's fine, I'll bring you out again tomorrow. I promise. As long as you're up to it. All right?'

You sigh and nod, breathing in the moist smells of nearby woodland, may blossom and rotted pine needles. Overhead the blackbirds dart, playing tag in the air currents. A gust of wind riffles through your hair from behind so you turn towards it, close your eyes and let it seduce your skin. Sue stands beside you, you can feel the heat of her body, but she says nothing. You open your eyes and she's watching you.

'What do you feel, Grace, when you do that?'

'Like I'm not here.'

'Where are you?'

'I've blended in, become part of it.'

'So you don't exist?'

'Not in this form. Close your eyes. Try it yourself.'

'Perhaps another day. Come on now, it's time for me to get back to work. Don't look at me like that. I've promised; you can come out again whenever the weather's good and you're not too tired. Okay?'

'Okay.'

1.17 p.m.

Back in your room you take the glasses out of their case and settle down in the chair by the bed. You take the metal box and shake it upside down until there's a familiar click. Turning it the right way up the lid opens. Inside are some letters, photos and a silver locket on a chain. They're going to move you soon so this may be your last chance to look at these in private.

Opening the letters you see the familiar handwriting, feel the blue fountain pen etching the words onto the paper. Brendan. Closing your eyes, you remember that first time, in the sacristy. You were fifteen years old and hiding from Mother again. Brendan wasn't meant to be there, he was supposed to be at the church hall for the Bring and Buy Sale. Mother was running the Tombola stall and you were supposed to be helping but you didn't want all the questions and concern from the other women about the bruises on your face—you were always punished more when people were nice to you.

Brendan had taken a short cut across the grass and was looking for a cloth to wipe his shoes when he spotted you hiding behind the bookcase. You should have stayed hidden, but he was younger than the other priests and you liked looking at him, particularly when he didn't know you were around.

'And what might you be doin' there, Grace?' he asked.

'Nothing, Father.'

'Come out, come out. Shouldn't you be—' He caught sight of your face. 'Mother of God, what's happened to you? Not another fall, Grace?'

'Yes, Father.'

'And what was it this time eh?' he asked, drawing you closer, your chin in his right hand. He looked into your eyes and you felt ashamed. Tears started to brim up and as they welled over he gently caught them with his finger and brushed them away. His voice softened as he pulled you close to his chest.

'You have to let me say something, child. This cannot go on. Your mother needs help and so do you.'

'I don't know what you're talking about,' you lied, struggling to be free, but he held you fast. He lifted your face up until you were looking into his eyes and you felt him harden against you. His face changed. Suddenly he let you go, rushing out, saying he had to get back to his duties. But you knew he'd be back. The voices told you.

You became his lover the following week, when he engineered for you to spend time helping him in the church. You were a willing participant, finding real peace in your times together. He, on the other hand, grew more and more troubled. Fortunately your mother never suspected, until you got pregnant and had to be sent away…

1.34 p.m.

A knock at the door breaks her reverie. It's Sue.

'I've just had a phone call from the police.'

'The police?'

'I'm sorry, Grace, but your grandson ran away from school and he's missing.'

'Adam? When?'

'I don't know the details but they're sending someone to interview you. You'll have someone in the room with you, you won't be on your own, but they do need to speak to you.'

'What about Jaynie?'

'I'm sorry, I don't really know anything else. You can ask when they get here.'

'When will that be?'

'I don't know but I'll come and get you when they arrive. I know it's easier said than done, but try not to worry.'

She leaves the door open as she walks away. There's a strangled cry from behind, then Grace screams, 'It's my fault, my fault,' repeatedly whilst banging her head against the door frame and has to be restrained and sedated.

2.56 p.m.

A female officer arrives to speak to Grace just as Sue goes off duty. Sue lets her into the unit, then shows her into Dr Norman's office. Dr Norman is suffering. She has a migraine coming on and divorce papers in her drawer that she wants to read over before she signs and sends them back to her solicitor. Having finally made the decision, she wants to get it over with as soon as possible. However, the matter of Grace is much more urgent and she forces her attention back to the situation in hand.

'Good afternoon. I'm Dr Norman and in charge of this unit. Grace Watson's one of my patients here and I understand you need to speak to her with regard to her missing grandson. Is that correct?'

'Thanks for seeing me, Dr Norman. I'd like to speak to Mrs Watson—'

'Ms Watson—she's never been married.'

'Sorry. I'd like to see Ms Watson and speak to her about her grandson. I understand he was a witness at his sister's death?'

'Yes. He raised the alarm.'

'I understand Ms Watson—Grace isn't it?—was sectioned at the time. How's she doing now?'

'Diagnosis and treatment is, of course, confidential. With regard to seeing you at the moment it will be difficult. Suffice to say that she is sedated and I'm not sure how much sense you'll get out of her.'

'I really need to speak to her. The boy's been missing for three days now and any information she may be able to help us with will be invaluable.'

'I realise your dilemma, but I do have a duty of care for Grace.' She pauses. 'If I grant you permission, I shall be present throughout the interview and I must insist that you suspend questioning if she becomes distressed at any point.'

'Of course.'

Dr Norman picks up the phone and dials.

'Ah, Darren. Can you bring Grace in here please? Thank you.'

Grace is calm again, but stares at the officer, not speaking or answering any questions. Dr Norman tries to engage her in conversation but Grace rocks and stares, rocks and stares, so the interview is terminated. Dr Norman promises to ask Grace if she could throw any light on Adam's whereabouts and will let the station know when she's more receptive.

3.13 p.m.

After Grace is taken back to her room Dr Norman studies Grace's file. She should have been on her way home by now but she needs a displacement activity to avoid going into a house devoid of Tim's things. This is what she wants, but it's still hard.

She is impressed with Sue, who has managed to track down Grace's notes from Ireland and the faxes arrived that morning. Although rather sketchy, Dr Norman is able to ascertain that Grace miscarried a second child. She had post partum haemorrhage and was given an emergency hysterectomy. Her daughter, Jayne, was placed in the care of the Church until Grace was discharged, almost two years later. There had been several suicide attempts in hospital, so Grace was moved to a more secure facility where severe depression was diagnosed and she was treated with ECT, water therapy and anti-depressants. There was no previous record of psychiatric disturbance and family history was not available.There was a mother somewhere in England but Grace had no contact with her.

As she skims through the pages a report catches her eye.

> 3 June 1980
> 'The patient demonstrates self-hatred and self-accusations, treating herself as a lost object. She has feelings about herself which are like the feelings of someone disappointed in love i.e. a pining sense of devastated loss and burning anger but she is unable to release her desire to regain the desired object (herself) or to acknowledge aggressive feelings towards it. She is prone to depression and melancholia, her self-esteem dependent upon her relations with others.

10 June 1980
Grace is becoming increasingly withdrawn from reality and her introversion prevents her from responding appropriately to social situations. As she lets her emotional ties with the world drop, so her relationships in it are lost.

17 June 1980
Withdrawal from emotions of the outer world have left Grace feeling locked away in an autonomous inner world where she is depersonalised. She feels she no longer exists insofar as her despair is solitary, unshared and unrelated to other people.

Further on Dr Norman discovers Grace developed some bipolar tendencies characterized by mixed episode, cycle acceleration, and chronic depression relating to the miscarriage. However, discontinuation of anti-depressants and the institution of treatment with mood stabilizers and atypical neuroleptics resulted in a sustained improvement and symptom remission. Grace was released into the care of the Church who had housed her previously. Follow up appointments were missed and no further records were found.

Dr Norman ponders over the information. Her stomach rumbles and she realises she has not eaten all day. Maybe she should get something at the Dog and Duck when she finishes?

3.49 p.m.
Custody suite, Carlisle

DS Hedley's computer screen has pulled up the photo of Alexander Freeman, AKA Sandy, and his rap sheet.

There is an outstanding warrant for his arrest for failing to turn up to court to answer charges on Child Benefit fraud along with his girlfriend, Sandra Murphy, brought by the CSA. There are several previous minor convictions for debt and cheque fraud going back ten years and he was released from an open prison in Acklington eighteen months ago. The address given at his discharge was a hostel in Alnwick and they had provided the girlfriend's address. Hedley needs to check all the bases then Northumbria police can have them.

3.52 p.m.

Sandy is hot and nervous. He told the stupid cow not to let her mother know where they were going and now look what's happened! That fucking Sandra's a liability. She even turned up at Jayne's looking for him! How stupid was that? Said she couldn't wait, needed to be with him, blah, blah, blah. How was he supposed to know Claire was dead? What did she expect him to do? It was his fucking daughter, for Christ's sake! He had to sweeten Jayne up, give himself time to get money from her, then they could go to Spain. That was Sandra's idea. She's got friends in Malaga running a car hire firm. They could buy themselves into the business—a right money-spinner—but he needed time. He'd taken Sandra to the pub to talk—to get her away from Jayne—but she did what she always did, got him all horny, then fucked his brains out in the toilet. She'll do it anywhere, anytime, if he let her. He couldn't go back to Jayne after that. He momentarily smiles at the thought, then frowns. But that doesn't make up for this load of fucking shite she's got them into. They'll send him down again, no messin'—go straight to jail, do not pass go—for jumping bail. When he gets out he'll definitely walk away from her. Permanently.

DS Hedley and DC Milligan enter. They introduce themselves to him and the duty solicitor, insert a cassette into the machine and record the names of those present, the time and date. Sandy's throat is dry and he's gagging for a cigarette. It's not like the old days—you could smoke then. Now all this health and safety shite means you can't smoke in the bloody building, not even your cell, let alone in the interview room, when you need one most.

Hedley clears his throat.

'Alexander Freeman, we've brought you here to ask you about the disappearance of your son, Adam Freeman.'

'What disappearance? I don't know about any disappearance. And he's not my son. I kind of inherited him when I got married.'

'Adam ran away from school two days ago and hasn't been seen since. Have you any knowledge of his whereabouts?'

'Two days ago? Is that what this is about? I thought—'

'What did you think it was about?'

Sandy licks his lips. Could it be possible they have no idea about the warrant? Maybe they don't know he's been inside? They must do. But then, he's always said the police were stupid.

'I didn't know. Your officers just said they had some questions for us. Two days you say?'

'Can you just talk us through your movements on Tuesday afternoon and evening please?' asks Milligan.

'What? You think I've got him?'

'I didn't say that. Where were you on Tuesday, Mr Freeman?'

'Let's see… Tuesday? I think I was… yes, I was with Sandra. We were in bed all afternoon, then went for a drink in the evening.'

'And where was that?'

'The Carter's Bog on Albion Road.'

'Can anyone verify that?'

'The landlord. I got into a fight with Sandra and they chucked us out just before closing. Then we went back to the digs.'

DC Milligan scribbles on a pad.

It's Hedley's turn. 'Have you any idea where Adam might have gone?'

'No, but why did he run away? That Gary hasn't been interfering with him, has he?'

'Gary?'

'Jayne's new boyfriend. He's far too involved with Adam for my liking.'

'Involved?'

More scribbling on the pad.

'Yeah. You know. Too feely touchy. Always hanging round. He brought him home from the funeral when Adam should've been in the car with us.'

Hedley and Milligan look at each other. Hedley asks, 'And how did that come about?'

'Jayne was in a right state so I was looking after her. When I turned round for Adam he was gone. Lizzie said he'd gone with Gary, but they didn't turn up till ages after we'd got back. Adam wouldn't tell us where they'd been or what they'd been doing. In fact, he wouldn't speak at all, just went to his room and stayed there. He wouldn't eat, wouldn't say nothing to his mam. Nothing.'

'Did you mention anything to Mrs Freeman?'

'Well, no, not really.'

'Why not?'

'She was too cut up as it was.'

'I see. And the next day you left with Sandra?'

'Yes.'

Hedley straightens in his seat. 'Let me get this right. Your child has just drowned. You suspect another child has been abused, and you abandon him and leave a grieving woman the day after your, and her, daughter's funeral?'

Sandy shifts uncomfortably in his seat before shouting, 'It wasn't like that. Sandra turned up at the door. What else could I do?'

'Why did you go back to Mrs Freeman?' asks Milligan.

'Well… I'd read about Claire in the papers.'

'That's not what Mrs Freeman says. She told us you didn't know about it till she told you,' contradicts Hedley.

'Er... When I went round I was cut up about it. I was in denial.'

Both officers laugh then Hedley comments, 'Wow. Denial. You were cut up, eh? How cut up? Obviously not cut up enough to stay and comfort your ex-wife. Just how much of Claire had you seen in the last three years? I understand you left when she was just a few weeks old.'

Sandy is getting hot again.

'It… er… it wasn't working out with Jayne. I needed some space, then I met Sandra.'

'I see. So nothing to do with you going inside then?'

Sandy's face drains of colour.

'What d'you mean?'

'I understand Mrs Freeman had no knowledge of your stay in Acklington. How did you manage to keep that from her?'

Sandy desperately looks around for inspiration. There is none.

'I think this interview's over, Mr Freeman. You'll be taken to your cell to await officers from Northumbria who'll take you away for questioning with regard to an outstanding warrant and a small matter of some bounced cheques from your B&B. Be aware that we may need to question you again, but we'll know where to find you. Interview terminated at sixteen twenty-two hours.'

Hedley and Milligan rise. Sandy is escorted out of the room.

4.27 p.m.

DCI Truman looks up as DS Hedley knocks and enters. 'What have you got on the disappearance, Billy?' he asks

'We've just interviewed Freeman and he's implicated the boyfriend, suggesting the boy might have been interfered with. Maybe it's sour grapes, but he confirmed the boy was taken home from the funeral by the boyfriend and that Adam was with him for quite a while and wouldn't talk or eat when he got back. Looks like there could be something in it.'

'Interesting. Keep me informed, will you?'

'Sure. I've asked uniform to pick him up now.'

'Thanks, Billy.'

'No sweat, sir.' Hedley leaves the room, closing the door behind him.

Friday 23 May

4.19 a.m.

Custody suite

Gary is shaking. He's still in the interview room, with its sparse walls, chipped table and coffee stains. They've left him for a break while they check up on a few things. He has been answering their questions off and on for hours. The solicitor told him after sixteen hours he is entitled to a proper break of eight hours but after that they can keep him another twelve hours authorized by a Superintendent before they have to go to court for an extension. He has been assured that so far the evidence is circumstantial, but he's terrified that there is even any 'evidence' at all. How could there be, he's done nothing wrong?

He can't believe what's happening to him, what they're accusing him of. Why on earth would they think he has molested Adam? Has Jayne accused him? Or is it just their twisted minds that conjured that one up? They know the reason Adam ran away—a fight with John—so why are they asking about this? They even suggested he used Kuma to help him abduct Adam, then killed Adam to stop him talking, and buried his body somewhere.

He feels sick just thinking about the questions they asked. They must be perverts themselves to ask those sorts of things. He likes Adam because he's Jayne's child, but not in the way they're making out. He wants a family of his own, sure, but he's more than willing to take on her kids—kid—he corrects himself. Jayne comes as a package, he's known that since he first started seeing her, so if he wants her, and he does, he takes the kids on too. How is that so difficult to comprehend? Not everyone wants to screw every female in sight and then move on to the next one. He wants to settle down with her, raise her family, maybe even have one or two of their own, although Jayne rules that idea out because of her age. Which is silly, as she's still young enough. Plenty women have children in their thirties. But he's not going to push it. Ever since Sharon… Just making Jayne happy is enough. He wants to look after her, not interfere with her son.

Hurry up and find Adam. He'll tell the truth.

5.00 a.m.
Mobile Unit, Mining Heritage Centre Car Park
The search resumes. DS Thompson is in charge of the underground search, whilst DS Hedley is co-ordinating the surface effort. Hedley is briefing the officers while trained volunteers painstakingly search the ground in co-ordinated lines covering squares of ground which he marks off on a grid map, writing the names of the officers involved in each grid. He feels frustrated. The lad has been missing for three days now and the likelihood of them finding him alive is getting more and more remote. Helicopters from Boulmer have covered every inch from the air but come up with nothing. It was decided not to use helicopter thermal searchers, which can track the direction of any footprints, because a) by the time it was realised that this was an abduction too much time had elapsed and b) even if the Force had enough money to employ them, they would have been ineffective because of the trees, thick heather and bracken. However, if there is a body buried, thermal imaging can pick it up if it has started to decompose, but at this stage it's too early for that kind of decomposition to show. Hedley hopes thermal imaging is not something they will need to consider in the future.

6.41 a.m.
Garrigill Farm, Nr Burnhope Reservoir

'What on earth!'

Mary Donkin shakes her head with the realization that Matthew's clothes have disappeared from the washing line. She is a small, round woman, her brown hair streaked with home-done blonde highlights giving the appearance of having an egg smashed on her crown, the yolk running down her hair. She forgot to take the washing in last night before bed because some of the new calves were having problems feeding with the drip system. She has been up most of the night with her husband, Mat, feeding them by hand.

-It's coming to something when you can't leave your washing on the line, all the way out here! And who on earth would want children's clothes? They aren't even his good ones, just old things he plays out in. –

It isn't worth reporting really, but she has to go into Alston to pick up the new fencing. Maybe she should see Doris? She'll know if anything funny's going on round here.

8.00 a.m.
Nr Martyn's Copse, Marshalldale

The searchers are hot and thirsty working in the open as the sun beats down on them and early morning midges nip their faces and necks. The forest is cooler, but the midges are worse in there. It is so easy to get distracted by them, but PC Moira Partington steels herself and concentrates only on thinking about a frightened little boy who needs their help to get him home. This is her day off, but it's her first child abduction case and she didn't realised how much it would affect her.

Someone to her left shouts, 'Over here,' and everyone stops what they're doing and waits for instructions. Forensics are called, then she and the others cordon off the area with tape ready for Forensics to process it. A pair of child's soiled underpants and a business card have been found. Her heart sinks. Please let him still be alive…

8.34 a.m.
The Rise

Jayne is on her fourth cigarette when the phone rings. She knows instinctively it's bad news. Her hands are shaking as she lifts the receiver.

'Hello, Mrs Freeman. PC Dickinson here. I've got the list of clothes you said Adam was wearing at the time of his disappearance. Can I just check that with you please?'

'Yes. What's happened?'

'I've been going through your statement and you said that Adam was wearing a royal blue school sweatshirt, grey trousers and white polo shirt with his school tie. What about underwear? It says in your statement "blue underpants". Is that right ?'

'Yes, I think so. I…I'm not sure which pair he had on. He dresses himself. I just put out clean shirts and trousers for him. Why? Is it important?'

Dickinson clears his throat, then continues. 'It may be. We've discovered a pair of child's underpants and were hoping you'd be able to identify them. I'll send a car for you, if that's okay?'

'Yes…yes…' A chill runs through her whole body. 'Oh, God, no. Please, not that.' She sits down heavily.

'There could be a number of explanations why his pants were discarded, but first we need to ascertain whether or not they're his. There'll be a car round to pick you up in half an hour at the most. Do you have someone who can accompany you?'

'Er…yes.' Dazed, she looks at Lizzie. 'My friend, Lizzie Waites.'

'Fine, I'll keep you informed of any further developments. Bye now.'

12.10 p.m.
Police Station, Alston

Doris Jamieson has three jobs, all of them equally important to her. It's what keeps her slim and sane, she tells everyone. She works Mondays and Fridays doing admin for Joe Dickinson in the police station, Tuesdays and every other Saturday in the post office, although it's looking more and more likely, despite their petition, that they'll lose the post office to Sainsbury's. And on Wednesdays and Thursdays she drives the mobile library. Toady she's holding the fort for Joe and is on the phone to her daughter when Mary rings the bell in reception.

'Sorry, poppet, I've got to go. Just soak in cold water; that should do the trick. I'll phone you this evening about eight, okay? Will you be able to get to the phone by then? ... Rightio. Talk to you then… Bye.'

She makes her way to reception. Opening the hatch she offers a cheery greeting. ' Hello, Mary. I've just been speaking to our Sheila. You'd think that by the time she got to university she would have learnt how to get bloodstains out of T-shirts. My, you're looking well.'

'Ha, I don't feel it. Been up all night feeding the new calves by hand. But that's not what I popped in for. I wanted to ask you something. It seems ridiculous now, but some things have been going missing from the farm and I wondered whether anyone else has had stuff taken?'

'What kind of stuff?'

'This morning I went to get the washing I'd left out all night and Matthew's old clothes were gone. They hadn't blown away or anything. Then I remembered that some horse feed, matches and batteries had gone the other week. I don't know if it's worth mentioning but it's really odd that, don't you think?'

'Might it be someone playing tricks?'

'Who'd go to all that trouble.? It's not as if we're accessible. They'd have to drive there and we hear anyone coming.'

'Unless they were on bicycles?'

'Well, there is that, I suppose. It just seems a lot of trouble to go to for a few items. Where's the fun in it anyway?'

'You never know. Nothing would surprise me these days. I'll have a word with Joe and see if he knows anything. He'll probably give you a call later. Now, I'll need a description—'

'Oh, don't bother. I'm sure Joe's got much more important things to do than chase a couple of old tracksuits and some underwear. Anyway, I'm off to pick up some fencing.'

'Just a minute, Mary. For the report. I need a description of the items.'

'Two blue tracksuits, one with red flashing down the sides of the arms and legs, the other's just plain blue. Two pairs of sports socks and three pairs of coloured underpants, boxer style.'

'Thanks a lot. 'Bye now.'

''Bye. Give my love to your mam.'

'Will do. You take care now.'

Mary leaves and Doris feels a surge of excitement.

-Boy's clothes, eh? Joe will be very interested in this.-

Doris picks up the phone again and dials Joe's mobile but gets the engaged tone. She is about to leave a message but another call comes in so she takes that, then looks at the time and decides to go for lunch. She has an elderly mother living with her who is a stickler for time. She is already late, so she makes a mental note to ring Joe and do the paperwork when she gets back.

They were his red Spiderman pants. What kind of mother doesn't know the colour of her son's underpants when he goes missing? I bought them as a pack of three at Tesco's last year for Xmas and thought he was wearing the blue ones. He was really into Spiderman and he and Claire played for hours making dens with the cushions off the settees so she could hide, then he'd demolish them and 'rescue' her. He's got a duvet set too, but there's The Hulk on the bed at the moment. I really can't bear this. If anything's happened to him...There's no point to being here anymore, if he doesn't come back. I carry this weight around inside me all the time. It shifts to my throat when I try to please Lizzie and eat, but usually it's in my stomach, dragging me down. Yet it's much more than just a weight, it's more like having to bear the sins of the universe—I think I know how Prometheus must've felt having his liver constantly eaten by that eagle, or whatever it was. There are sounds in my ears, like the edge of ticking clocks. I can't quite make out what they are or where they come from, but I know they're there. They don't scare me any more—I think I'm beyond any fear other than for Adam—but they annoy me because they won't go away. It feels a bit like when there's a mozzie in the room. You can hear it, often it buzzes right past your ear, but you're buggered if you can see it, until it lands somewhere. Maybe I've got tinnitus?

Gary's still in custody. I can't believe they've kept him in so long. They wanted to know how he got on with Adam, did I think he was too attached to him for such a 'short acquaintance'? How did Adam behave after he'd been with Gary? Did he spend too much time alone with him? Did I think it odd that Gary had been so keen to accept the kids and be involved with them as soon as we started our relationship, and all that kind of thing? They found his business card with the underpants so they must think he's involved or why else don't they release him? Oh, God, what if he's been...all the time...and what if he touched Claire?... I can't take it in. I just can't think any more. If there's any God or Justice in the world, please bring Adam home. Please...

12.55 p.m.
Mobile Unit, Mining Heritage Centre Car Park

The mobile Incident Room is crowded with the next shift of uniform, army and forestry volunteers drafted in for the search.

'Let's make a start. We've covered all these quadrants from here,' DS Hedley indicates on a large map of the area, 'to here. The red markers are where items of Adam's clothing have been found. These relate to his tie and buttons, this is the barn where a scrap of sweatshirt was found on a nail on the door frame, blood, hair and skin on the hatch of the woodstore, and this,' he points again, 'is where the underpants and Hindmarsh's business card were found this morning. We've had to let Hindmarsh go because so far everything is circumstantial and we really need something to directly tie him to the evidence.'

‘There were no signs of vehicle tracks or of him being dragged, so do we assume he was carried, Sarge?’ asks Caroline.

‘Probably, but it’s a long way between where we believe he was abducted, and where the card and pants were found. Of course, there’s nothing to say he couldn’t have been carried somewhere else and the abductor left these items to lead us on a false trail.’

‘Are there any footprints which might suggest someone was carrying a heavy load?’

‘You’ve been watching too much *CSI*, Caroline,’ Carter laughs, but he’s stared down by Hedley and coughs, awkwardly.

Hedley continues, ‘It’s hot and there’s been no rain for days so the ground is dry and hard. We found one set of footprints down by the stream, here,’ he indicates, ‘but that could have been from a walker, or farmer, or anyone. The tread suggests hiking or army boots, so we’re keeping that in mind, particularly since it’s not too far away from the crime scene areas.’

‘Are we assuming the boy’s still alive, sir?’ asks a young army cadet.

‘Officially, yes. But the longer he’s missing, the greater the possibility he’s dead. Any more questions? No? Right, let’s get into teams again. DS Thompson wants Blue and Yellow teams with the Cave Rescue volunteers to search this underground area.’ He indicates with his finger. ‘You’ll need to report to him here,’ he stabs a finger at the map again, ‘to sign in and get your kit. Reds, can you go here with the forestry and half the army volunteers and search this area?’ there’s another stab with the finger, ‘and Greens, I’d like you to join with the other half and Mountain Rescue and cover this area here. Good luck, everyone, and let’s hope we can find this lad alive somewhere.’

1.13 p.m.
Merry Farm

They released Gary at midday without charge but he has been asked not to leave the area as they may need to question him further. Opening the door he is almost bowled over by the smell. There's a pile of dogshit in the kitchen and the place reeks in this heat. There are also puddles of urine, so he opens the back door then begins the task of cleaning up the mess. He rang Scottie late last night to pick the dog up, but obviously he wouldn't clean up the mess.

Gary is tired and angry so he puts the kettle on and moves into the lounge where his computer and all the disks used to be.

-Bastards! What do they think he is? Some sort of paedophile involved in a child porn ring? Christ Almighty! That kind of thing sticks. He's often said, 'There's no smoke without fire,' but now the shoe's on the other foot, isn't it? Well, he's nothing to hide, so they won't find anything, will they? That's probably why they had to let him go. But he's still their main suspect and that's scary. What he wouldn't do to have his mam and dad here right now. What're his friends going to think? And Jayne. What about her? Well there's one way to find out.-

Gingerly he picks up the phone and dials Jayne's number. The call is intercepted by BT and he puts it back down.

-What if he goes round? Will she see him? How will that be construed by the police? -

Feeling impotent and frustrated, he gives in to tears. The chaos of his business—the missed appointments, disappointed customers, irate phone calls—will have to wait till he's strong enough to deal with them.

He makes a decision. Right now, he needs to get the dog.

10.00 p.m.
BBC Television

'Good evening. In Cumbria today the hunt for missing schoolboy Adam Freeman was stepped up when an article of his clothing was discovered in woods near Martyn's Copse. Police are not at liberty to provide further details, but a spokesperson said that they are "gravely concerned" about Adam's whereabouts and cannot rule out foul play. The boy's mother, Mrs Jayne Freeman, was said to be too distressed to comment. Tragically she lost her three-year-old daughter, Claire, in an accident less than two weeks ago. Mrs Freeman is at home being looked after by friends. The police are appealing for witnesses, or anyone with information of the whereabouts of Adam Freeman, to contact them. All information will be treated confidentially.

If you have any information at all which might help find this little boy, please contact the police on the number coming up on your screen. That's 0800 275 6699.

Now, over to our correspondent in Beijing for the latest news on the merger—'

Sat 24 May

10.22am
Fletcher Ward

It hurts to remember those drips of time and memories. You want to go back to that day and change it. If only you ha-d listened, had let them in. Would it have ended differently? Who can you ask, who will know? Brendan used to tell you that everything was pre-ordained and that knowing an outcome wouldn't change it, but you never really believed that. Oh, Brendan.

Suddenly, the dream returns…

The light has turned red and feels like syrup on your skin. It sounds like melon. It smells smooth and silky, like a black, glossy horse and tastes like peace. In front of you is a large door, which is open. You can see through to a cathedral of trees, where early morning mists swirl and rise to greet the lances of sun, slicing the dark shadows. There's a small deer ahead in a clearing. You want to walk towards it but notice that your feet don't seem to be touching the ground. Or if they are, you can't feel it. This is very strange. But the strangest thing of all is that you're not afraid. For the first time since you can remember, you're not afraid. Does this mean you're dead?

The light is hot on your eyes. It has changed slightly in texture and the colour is now orange. On your feet you have soft leather bindings; your skirts are long and splashed with mud. As you make your way through the lines of trees there is an urgency in your steps, but your purpose hasn't formed fully in your mind yet. It's like a half-remembered dream that whispers to you on the periphery of thought.

You increase your speed a little and notice your hair is corn yellow, long, in tight curls matted into ringlets, swinging down your back. Strands of it are stuck to your forehead with sweat and you brush them away with a grimy hand. Your nails are dirty, the knuckles slightly swollen and you have calluses on your palms. The tips of your fingers are numb and you notice there are no fingerprints there, they seem to have been burnt away.

The forest is getting thicker, oak and pine trees veer to your left and right, so you slow down and take more care not to trip over the roots that lie in wait for your feet. The smells of rotting leaves and pine needles cling to your nostrils, mixed with the aromas of loam and peat. The texture of the light is changing, getting thicker as the colour spreads; it feels like glue now. You have to fight your way forward through a stickiness that is threatening to suffocate you, yet there is no fear. The boulders in your chest are still.

The light begins to smell like passion and tastes like pansies. Ahead there's a clearing. You must reach it to warn…who? The trees are thinning out slightly, bending backwards to let you pass and you're grateful to them. Underfoot the roots rise up and clear a path for you as you're propelled forward. You experience a lightness of being, unhobbled and free.

You enter the clearing and see a tall man dressed in black as the light changes to yellow. Suddenly it darkens around you. He's snapping the necks of rabbits, putting them into a sack. You see a gaping hole and watch as two small arms stick out from it, waving frantically as earth tumbles down on them until only the fingers are visible, and still. The air is chilled, you taste dirt and death on your tongue, then it's over.

-You have to tell them. Adam needs you to tell them.-

-But I don't know how to. Not anymore. It's been too long. I just can't. -

-Can't or won't?

-Who could I tell? Who would believe me? They haven't in the past—why should they now? -

-You have to try. Try China Blue. She might believe you…-

2.10 pm
Under Garrick's Fell

Dom Hargreaves and the team are painstakingly searching along the horse levels, which is slow and tiring work. Dom is in the lead and carries the ultra-low frequency radio, to make contact with the police searching above. He has an obsession with extreme sports and despite the fact they search is for a missing boy, he's enjoying himself. He shuffles his way forward—this is a tricky bit because it's very narrow and full of 'deads', which is waste material left over from when the mine was worked. There has also been a recent rock fall, making it even narrower and more difficult to reach the shaft ahead. He puts aside some rocks and pushes himself through into the shaft. He shines his beam upwards and almost misses the plastic bag. Carefully, he pulls on plastic gloves, removes it from its hiding place and peers inside. He is straight onto the radio.

'Charlie Blue One to Charlie Blue Two. Come in please.'

The radio crackles a response. 'This is Charlie Blue Two'

'We've got something here. It's hidden in the rise of Stephenson's Shaft, in a small pocket where it connects with the level above. It looks like supplies of dried meat and fish in plastic bags. It must be someone's emergency supply.'

'Right-o Charlie Blue One. Bag them and send someone out with them. And be careful not to obliterate any fingerprints. The rest of the team continue with the search and see if there's anything else down there.'

'Message understood. Over and out.'

Dom bags the items and passes them through to the last member of the team, Greg Hardy, to take up to the surface, and he and Jimmy Anderton, his rock-climbing partner, carry on searching. There are still five miles of tunnels ahead.

4.55 p.m.
Police HQ

'So what do you make of it, sir, and where does this leave us with Hindmarsh?' asks DS Thompson. Hedley stands beside him.

DCI Truman studies the board in front of him, which is covered in photos, maps and information. He doesn't answer for nearly a minute, then says, still looking at the board, 'I'm not sure. It could be he's been preparing this for a while, although there's nothing to suggest he's familiar with the tunnels. Or it could indicate someone else is involved, an accomplice, or we've been looking in the wrong place. Or the supplies could belong to someone totally unrelated to the enquiry. We'll have to keep an open mind and see what else turns up. We'll see what forensics say about the age of the stuff and how long it's been there and also if they can find any fingerprints. You never know, we may have them on file.' He turns and looks at his officers, smiling grimly, 'It may turn out to be nothing but we can't rule anything out.'

Thompson and Hedley nod in agreement and Thompson adds this latest piece of information to the board whilst Hedley updates SLEUTH.

6.00 p.m.
Radio Cumbria
' OVER TO JEAN IN THE NEWSROOM.'

'THANK YOU, GARETH. WE'VE JUST HEARD FROM SOURCES AT THE SCENE THAT THE SEARCH FOR MISSING SCHOOLBOY ADAM FREEMAN HAS THROWN UP NEW EVIDENCE AFTER THE DISCOVERY OF SOME ITEMS IN ONE OF THE MINE LEVELS UNDER GARRICK'S FELL. THESE MINE WORKINGS WERE ABANDONED IN THE 1950S AFTER A SLUMP IN THE DEMAND FOR IRON ORE. MANY OF THE TUNNELS AND SHAFTS HAVE COLLAPSED BUT THERE ARE STILL A LOT OF ACCESSIBLE LEVELS RUNNING ACROSS THE WHOLE REGION. IT'S NOT KNOWN YET WHAT THESE NEW DISCOVERIES ARE BUT AS SOON AS WE FIND OUT WE'LL LET LISTENERS KNOW.

AND NOW FOR THE REST OF THE NEWS...'

9.27 p.m.
The Rise
Jayne takes the sleeping tablets Lizzie gives her without a fuss. She has thought of saving them up and taking them all together, if anything has happened to Adam, but her bones are liquid and she has no strength even to get into bed. Lizzie helps, then tiptoes out the room.

I can't even cry. I just lie here, waiting for oblivion. If only I could sleep, forget about it for a while. But even in sleep I see Adam, lying somewhere in the dark, hardly moving. I've been having these same pictures of him even when I'm awake. In my dreams I call out to him but he doesn't hear me. I call and call frantically, then there's a glimmer of light off to the left of him, flickering like a candle. Momentarily I see wooden boards, a strange kind of bed beneath him, animal skins over him, then he's gone.

11.56 p.m.
Crofter's Wood

Johnny feels the time is close to midnight and sniffs the air. The cool breeze ruffles his hair as well as the leaves on the trees above his head. He is troubled. Stealthily making his way towards the river he is suddenly incapacitated by one of his headaches. He falls to the ground convulsing. When it's over he sits for a while, unable to remember where he is or why he's there. Slowly memory returns in splashes of colour. The boy. They'll find him soon. If Johnny doesn't get away, there'll be trouble. He has been listening to the search on his wind-up radio, so knows it's just a matter of time now. The old warrant for his arrest might still be on file and if they find him… He doesn't want to think about that.

It isn't his fault. He always gets the blame, but it's not his fault. The boy made a lot of noise at first, but he's silent now. Johnny hates noise. It hurts. Just like bright light does. He used to have to wear special glasses in prison but he's okay here; he mainly only goes out at night, on dull days, or first thing in the morning before the sun gets too bright.

Spotted moonlight shining through a break in the tree cover glints off the metal shovel as Johnny digs. He places a soiled bundle in the hole, then covers it with earth and dried leaves. He shudders.

Suddenly, to his left he hears the distant call of a vixen and he sniffs the air again. The wind's blowing from the south, bringing with it the scent of garlic and rain. Silently he changes his position and puts the spade in his sack. He needs to wash his hands now.

Sun 25 May

2 a.m.

The Rise

Jayne is soaked in sweat. The dream tonight is much more vivid and she screams out, loud enough to wake Lizzie who rushes into the room.

'What's wrong. What happened?'

'It's …nothing. Just a dream.'

'What kind of a dream?' Lizzie asks as she plonks herself on top of the bed.

'A dream. Just a dream.'

'What happened in the dream?'

'I saw Adam. He's lying down, not moving. Maybe he's dead, maybe just sleeping. It's dark, very, very dark, then someone comes with a light and bends over him.'

'What kind of person? A man? What does he look like?'

'I couldn't see his face. Everything about him is dark. Black even.'

'What? As in…he's black? Asian? Afro-Caribbean?'

'No. He's surrounded by blackness. It's not just dark, it's black. No light can penetrate it, even when he's holding the candle, the light doesn't shine on him.'

'What d'you think it means, Jayne?'

'I don't know, do I!' she yells. Then more reasonably, 'It's probably just a reaction to the tablets I'm taking. Some sort of hallucination. But…'

'But what?'

'Well, it's a bit like when I was away with Gary. I suddenly knew there was something wrong with the kids, but he didn't believe me. And with this dream, I know it's Adam.' She starts to weep. 'I just keep thinking, if he's not found soon… Oh, Lizzie. What am I going to do?'

‘Didn’t Grace have funny dreams?’

‘Why bring her up?’ Jayne snaps.

‘I don’t want us to fight again, but you’ve told me yourself—’

‘No! I’m not like her! I’m not!’

‘I didn’t say you were. Look, love, will I phone and speak to her? Tell her I’ve had this dream and what does she think? It’s got to be better than sitting waiting for the phone to ring. And if it’s nothing, then there’s no harm done. Surely it’s worth a try?’

‘And what if she says he’s dead? Or being tortured? Sexually abused? Do I believe her? And what hope will there be then? She used to tell me that once something’s spoken, it becomes a reality. Well, I don’t want my darkest fears to see the light of day. I have to stay positive. I have to believe he’s coming back.’

Jayne lies back and covers her head with the sheet. At first Lizzie is lost for words, then she recovers herself and suggests, ‘Look, you get some rest and we’ll see how you feel in the morning.’

‘Thanks, Lizzie. I don’t know what I’d do without you. I hope that man of yours appreciates what a good wife he’s got.’

‘Don’t talk shite! Look, you get some sleep. You never know, there may be good news tomorrow. Which reminds me, I start work tomorrow at the Estate Office. I’ll need to be up and out early.’ Jayne doesn’t respond so Lizzie slides off the bed, and returns to Jayne’s room, leaving Jayne huddling in the comfort of Adam’s bed.

2.06 a.m.
Fletcher Ward

It is still dark when Grace wakes and sits bolt upright in

bed. The dream. She's had the dream again. This time she knows exactly what it means and what she must do. If only she had understood the warnings about Claire.

Closing her eyes she lies back against the pillows and lets the voices return. She's going to need them again.

2.18 a.m.
Craft Room

Normally no-one is allowed in without a therapist but it's still early, so no-one will miss her just yet. Fortunately for her, the door is unlocked and made of solid wood so no tell-tale light shines through, although if anyone comes down the corridor they will probably see the light shining under the door. She just has to take the chance.

The smell of paints and glue momentarily arrests her, taking her back to the log cabin, but then she remembers where she is and why she's here. The room is large with huge cupboards along three of the walls, the fourth has a bench running along its length and above the bench are three wide windows looking out on the garden; they are locked.

Opening the cupboards Grace finds what she is looking for. Selecting a large canvas she places it on an easel that she sets up in front of a window. She then searches for the tubes of oil paints, brushes and some solvent. She finds them in the third cupboard and takes them over to the bench beside the easel. She needs natural light but this will have to do till the sun comes up.

Closing her eyes, she recalls the details of her dream and starts mixing paints to translate them onto the canvas. This time, however, she leaves her clothes on, a concession for where she is, and covers herself with one of the aprons hanging on hooks inside the cupboard by the door.

She begins under-painting with a first layer of one of the 'earth colours', raw umber, which she mixes with ultramarine and solvent to provide a dark brown tone for the background. This is fast drying, enabling her to add the next layer. Using less solvent this time,she creates depth to the painting. She must wait for this layer to dry before applying paint from the tube for the characters. The next two layers are mixed with increasing amounts of linseed oil to make them 'fatter', adding texture and definition to the brush strokes.

Grace works on, oblivious to anything else, unaware of the time. As she stands back to wait for the last layer to dry she hears the tea trolley arrive and slips quietly back into her room unnoticed.

8.32 a.m.

After breakfast Grace asks for Sue but is told she's not in today. Grace is disappointed and mutters softly to herself as she returns to her room. A few minutes later she comes back out and makes her way to the craft room. There is one detail she needs to add, then she can let it dry completely.

8.34 a.m.

South Row, Nenthead

Lizzie is back home and snuggling up to Derek. This running back and forwards is killing her, and she misses the security of lying next to Derek in bed. She has no idea what to make of Jayne's dream. Lizzie has always had problems with the New Age philosophies and therapies that Grace and Jayne bought into—they are not scientific and she believes there are always rational explanations for things—but her instincts, which she has never trusted before, tell her that Jayne needs to see Grace. But Jayne has categorically refused to have anything to do with her mother.

-Perhaps that woman at the hospital might be able to help?-

Throwing back the sheets she disturbs Derek reading his *Sunday Observer* and goes downstairs to telephone.

10.46 a.m.
Merry Farm

Gary has been up and out with the dog and is now considering how to fill the rest of the day. If he and Jayne were still together he would suggest a picnic at Talkin Tarn, or perhaps a trip to Hexham. He used to love his Sundays, even before he met Jayne. The precious lie-in; pub lunch; time with his mates. After Jayne his Sundays took on a different face, but now that's gone too. Is this all there is to life? All this hassle and pain? Maybe his dad's right. Maybe he should make a fresh start somewhere else…

6.55 p.m.
Coglin Mews

Sue has the weekend off and is meeting Darren tonight. He invited her over to his flat for a celebratory meal at eight o'clock and she is so excited she's almost peeing herself. He wouldn't tell her what the celebration was, but she hopes it has to do with her.

-Maybe he's going to tell me he's fallen in love with me? Maybe he wants me to move in with him? Have his babies? Hold on, hold on. Not too fast, girl. Get a grip of yourself. What happened to the woman who didn't need a man to give validation to her existence?-

She has changed clothes about ten times and the discarded garments litter her bed. What to wear? What to bloody wear? He said she had a nice cleavage, so something to show her breasts off. Her basque holds them up nicely—underwear has never been a problem, it's the top stuff she has difficulty with. She moves her attention to her hair. He said he likes it down, on her shoulders and neck. If only it was long enough to wrap round her throat like that advert he showed her. That would be something, wouldn't it? Ah, well, she will have to make do with a nice silver necklace and her hair falling forward onto her neck.

Looking at the time she realises if she doesn't make a decision soon, she's going to be late, so she plumps for a copper-coloured silky top and skirt. With any luck she won't have them on long. The excitement and anticipation is so great her heart flutters and she has to sit down. If she carries on like his she's going to have a heart attack. It's not as if he's a stranger or anything. Maybe it would be better if he was. She always has difficulty with people she really likes. Anonymous men are easy—you don't have to see them again, so if they think you're crap it doesn't matter. But it matters what Darren thinks and she starts trembling all over again.

-This is just stupid- she tells herself.

- Pull yourself together or he really will think you're crap. A few drinks will help. You can have a couple to calm your nerves and still be able to drive there. He'll obviously have wine for the meal but you're taking a bottle anyway, just in case. With a bit of luck you'll be staying the night and can drive home in the morning.-

She pours herself a large measure of vodka, adds some cranberry juice and slugs it back, then she makes her way to the door, checks herself in the mirror, smiles and repeats, 'Whatever happens, I can handle it.

Whatever happens, I can handle it,' goes out and closes the door. She hears the phone ring but ignores it, not wanting to delay any more. If it's anything important they'll leave a message or phone back.

7.32 p.m.
North Parade, Whitley Bay
Darren's flat is in a residential area of Whitley Bay, just round the corner from Lisa's, overlooking the sea. Standing in the huge bay window Sue is impressed with the views over the links to the lighthouse. It is rented, Darren tells her, when she remarks on how its value would increase if he did one or two alterations. She is not sure what to say after that, so asks for another drink. He obliges with another glass of wine from the bottle she brought, and smiles at her.

'So…what's to eat?' she asks.

'At the moment, you.' Smooching in close he starts nuzzling her neck, his tongue skimming the surface. She responds to his caresses with a few of her own and feels him harden.

'I thought we'd eat later—I hate having sex on a full stomach, don't you?'

There is no answer she can give because his tongue is in her mouth. He has started to undress her, sliding the zip of the top down her back. She assists him and the top is quickly discarded. She removes his tee-shirt and undoes his jeans as passion starts to take over. Soon they are on the floor and 'carpet burns' momentarily flits across her mind but is quickly forgotten as he prises her open with his fingers. Their breathing is becoming ragged and she surfaces for air to ask if he has a condom. Reaching for his jeans he searches the pockets and produces one, which she expertly positions around the shaft of his penis. She has heard you can do this with your mouth but she uses the old tried and tested method of hands, masturbating him with one whilst the other plays with his balls.

Turning over, she straddles on all fours and he enters her. He licks his fingers and starts massaging her clitoris. She moves her arms till her elbows are resting on the floor, making her buttocks more prominent so he can penetrate deeper. She has her back to the door and is vaguely aware of a shift in air, or a slight draft, but she has her eyes closed, losing herself in the feelings he is generating. Boy is he good. One hand is raking her back, forcing her to arch involuntarily, while the other is still working on her clitoris. Then a third hand and nails starts raking her legs.

Confused, she turns her head sideways and sees Lisa, naked except for a cross-over dress that is hanging open. Lisa kneels beside her, kissing Darren whilst raking her nails over Sue's leg.

Shocked, Sue tries to turn over, knocking all three of them into a sprawl on the carpet.

'Hey!' yells Darren, sitting cross-legged, inspecting his penis for signs of damage.

'What's wrong?' asks Lisa, innocently. 'I thought this would be a nice surprise for you.'

'A nice surprise? I told you I wasn't interested in another threesy.'

'Ah, come on, Sue, lighten up,' Darren says irritated, 'it's not as if we haven't done this before. You really enjoyed last time,' and he moves closer to kiss her, but she pulls back from him.

'I thought tonight was about you and me, Darren.'

'What do you mean?'

'Well, you and me. Going out together. Properly.'

Stunned, Darren asks, 'What gave you that idea?'

'You asked me to come for a celebration—I thought it was about us.'

Lisa bursts out laughing at the sight of Darren's face. Sue blushes deeply and starts to find her clothes and put them back on.

'Oh, that. I was going to tell you later. Look, I'm moving to Dumfries in six weeks. A mate of mine works there and they're looking for nurses for their psychiatric unit. I've got one of the key jobs so I'm handing my notice in at the end of the month. I thought this would be a good way to celebrate.'

'Did you know about this?' Sue asks Lisa.

'Of course. We thought after the other night that it would be a nice way to celebrate, before he moves away.'

'We? Do you two sit and discuss me?'

'Stop being—'

'Being what? Hurt? Feeling betrayed? I told you my feelings in confidence, Lisa, not for you to plot to get me into bed with the two of you. How long have you been seeing each other?'

'We aren't "seeing each other". We just have sex, hang out, get drunk, do a bit of coke. You know.'

'No, I don't. We work together. We're on the same shift. How can I work with you now?'

Lisa stands up, pulling her dress closed. 'Stop being so melodramatic. Get over yourself. I'm leaving.'

'No, Lisa. Stay. We haven't finished what we started yet,' says Darren standing up. He removes Lisa's dress and starts to play with her breasts as Sue finishes dressing and leaves, mascara running down her cheeks.

8.04 p.m.
North Parade
Outside Sue is distraught. She opens the car, collapses inside and sobs until she has nothing left. Bastards. Bloody bastards. How could they do this to her? And Lisa? How had she ever considered her a friend? She turns the ignition, then a glimmer of common sense kicks in. She has had far too much to drink. She turns the ignition off, reaches for her mobile phone and presses a number.

'Cassie? It's me. Can you do me a favour please?' she asks then starts sobbing all over again.

'What's wrong? Where are you?' asks Cassie.

'Can you get a taxi to Whitley Bay—I'll pay for it—and drive me home please? I've had too much to drink and—'

'Where in Whitley Bay?'

'North Parade. Beside the Avon Hotel.'

'I'll be there as soon as I can.'

'Thanks. You're a star,' and Sue smiles despite herself, for using Grace's expression. Grace is right, he's not worth it. She'll just have to find someone who is and get over her phobias. She can't live like this anymore, she needs a change. Blowing her nose she waits for Cassie.

Monday 26 May

7.00 a.m.
Nenthead

Joe Dickinson knocks on the door of the big house. It has been called that for as long as he can remember but its real name is Whitfield Manor. It was built in 1727 by Lord Longstaff as a retreat for his painter sister Emily, who died of consumption the following year. After that it was sold to a local historian, Sir Robert Enfield, and had once even belonged to one of King George V's minor cousins. Sadly it has seen better days and the current owner, retired soldier Major Cartwright, keeps himself to himself while the property crumbles around him.

His knock on the door produces no answer so Joe moves round to the back of the house that once was the servants' and tradesmen's entrance. He tries the large oak door that leads into a tiled kitchen and it opens. Stepping inside there is an overpowering smell of decay and flies buzz furiously at him as he disturbs their foodfest. There are empty cartons and rotting food in the bin, mouldy cups and plates in the sink. Gagging a little he calls out, 'Major, it's Joe Dickinson. Can I have a word, sir?' to which there is no reply. Undeterred he calls again, moving through the kitchen and into a large entrance hall where the smell grows even stronger.

'We've been trying to get hold of you for the last few days…'

His voice trails off as he comes across the maggoty figure of the Major at the bottom of the stairs. He doesn't need to check for a pulse.

Pulling out his mobile he phones the station. Doris answers.

'Doris, it's Joe. I'm at the big house. Look, Doris, the Major's dead—he's been dead a while by the looks of it. You'll need to organise an ambulance and let DCI Truman's mob know.'

'Will do,' Doris replies. Her voice sounds strained, then Joe remembers.

'By the way, how's your mother? I heard she had an accident and you found her.'

'She's fine now, thanks. They've kept her in till the leg heals. Daft bugger tried to chop some sticks. We've got bloody central heating! She'll be the death of me yet.'

'Ah, well, maybe the rest will do her some good.'

'It'll certainly do me good, I can tell you.'

Dickinson laughs, then Doris continues, 'There was something, Joe. I meant to tell you Thursday afternoon but when I found me mam like that, it went clean out of me head. You mentioning her has reminded me.'

'What was it?'

'Mary Donkin was in and wanted to ask if other people had reported things going missing lately. She's short of horse feed and her Mat's old clothes. I thought with the boy missing—'

'You'd better fill in a report, Doris, and pass that on to Truman. It might be good news. God knows, we need it.'

'Right you are. No sooner said than done,' and she cheerily puts the phone down while Joe waits for the ambulance.

7.13a.m.
HQ, Penrith

'How long's he been dead?' asks DCI Truman.

'Looks like a couple of weeks, sir,' Hedley replies.

'Why wasn't this picked up sooner? Dickinson's lot were supposed to be contacting everyone in the area to check their land and outhouses.'

‘Yes, sir. But he didn’t answer the phone or the door when they called at the premises’

‘He couldn’t very well if he was dead, now could he?’

‘Apparently he was a crotchety old sod and gave short shrift when anyone disturbed him. He went out walking a lot, so that’s where they thought he was.’

‘That’s no excuse. Now, what about his property? Has it been searched yet? It’s near the crime scenes and there’s a set of old buildings here,’ he peers at the map, ‘which look interesting.’

‘We’re already on to it, sir.’

‘Good. And no more cock-ups, okay?’

‘Yes, sir. Oh, one more thing, sir. There’s been a report of some missing child’s clothes from a farm near the reservoir. It’s not exactly in the vicinity, but...’

‘Right, I want that one followed up immediately. With a bit of luck, the lad might still be alive…’

7.22 a.m.
Crofter’s Wood

After a five-mile walk through the forest and over the fell to reach the wood from a track where they parked the vehicles, the search party with dogs approaches the wood from the north side. The team are tired but a pep talk from DS Hedley before setting off reminded them about the urgency of their purpose. About a kilometre in they make a discovery. Earth has been disturbed.

Taking care to preserve the area around the disturbance, one of the officers takes a photograph of the site, then scrapes away at the loose earth until some navy-blue material is exposed. Another officer phones through the report to HQ then makes a rough sketch of the crime scene and its geographical relationship, whilst the others cordon off the area and wait for Forensics.

7.30 a.m.
Coglin Mews

Mondays are never Sue's favourite but today she is even more reluctant to get out of bed. She has a thunderous headache, despite the painkillers she took at 2 a.m. and the gallon of water she drank, so her mood is tetchy, to say the least. Bloody Darren. Bloody Lisa. She'll have to look for another job now. Even if Darren is leaving, there's still Lisa, isn't there? How the hell is she going to cope with those two bitching and laughing about her behind her back?

She throws back the covers in a temper, only to be rendered useless when another paroxysm of pain makes her head feel like it's being sliced off by a machete. Not that she actually knows what that feels like, but she always prides herself on her imagination. It's no use, she'll have to phone in sick. But then, that would only look like she was a wimp and trying to avoid them. Like hell she is! She'll go in there and show them. Just as soon as she can get rid of this bloody hangover. Never again…

8.27 a.m.
St Julian's Hospital

Sue makes it just in time. She had to stop twice en route to be sick, but now there is nothing left to bring up she feels a little better. That is the last time she drinks on an empty stomach. She had been so nervous about seeing Darren that she was unable to eat anything the whole day. No wonder she got drunk so quickly! The headache is still there, but if she moves her head carefully she can just about cope.

-Let's hope there's no temper tantrums from Gina today. And Harvey's music will have to be turned down. Yes, I can do this. Only eight hours to go. Easy.-

Checking her pigeon-hole she discovers a message from someone called Lizzie. Who the hell is Lizzie? She turns the scrap of paper over but it has nothing on but the name and a phone number. Not ready to face people quite yet she makes herself a coffee as she ponders over who Lizzie might be. Still none the wiser she decides to phone this Lizzie at lunchtime—at least that will take up some spare time so she doesn't have to bump into You Know Who in the staffroom. Now, what's on the board for today?

8.45 a.m.
Fletcher Ward

Grace is in the day room, standing looking out the window again when Sue finally finds her.

'Hello, Grace. You're looking well this morning. Had a good night's sleep?'

Grace doesn't turn round. 'They said you were off,' she states flatly.

'I had the weekend off but I'm back now.'

Grace turns to look at her, staring into Sue's eyes for quite a few moments until Sue begins to feel uncomfortable. Turning back to the window she says, 'You found out then? He isn't worth it. Nor is she. Don't worry, you'll be fine.'

'How do you do that, Grace? How do you know things?'

Grace shrugs. 'You wouldn't believe me.'

'Try me.'

'No. You'd tell them. They'll keep me here and …it's not important. But I do see things. I always have. I'm not a fortune teller, I can't see beyond a week or two, I'm just sensitive to energy shifts. Peoples' auras. The Universal Conscience—'

'What?'

'It's too difficult …'

Sue waits, until Grace goes on, 'You've heard of Einstein's theory of relativity?'

'What, "*for every action there's a reaction*"?'

'No, that's Newton.' Grace sighs, then continues, 'All over the world scientists tried to freeze glycerine. They tried for years but all failed. Then someone had a breakthrough and knowledge entered the Universal Conscience. Suddenly everyone was discovering how to do it. The knowledge was available so people tapped into it.' She turns back to face Sue, her eyes intense, willing the other woman to believe her. 'People find it scary, but I tap into what's out there.'

Sue nods, wondering what Dr Norman will make of this. As if reading her mind Grace says, 'I know I'm ill, but this has nothing to do with it. I have a gift. My mother tried to beat it out of me. My daughter has it too. We've never talked about it, because…because… I don't know how to.'

'But you're talking to me, Grace.'

'Because I have to. I have to show you something. It's too important not to. I need to trust you. I don't want them in here… with their sedatives. They'll think I've gone crazy again.'

'You know I can't promise that. I have to report everything we discuss. It's my job and it's for your own good.'

The stuffing seems to have left Grace's body. Sue waits. After several minutes Grace speaks, her voice sounding slightly disembodied.

'Okay. Whatever. It's Adam—I know where he is.'

'Shouldn't you be telling the police, not me?'

'They won't believe me, not with my history. But you could.'

'I can't do that, Grace. I can't interfere like that.'

'Not even to save Adam?'

'Grace, there are proper procedures, proper channels for this kind of thing. I can call the police for you, but you'll have to give them your information and make a statement. I can't do that for you.'

Grace is visibly distressed so Sue offers, 'Look, why don't you let me see what you have to show me and we can talk about it?'

Grace shakes her head and leaves, moving slowly along the corridor to her room.

8.53 a.m.

Hilary Norman is in her office looking at the pile of paperwork that has accumulated, when Sue knocks on the door.

'Come in. Yes, Sue?'

'Can I have a word about Grace? She's been speaking to me just now and I don't know what to make of it.'

Sue pulls up a chair and sits down. Dr Norman looks for Grace's file, pulls it out and opens it. Attaching a fresh report sheet she then looks at Sue.

'Go on.'

'It was really odd. She spoke the most she has in one go since she's been here. She wanted to show me something because she thinks she knows where her grandson is.'

'How? She was in here when he went missing. Has she been watching it on TV?'

'Not that I know of. But she's convinced she knows where he is. She wants me to tell the police. I told her that wasn't what we do and then she walked away.'

Dr Norman makes a couple of notes then asks, 'What did she want to show you?'

'I haven't a clue. When I said I couldn't help, she walked away. What do you think?'

'Well, she's clearly delusional but it would help to know what she wanted to show you. Go back and give it another try.'

'What if…what if she does know where the little boy is?'

'Sue, she's on medication and suffers from paranoia and delusions. See what it is she thinks she knows and we'll discuss it. I've to go out at eleven but I'll be back this afternoon. Fill in the report and we'll see what there is to do when I get back. By the way, how's Gina this morning?'

'Fine. She wants to go home, but hasn't yelled at me yet.' Sue laughs, wishing she hadn't when her headache explodes again.

She is half-way to Grace's room when she remembers who Lizzie is. Making a mental note to call her when she is finished with Grace, she knocks on Grace's door and enters. Grace is lying on her back on the bed, staring at the ceiling.

'You wanted to show me something.'

There is no response from Grace. Sue moves closer, checking whether she has gone catatonic again. Grace's head moves and she looks Sue in the eye.

'I haven't taken myself away again.'

'Is that what you do? Take yourself away?'

'Not always. Sometimes it just happens. Like with Claire. Sometimes I can make it happen. Not always, just sometimes.'

'And why do you do that?'

'Isn't it obvious?' She waits for Sue to comment. When she doesn't, Grace continues, 'Because I don't want to be here. It's too painful. If I stayed, I'd try to kill myself again. That's a sin, so I go away.'

'You've tried to kill yourself before? In Ireland?'

Grace nods.

'What happened?'

Grace doesn't respond so Sue tries again. 'You were in hospital, weren't you?'

Still nothing.

'What happened there?'

'They took everything from me.' And then Grace is sobbing, her body shaking with the effort.

Sue sits down on the chair beside the bed, watching her. After a while the cries subside. 'What did you want to show me, Grace?' Sue asks.

Wiping her eyes and nose Grace rises from the bed and takes a large A2 size canvas from behind the wardrobe. It depicts what seems to be a dark room with a boy in the foreground lying on his back on the floor. A figure in black stands over him. The boy is wearing a navy tracksuit with red flashing down the sides of the sleeves and trouser legs. His feet are bare and his eyes are closed. The black figure stands to the side of him holding a lamp of some kind, which gives off a faint light, illuminating the child and parts of the room, but not the black figure. He is completely in the dark and there is a small container on the floor beside his foot. In the background is a circle of oblong stones.

'Who's that?' Sue asks, pointing to the man.

'Someone who has him. But… he also represents a threat. Death maybe. Like in Claire's picture.' She faces Sue and confesses, pointing to her head, 'I saw Claire's death, but I didn't recognise it. You can see for yourself. In the annex next to my workroom.'

'See what for myself?'

Grace steels herself and continues, 'I painted a picture. Before the accident. I didn't understand it so put it away. It's still there.'

The memory upsets Grace so Sue changes the subject. 'What's that?' pointing to the container.

'Water,' Grace replies.

'And this is Adam, is it?'

Grace nods.

'So where is this? A cellar somewhere?'

Grace closes her eyes and concentrates. 'No, but it's underground. There's a concealed door somewhere.' She opens her eyes and looks at Sue. 'Near those.' She points to the stones.

-Believe me. Please, just believe me- her eyes seem to say. Urgently now, she grabs Sue's hand. 'I saw earth falling, hands sticking out. I think it was a cave-in.' She is sobbing again. 'But they won't believe me. No one ever believes me.'

Grace is clearly distressed so Sue lets her cry so that she has time to think. There is nothing she can do other than write it all down in a report, but her conscience tugs at her. Grace is right; no one will believe her, even if she did have—not that she thinks she has, mind you—an uncanny gift. But if there is the slightest possibility that it might help? She has to report this; thankfully Hilary is out from 11 o'clock and won't be back till this afternoon.

'Grace, I have to go now and see to something, but I'll be back in a little while. I'll leave the door open so we can check on you. I can't promise anything, but I'll try my best to help in some way. I won't be long,' and she heads for the staffroom and her pigeonhole. Now where was that piece of paper?

9.07 a.m.
The Rise
Jayne is sitting in the garden, smoking. Lizzie doesn't smoke, so Jayne smokes outside now whilst Lizzie is staying there. Maybe she should do that when Adam comes home. She hasn't really thought much about passive smoking and how it will affect Adam. But she will be a much better mam when he comes home. She will give up again—they could use the money to go to Disneyland or somewhere, just the two of them. And she'll buy him some nice new clothes and toys. He'll like that. They found his old clothes yesterday, so he'll be needing something to wear. It's a good thing the weather is warm at the moment, otherwise he could get cold out there. She had to identify the soiled clothing the police found buried in the forest. At first she knew they weren't his, how could they be, in that state? But then she recognised the school logo on the sweatshirt…There's a reason he took them off and buried them. She doesn't know what it is, but Adam will tell her when he comes home. It won't be long now. She is not aware of the cigarette burning her fingers until the ringing of Lizzie's mobile reaches through to her.

9.09 a.m.
Lizzie takes the call into the kitchen. She should have been at work by now; fortunately they were sympathetic. She phoned NHS Direct for a doctor and thinks it is them ringing back.

'Hello, it's Sue Johnson from St Julian's. You left a message to ring you.'

'I know. I'm sorry. It was just that…. Well, anyway, it was nothing.'

'What was?'

‘Jayne’s dream.’

‘Jayne’s dream? You’ve lost me.’

‘Jayne had a dream on Saturday night about Adam. I know it sounds crazy, and I don’t really believe in that kind of thing, but Grace sometimes had …er… premonitions. So I wanted to see if it was possible for Jayne to visit her so they could talk…but that’s not possible now.’

‘Why not?’

‘They found Adam’s clothes yesterday, buried in a forest. Jayne had to identify them…she’s losing it. I’ve just rung the doctor.’

‘How do you mean, losing it? What is she doing?’

‘She keeps thinking Adam’s coming home, just sits there expecting him to walk through the door any minute. She’s so calm, it’s frightening. The other night she was screaming he was going to die if he wasn’t found soon. I think that’s already happened.’ Lizzie starts to cry. ‘Look, I’ve got to go. I’m sorry to have bothered you.’

Sue’s ear resounds with the click of disconnection.

9.20 p.m.
Coglin Mews

It has been bothering her all day. When she finished her shift she drove out to Grace’s house. The keys were still in the safe so she borrowed them and let herself into Grace’s cabin. The workroom was easy to find and on the floor against one wall in the annex were a lot of canvasses covered by old curtains and sheets. She riffled through them, admiring Grace’s obvious talents, and there it was. As Grace had said it would be. A blonde child with a red hoop around her ankle.

When she gets home Sue plucks up the courage to ring the police; they have made another appeal on TV for people to come forward with any information. The police officer on TV described the approximate area where the clothes were found. They had been buried, so perhaps she was too late. But if they can find him, then at least his mother will have some sort of closure, to be able to say goodbye to him. When Sue's parents and brother were killed, she hadn't been given that chance. She was in the car with them when they were involved in a stupid motorway pile up. They were overtaking in the outside lane when an idiot had tried to do a U-turn. Their car was hit by the lorry that swerved to avoid him, then other vehicles ploughed into the back of them. Sue survived, but was unconscious and seriously ill for months. She never even got to go to the funeral.

Feeling her face wet, Sue wipes away tears she has only just become conscious of. There is such a lot of shit in the world, her disappointments in the man department fade by comparison. She thinks her relationship with Grace, a patient, is creepy. She has always been able to divorce work from home and, unlike lots of colleagues, leave her worries about patients at work, not bring them home with her. This is crazy. And what about ethics? Should she really be doing this?

For a while she stares at the phone. Oh, bugger ethics. If it's able to give some sort of resolution to someone then she's doing the right thing. It might not be professional, but there you go. It's hardly professional to have sex with your colleagues either. Not that she's saying that's all right…oh, God, what was she saying? Just shut up and get on with it.

9.47 p.m.
Police HQ, Penrith

'This has just come through from North Shields, sir. A woman thinks she may have information but says she needs confidentiality. She's committing a professional transgression, but feels the circumstances warrant it.'

DCI Truman looks up from the piles of papers in front of him to DS Hedley holding a fax report. 'What's she got?' he asks.

Hedley summarizes it for him. 'She needs guarantees of confidentiality first. The desk tried to assure her but she wants to speak to someone in authority. She said she may have information about where the boy is. She wouldn't say what that information was though. She's very nervous but said she'd go in and make a statement. She's on her way.'

'Did they get her number?'

'Just her mobile.'

'Good. Thanks.' Truman takes the report and studies it, then puts it on one of the piles. Turning to Hedley he says, 'It's a week tomorrow, Billy. I think we need a reconstruction to try to jog people's memories. Can you get onto Sheila in the press office and get that arranged?' Turning to DS Thompson he asks, 'Harry, have any more plans of the underground tunnels turned up yet?'

Thompson shakes his head. His eyes are red rimmed. 'It's a bloody nightmare, sir. There are hundreds of old shafts and tunnels. We've got recent ones of the water systems but a lot of the very old tunnels are disused and caved in, so we haven't got accurate records of them. I found a guy called Norris who did a PhD on pipes and sewers in the area—he's a caver, actually. Apparently he's got the most accurate records. Unfortunately, he's away in the Lakes for the week walking. A colleague has tried to contact him, but the phone seems to be switched off and he doesn't know where Norris is staying. He's not sure if it's B&Bs or hostels, so I've sent the information to our lads in that area and they're trying to track him down'

Truman nods appreciatively. 'Good. Let's hope it's sooner, rather than later.'

'Yes, sir. The volunteers from Cave Rescue are doing a tremendous job but it's slow work. It's easy to miss something and there are several levels in some places, so they have to keep going back over the tunnels. There's evidence of the tunnels being used but they can't ascertain when or by whom. However, the good news is that there aren't any new cave-ins and water in the shafts is low due to the weather, so that's something at least.'

'Right.' Turning back to DS Hedley he asks, 'Anything back from forensics on the clothing or the dried food?'

'Not yet, sir,' replies Hedley.

'We need that a.s.a.p. See if you can hurry them along, Billy.'

'Yes, sir.' Hedley leaves and Truman picks up the telephone report from his pile.

Tuesday 27 May

12.44 a.m.
Coglin Mews
It's way after midnight before Sue gets home. She feels foolish. The policeman didn't exactly laugh at her but she could tell he thought she was wasting their time. Answering his questions she realised how silly it all sounds and now she regrets ever having contacted them. Trust her to cock things up. Will she never learn? And if this gets back to work…Where's that bloody vodka?

8.24 a.m.
Angle Tarn, Nr Langdale, Lake District
Stuart Norris breathes deeply. The air is heavily scented with early summer and he feels great to be alive, in this moment, in this place. Long brown grasses, dead from last season, contrast with the new, lush green ones that have sprung up. Above him the peaks of Bow Fell and Esk Pike dominate the sky and are reflected in the clear, still waters of the tarn. He definitely should do this more often. How long has it been? Christ, too long! He used to go away every weekend when he was at uni. What happened? Life happened. Well, now he's reclaiming it. There's nothing like a cancer scare to get you to review your life. This is his time and he's making the most of it. And now he's not having his balls removed, well, life's for living, isn't it!

Shifting his backpack a little he breathes deeply again, smiles and sets off along the track. This is great. He will reach Ill Crag soon and then the real climbing begins. There will be time for a short break when he gets there, then it's scrambling over the boulder fields to Broad Crag and on to Scafell Pike itself; the amazing views from the summit are more than enough compensation for the discomfort of the climb. After that he is following the becks and using his orienteering skills to get back to base in Holme Wood, Loweswater via Sourmilk Gill Waterfall, Scale Force and Carling Knott. He'll have fantastic views of Crummock Water on the way back and be well away from the main drag and other walkers. Just what he needs to get back in touch with nature.

The weather forecast is good; not too hot, just enough cloud to keep from burning, but warm enough to make walking pleasant. This is great, and there are still five days left! Maybe he should contact the lads and see if they're up for a biking weekend? He'll have to give the bike a good checking over and a make a few practice runs—maybe on the black runs on the Seven Stanes over in Dumfries and Galloway—before he commits himself to a weekend with the lads. He needs to get his fitness levels up again—he doesn't want to show himself up, now does he?

Happy with his lot he whistles and starts climbing.

6.04 p.m.
Rose Cottage, Holme Wood, by Loweswater

Norris told the landlady he would there at six, in plenty time for the evening meal, and is looking forward to a few pints at the local afterwards. There is a police car parked outside and as he approaches the front door, an officer gets out.

'Excuse me, are you Dr Stuart Norris?'

'Yes. Why, what have I done?' he asks more cheerily than he feels.

'Can I have a word inside, sir?'

'Er…yes…of course,' he stammers, then turns to see the door open. Mrs Lockhart holds it open for him and the police officer, indicating they go into the lounge.

‘I’ll bring you a nice cup of tea, Mr Norris. Would you like one too, officer?’

‘No thanks, I’ve just had one about half an hour ago.’

They go into the lounge and sit down.

-What is it about police officers?- wonders Norris. -Why do you always feel you’ve done something wrong? It’s a bit like whispering in church; there’s a sense of judgement looming over you somewhere.-

‘Don’t look so worried, sir. I’ve just come to ask for your assistance.’

‘Me? I’m not from here. I’m on holiday.’

‘I know, sir, but are you aware of the recent disappearance of Adam Freeman?’

‘The lad from Nenthead? Yes, it’s been on the news. But how can I help…’ The colour drains from his face. ‘You don’t think I…’

‘No, sir, nothing like that. It’s just that he went missing in an area that you’re very familiar with. I understand you have plans of the old lead mining shafts and tunnels from your PhD?’

‘Yes, but they’re at home. The university have copies from my PhD. Why do you need me?’

‘We understand you’ve got more plans than the ones submitted for your PhD. We’re particularly interested in the shafts that have collapsed and are no longer in use.’

‘Of course. Yes, I’d be happy to assist. When do you want them?’

‘Now, sir.’

‘Now?’

‘Yes, sir.’

‘Okay, but I’ll need to access my web page to download them.’

‘No problem, sir. You can do it down at the station and maybe answer some questions if they arise.’

'I'm more than happy to. Can I quickly have my cup of tea before we go?'

'You can have one as soon as we get there.'

6.32 p.m.
Police HQ

DCI Truman reads the forensic report. The underpants were soiled with faeces, and the business card is too deteriorated for any fingerprints. A tox report is to follow in the morning, along with the initial findings of the clothing but DNA will take a few more days. DCI Truman calls everyone in the room over to the incident board.

'Right, folks, here's what we've got. The Forensic report says Adam shat himself; I'm guessing through terror but we'll have to wait for further forensics to confirm that. The business card belongs to Hindmarsh. He was in the area at the time of the abduction, he's got no alibi for that time, and had the perfect excuse of the dog to lure Adam away. We've only circumstantial evidence at the moment and there's nothing to suggest he's familiar with the tunnels, but he could have an accomplice. Freeman thinks he's been interfering with the lad and it's common for paedophiles to work together. Hindmarsh can't really account for the time after the funeral when he had the lad in his car. He says they were 'just talking', but the neighbour corroborates Freeman's story that Adam was away over an hour and since then has been moody and wouldn't talk to anyone. I think I need to have another little chat with Hindmarsh, so Billy, can you arrange to have him brought in? With a bit of luck we can charge him in the morning and hope he tells us where the lad is.'

8.37 p.m.
Garrick Fell, Nr Meldon Rigg

The derelict house stands prominently in the clearing. Once built by subsistence farmers who later tried their hand at lead mining, it now stands empty and broken. Built of stone quarried from the hills nearby in a traditional design of one up, one down it was used to house the farmer, his wife, their seven children, a lodger, three sheep and a horse. It is one of four in the clearing, each one set apart from the others on its own land. But the ravages of time, and the robbing of stones, have more or less demolished the other three, obliterating all but a few foundations to show they had ever existed. Skeletons of wooden slats, to which horse hair still clings, stick out at odd angles and bear the marks of time and inclement weather.

At the back of the building, some new potato shoots grow haphazardly beside weeds, sheep droppings and broken branches and to the side there is a small area where a new crop of dark green shoots poke through. To the inexperienced eye this looks like the crops are remnants from previous inhabitants, long dead or departed, but Jethro Monihan, a short, stocky man with a shock of sun- and sea-bleached hair, sees something very different. Before he left the army he was a trainer in survival methods. He has got his own outdoor equipment and clothing shop in Ambleside, but is also a part-time trainer in the TA. Monihan recognises they are fresh crops, and for a current inhabitant, wherever he may be.

He calls to PC Gibney, the most senior officer there.

'Someone's living rough hereabouts, probably has been for quite a while, and he has survival knowledge. He's probably from one of the forces, and I'm guessing army.'

PC Gibney writes in his notebook.

Monihan continues, 'We need to spread out and look for signs of any kind of cover—a makeshift tent, cave, hollow, whatever—something that gives shelter from the weather as well as from sight. Look for the remains of camp fires, for freshly dug patches of earth where he'd bury things. You also need to look for signs of latrines—logs or stones laid across a trench about four feet deep, with a hole in the top for ventilation. This could be a hollow piece of wood or a pipe sticking out of the top. The latrine might also have a lid of some kind. There'll be a urinal nearby, probably an area where stones have been covered with earth, with a funnel of some sort in the middle. This guy knows what he's doing—he's hidden the crops to look like they've been part of this homestead so his latrine and urinal will look a natural part of the landscape too. But it won't be far away from his shelter and if he's got the boy, that's where he'll be. Try the locals. They'll probably know about someone living rough, or if anyone, local or otherwise, likes to come out here for long periods at a time.'

PC Gibney acknowledges the information, makes sure he has it all, then phones it through to HQ. Meanwhile the rescue team and dog handlers spread out and resume the search, all thoughts of tiredness extinguished in the excitement that they are closing in. If only they can find the child before the light goes.

8.45 p.m.
Custody suite, Carlisle

DCI Truman is thoughtful. This latest news is interesting. If Hindmarsh has an accomplice he could be holding Adam somewhere. An army or forces connection? Sanderson is good at tracking down that stuff; he'll get her on to it straight away. He scribbles a note and passes it to DC Milligan who leaves the room, then Truman looks back through the notes in the file. If only he can break this bastard and find out where Adam is…

8.50 p.m.
Police HQ

Stuart Norris doesn't go back to the Lakes. He has not had this much excitement since he was canoeing near Pitlochry and got stuck in a stopper. He managed to get himself out with the last reserves of energy he could muster, and never felt so alive as when he was coughing and spluttering on the river bank. He feels like that now. His life has a new purpose, a new direction. He has been given a second chance and he is grateful. If he can help find that lad, well, it'll be an opportunity to give something back for his good luck. He can holiday anytime—after all, he's got his life back now. He has never been a religious person but he doesn't mind admitting there are times when he prays; this is one of them.

The sketches are laid out on the table in the Incident Room, alongside the council maps of the area and the ones from his thesis. Norris looks at them intently, comparing the areas covered that are marked off on a grid on the wall. He has been at it for three hours when he finds what he has looking for.

'This one hasn't been checked,' he points out to DS Hedley who is cross-referencing reports. 'It's one of three that are disused and dangerous because they've collapsed through cave-ins, but the only one in your immediate search area. The other two are here, and here,' he indicates on the large map on the wall.

'Cave-ins? Where have I seen that?' Hedley wonders aloud. Going back to his pile of reports he rummages until he finds it. It is the one from Northumbria Police, about a Susan Johnson, psychiatric nurse, who reported one of her patients thought the boy was being held in a tunnel and was afraid there was going to be a cave-in.

Picking up the phone he calls Truman and reads the rest of the report whilst waiting for him to return the call. The phone only rings once before Hedley picks it up.

'Sorry to interrupt your interrogation but I thought you'd like to know that Mr Norris has found a tunnel he sketched that isn't on any of the maps we've got and it's right in the middle of the search area.'

'That's great. When were the sketches made?'

'Eleven years ago, sir. That particular tunnel was dangerous because it had collapsed through cave-ins, so I don't know what state it'll be in now. However, it's all we've got left to search.'

Truman considers this then continues, 'Okay. Get Cave Rescue onto it and send Norris as well, if he's willing to go, seeing as he's the only one who's been in the tunnel. He's a caver too, I gather.'

Hedley beckons Norris over to his desk. 'Yes, sir, although he told me he hasn't been down one for a while.' Hedley looks at Norris who nods furiously. 'He's keen to help though, in any way he can.'

'Good. Get onto it. Where's Harry Thompson?'

'Having a kip somewhere. He's not been home since this started.'

'Well wake him up. We'll need his contact list of cave volunteers. Has Joe Dickinson been able to find anything out about someone living rough?'

'Not yet, sir. He's contacted Farm Watch and they're ringing round all their contacts. He's waiting for one of the keepers to get back to him and he's going through reports of small items missing from farms in the area to get an idea of geographical boundaries the guy might be working in.'

'Good. Get admin support for him.'

Hedley grabs a pad and makes notes whilst he continues, 'Yes, sir. There was something else.'

'Go on.'

Finished note-making Hedley puts the pen down and sits on the edge of the desk. Norris moves away, back to his plans, out of earshot. 'Well, it's probably nothing but... it was just odd. It jumped out at me when Mr Norris mentioned cave-ins.'

Truman is curious. 'I'm listening.'

'That woman from North Shields.'

Truman nods to himself, 'The psychiatric nurse? Looks after the grandmother?

'Yes, sir. In her statement she said the old woman had painted a picture of where he was being held. She describes the picture as being of somewhere below ground with Adam on the floor and a man leaning over him. She described his clothing as dark, having a red stripe down the outside of the leg, and mentioned that Ms Watson had told her there'd be a cave-in soon if he wasn't found.'

Truman laughs, 'God, Billy. Surely you don't believe in all that mumbo jumbo?'

'Not really, sir, but I do notice coincidences. And sometimes they turn out not to be coincidences when you look at them a bit closer.' He finds the report and scans it as he speaks. 'The Johnson woman goes on to say Ms Watson told her she'd had a vision of what was going to happen to the granddaughter and had painted a picture of that too. Miss Johnson went out there and found it beside the woman's workroom.' He puts the report back. 'As I say, sir, it's probably nothing, but then stranger things have happened.'

'Sounds like a load of crap to me, but take a trip out to see her and the grandmother tomorrow morning. Get some sleep first and take a look at that painting. By the way, has the Forensic report about the clothes come back yet?'

Hedley shakes his head and picks up a fax he's just finished reading. 'No, sir. I've rung again and they said they're still working on them. They've faxed an initial description of the clothing; navy-blue child's tracksuit with red flashing down the arms and legs—that's pretty much the same as in the Johnson statement—two pairs of red boxers and a school shirt minus two buttons. Analysis of substances, fibres etc. on them will take a couple of days. Apart from the shirt, the other clothes match the description of items stolen from the washing line at the farm near the reservoir.'

'Good. Keep me informed the minute it comes in.'

Hedley puts the phone down, grabs his coat and goes off to look for DS Thompson and his list of cavers. Norris studies his sketches, rolls them up and is ready to go.

9.45 p.m.
Meldon Rigg

PC Steven Miller has always wanted to work with dogs, ever since he was very small. He's a big bloke now, almost six feet two, with dark wavy hair and shrewd blue eyes. Landing this job felt like his dreams come true. His dog, Pebbles, a four year old golden retriever, has won more awards than any other in the Division, so when she starts barking, he knows they are onto something. The light is fading quite quickly now but he can see a pile of old logs arranged neatly in rows and covered with moss. Lifting the moss he sees a grey plastic pipe sticking out from the pile of logs. He is tempted to remove some of the logs to make sure, but his training stops him disturbing anything. He calls to the others, 'It's the latrines.' The shelter can't be far away now!

9.50 p.m.
Police HQ

DS Hedley takes the call, which simultaneously raises both his adrenaline and blood pressure levels. He quickly yells the good news at DS Thompson who is passing the door and phones through to DCI Truman in the Custody suite who suspends his interview and takes the call outside the suite.

'They've found latrines up Meldon Rigg, sir. One of the volunteers, Monihan, is an ex-army survival trainer. He says it's text book survival stuff so the shelter won't be far away.'

Truman tries to hide his excitement. 'Recall everyone into that area and issue lamps and torches. Bring in anyone who's on leave or at home. We've got to find him. Proceed with caution though. I haven't been able to get Hindmarsh to tell me about his accomplice so we don't know if the lad's alive and being held or even if the accomplice is armed. Get a couple of guys from the armed response team there a.s.a.p. Close all the roads and as much of the area as you can cordon off.'

The news quickly brings everyone into the room. Hedley holds his hand up in the air for silence as he continues the call.

'Yes, sir.'

'And where's that man Norris? Is he still there?' asks Truman.

'He went to join the cavers.'

'Well get him on the radio and see if there are any tunnels that bastard could use to escape. We can't let that happen, Billy.'

'No, sir. I'll speak to him and get back to you.'

'Good. Meanwhile I'll get what I can out of Hindmarsh. He's still snivelling and protesting innocence, but hopefully it won't be long before he breaks.'

There is a rush of activity as Hedley puts down the phone and contacts admin to round everyone up.

10.12 p.m.
Crofter's Wood

The night is still, with only the gentlest of breezes soughing through the trees. The skies are alive with stars and in any other situation Stuart Norris would feel relaxed and content with the world. But not tonight. He and Dom Hargreaves are looking for the entrance to a series of collapsed tunnels that Norris recorded when he was still pursuing academic success. Strange how he ended up in the Civil Service. That's another thing he wants to do when this is over—new life, new start, new career. It's never too late, so they say. Let's hope they're not too late in finding the boy.

Jethro Monihan and his team are nearby helping with the search and they hear a yell of pain from one of the forestry volunteers, Aaron Spitz, a big, bulky-looking lad of eighteen. He has found an adit, a horizontal access tunnel often used for drainage. Hidden by an elaborate screen of wood and ferns it would have been virtually impossible to spot unless someone tripped over it. Which is what Spitz has done. A root caught his foot and he was catapulted against the screen. His weight broke the uprights and he fell against the stone archway of the entrance.

Norris and Hargreaves re-check their equipment: flask; food; ropes; carabinas; harness; first aid kit; whistle; knife; waterproofs; gloves; spare batteries; photographic equipment; small yellow box containing the harephone, a low frequency radio system. They confirm the codes for the radio channels—condition zero and foxtrot—take two experienced cave volunteers with them and set off, grim-faced, down the tunnel, each aware of the dangers ahead and secretly praying that the bastard is unarmed and the boy is alive.

11.12 p.m.
Tunnel under Crofter's Wood

Well, this is it. No going back now. Johnny uses all his strength to dislodge the wooden beams. He erected them years ago, to keep the roof up because this tunnel connected with the others he dug and enabled him to move, unseen, across the fells. The timbers are showing signs of decay and rot so it doesn't take long. Further down the tunnel he hears the crash of another part of the roof falling in and smells the acrid dust. Soon the whole lot will have gone. The sound of rocks cracking is thunderous to his ears. He has to get out, and quickly, before he is buried alive.

11.14 p.m.
The other side of the Tunnel under Crofter's Wood

They are busy retreating as quickly as they can when the third rock fall gets them. Norris and the other two volunteers manage to scrabble clear and use their headlamps to check on each other.

One of them yells, 'Dom! Where's Dom?'

Looking back into the tunnel they see a pair of arms sticking up out of the rubble and rush to his assistance, pulling him clear. He is shaken and bruised, but very much alive.

'Fuck me,' he yells, 'who farted? Next time wait till we're outside—we don't need any more rocks dislodged, thank you very much.'

The men laugh heartily as they dust him off, then continue on their way back up to the surface, radioing their actions to the police above.

11.18 p.m.
Police HQ

DS Thompson is relieved to hear the men are safe, but unhappy about how DCI Turner will take the news; he is still interviewing Hindmarsh and Thompson is loathe to interrupt him again. He leaves a message with members of staff in the custody suite for Turner to contact him during a break, then he contacts Monihan at the scene.

'Have the men come up yet?' he asks.

'It'll take them at least another hour and a half,' replies Monihan.

Thompson swears, then continues, 'Get Norris to call me as soon as he's out. There must be another way for our guy to get out.'

'Will do. What do you want us to do in the meantime?' The tiredness is evident in his voice.

'Get some rest,' Thompson urges. 'You'll be needed if Norris can locate the exit area and an hour's shut-eye can make all the difference. Call me when Norris is out.'

Monihan affirms and signs off. Thompson returns his attention to the incident board and hopes for some Divine intervention.

Wednesday 28 May

3.47 a.m.

Nr Burnhope Reservoir

Johnny dumps the bundle and runs, reaching the reservoir in a couple of minutes. The water level is low, and the sound it makes lapping over the stones at the shore is quite hypnotic. In the moonlight he can see the ghostly shapes of trees, bracken and moss, murky shades shadowed in greys and blacks. He is going overland to avoid being stopped. He has been careful to ensure they will never find him.

Brushing the few remaining bits of earth and dust out of his hair he pulls a cap firmly down on his head. It was touch and go a couple of times back there but he managed to collapse the tunnels to prevent them following him. He also buried everything in different places, quite far apart, so it'll take ages to piece it all together. And by then he'll be long gone. He can't…he just can't go back to prison.

What was just as bad as his failure with women was the fact that people at home didn't understand what he'd been through. How could they? They'd been keen enough for him to go, to "do your bit for queen and country" bollocks, but where were they when he needed them? Who came to visit him in hospital, eh? No-one, that's who. Not even his mother. She was too busy getting shacked up with another bloke and being used as a punch-bag again. And those in the pub used to wind him up something rotten.

He met up with a couple of mates from school, well, tossers really, Alan and Roger, who took him in. But after a couple of weeks they said they were sick of hearing about the Falklands. Sick of hearing about it! They were lucky they didn't have to live it every fucking hour of the day like him. Alan called him a whinger and told him to get over it, so he'd broken Alan's jaw and several ribs before Roger hauled him off.

He wasn't to be trusted, the magistrate said. He was sent down for six months, but he ended up doing three years for 'bad behaviour' inside, most of which he spent in solitary, sometimes to stop the others attacking him for screaming night after night when the medication didn't work.

Taking a last look round, Johnny shifts the rucksack into a more comfortable position and strides purposefully forward.

4.30 a.m.
Garrigill Farm
Matthew and Mary Donkin are astonished to discover a bundle at their back door. Mary almost trips over it on her way to the milking shed and further inspection reveals it to be a small boy wrapped in animal skins, dressed in their son's old boxer shorts tracksuit jacket. The milking has to wait while they carry the youngster indoors and phone for the police and an ambulance. The lad is weak, unconscious and a terrible colour. He is also filthy and smells, but at least he's alive…

5.10 a.m.
Adam is carefully wrapped in thermal space-blankets and loaded into the back of the ambulance. WDC Sanderson climbs into the back to accompany him to hospital. He is feverish and moaning. The paramedics have put a saline drip in his arm but it's urgent they get him to hospital, quickly. They head off, sirens blaring and Sanderson hangs on, expecting a bumpy ride.

It has been a long night for Sanderson but this is what she has been working towards and is relieved to find Adam still alive. She was trawling though the databases looking at other missing kids and re-checking paedophile lists, statements and alibis when the news broke. She volunteered to accompany Adam to hospital and to take his statement as soon as he is well enough. Joe Dickinson is meeting them there with the mother. The abductor has still to be found, but after this, Sanderson promises herself a long sleep, around the clock.

5.19 a.m.
Police HQ

The teams are ecstatic that the boy is alive, but their celebrations are curtailed until the abductor is found. Forensic reports have finally come in from the clothes unearthed and the bag of dried food found in one of the tunnels. DS Hedley reads it eagerly. Faeces from the underpants show traces of a toxin, gyromitrin, and a scrap of material was found to contain semen. DNA from this has been matched to a Sergeant John Henry Medhurst, formerly of the Royal Engineers, so that confirms Monihan's assessment of an army connection. Disappointingly, no fingerprints were found on the plastic bag of dried food, which turned out to be smoked rabbit and fox.

Someone in admin has pulled up everything they have on Medhurst and as Hedley reads the copy of Medhurst's army record he realises that finding him is not going to be easy. There is also an interesting report from Medhurst's prison record and Hedley quickly gives the warning to all personnel confirming him to be dangerous, desperate and probably armed. Hedley also makes a note to contact the media and warn the public not to approach him. This nightmare isn't over yet. Not by a long chalk. They've got to get him before he molests another child. The next one might not be so lucky.

DCI Truman hasn't broken Hindmarsh; so far he is still holding out. Maybe with the news of his accomplice being identified that might change. Hedley picks up the phone and dials the custody suite.

8.33 a.m.
Carlisle General Hospital

Dr Roshana Newari has been on duty for eleven hours. It has been a busy night in A and E and she still has several patients to attend to before she can finish her shift. Her glossy, almost-black hair is swept up at the back of her head and secured in place with a biro. Loose tendrils frame her face and she unconsciously brushes them away as she checks the notes carefully before answering WDC Sanderson's question.

'Adam's stable now, we're giving him plenty fluids to prevent further dehydration and he's being treated for hypothermia. Initial tests show he has intravascular haemolysis,' she looks up at Sanderson and explains, 'destruction of his red blood cells,' then returns to the notes to continue, 'and hypoxia, which is a deficiency of oxygen getting to the tissues. His blood sugar level is very low. He has further complications of convulsions, which have been caused by the hypoxia and acidosis, that's an excessive acidity in his body fluids and tissues. He's jaundiced, indicating liver dysfunction and may have cerebral oedema, that's a watery fluid collecting inside his head. There may also be some renal problems.'

She closes the folder and looks directly at Sanderson. 'It looks like poisoning, but with what and to what extent it has damaged him, we don't know yet. We've started correcting the hypoglycaemic and electrolyte imbalance and put him on a course of penicillin. However, before we can make any firm diagnosis we need the results of his toxicology tests. He's probably not going to be conscious for a while and there is the danger of seizures, so a statement is out of the question. I'm sending him to ICU and I'm afraid only Mrs Freeman will be able to sit with him. We'll ring as soon as we know anything.'

'Thanks. Is he going to be all right?'

'As I said, at the moment he's stable. He's young and the young have great powers of resilience. But until we know what poison it is I'm afraid I can't say more than that.'

Sanderson nods and Dr Newari replaces the folder of notes in a tray at the nurses' station and picks up another set, making her way to the next cubicle.

Sanderson makes her way out the front door and calls in her report. A car will be sent as soon as one is available to pick her up so she goes back inside and settles down to wait.

10.15 a.m.
Intensive Care Unit

Adam is in a bed in the corner of the room. There are four beds in this part of the ward and each are occupied; two by patients recovering from brain surgery, a baby with respiratory problems, and Adam. The nurses are efficient and caring, but Jayne's whole focus is on the bed in front of her and the yellow-faced child she gave birth to. Her last remaining child.

Jayne grips Adam's hand as Dr Tim Penshaw approaches. He is a short, tubby man in his sixties with thin faded red hair in the shape of a monk's tonsure. She prays it's not bad news. How much more is she expected to take? The doctor draws up a seat and sits facing her.

'Hello, Mrs Freeman. I'm Dr Penshaw and I specialise in drugs and poisons. We've been able to identify the toxin Adam ingested. It's called gyromitrin.

'What's that?' asks Jayne

'It's found in false morel mushrooms. From the lab results I think Adam ate these a few days ago and he's a very lucky boy to have been found.'

'What does it do?'

'Well, usually the onset of symptoms occur between six and ten hours after eating the mushrooms. It's a haemolytic toxin, which means it destroys red blood cells. It can damage the gastrointestinal tract and the liver, so we've started treatment to reduce the effects of that.'

'Oh my God!'

'I know this is all very worrying and I won't minimize the seriousness of it. Children are particularly susceptible to this toxin and the dose required is very small. For instance, they can be affected just by smelling the mushrooms cooking—they have a sort of chocolate smell that children find attractive. But the good news is that Adam was suffering from hypothermia when he was brought in—'

'How's that good news?' Jayne interrupts.

The doctor smiles at her. 'Because it means that his body functions slowed down and prevented the toxin from doing more damage.'

Tentacles of fear clutch at Jayne as she asks, not wanting to know the answer, 'More damage?'

'I'm afraid at the moment it's difficult to say what the full extent of damage is. We'll need to do lots more tests, but there's a severe depletion of his red blood cells, and it looks like there is some liver damage.

Gyromitrin also affects the central nervous system, which is why Adam is having tremors and seizures. Convulsions are common with this kind of poisoning but these will probably pass once he starts to get better. However, to rule out all possibilities we've given him an MRI scan just to make sure there aren't any fluids collecting in the brain, and that, I'm pleased to say, is negative.'

Jayne lets out a small cry, 'His brain?' and clutches Adam's hand tighter.

'Mrs Freeman,' Dr Penshaw reaches for Jayne's hand and covers it with his own, 'he's responding well to treatment so far, and he seems to be a fighter. I can't understand how he's survived all this time without treatment, but that's kids for you. They're always making medical history.' He smiles encouragingly at Jayne.

'How long before he wakes up?' she asks, looking at Adam, the drips in his hand, oxygen hissing into his nostrils and a catheter draining urine into a bottle at the side of the bed.

'Now that, I don't know. He's very weak, but all being well, with no further complications, it shouldn't be long once we've got him re-hydrated and his electrolytes balanced. I'll be back in to see him later.' He sees the misery on Jayne's face then adds, 'The nurses here are excellent and he's in the best place possible, so try not to worry.'

Jayne nods and gives him a weak smile before turning her attention back to Adam and her prayers for his recovery. Dr Penshaw quietly leaves her to it.

11.30 a.m.
Dr Norman's Room, Fletcher Ward

DS Thompson looks rough. His eyes are bloodshot

and his face is slack with lack of sleep. He is also in no mood for bullshit. Which is what he feels he's getting from the woman in front of him.

He asks again, 'Look doctor, can I please see Grace Watson. I've good news for her and there are also some questions I need to ask her.'

Dr Norman, by comparison, looks remarkably fresh. Dressed in a cool daffodil-yellow linen suit, She smiles indulgently at the officer, saying, 'I'm sorry, but as I've already told you, Ms Watson is in a very agitated state and is certainly not up to answer any of your questions. Any good news you have I'll pass on personally. Now if there's nothing else—'

'There is actually. You have a Susan Johnson working for you?'

'Sue? Yes, she works here.'

'Is she on duty at the moment?'

'She is, but—' Dr Norman is interrupted as DS Thompson stands up and looks down at her.

'Then she'll have to do. Where can I interview her? Unless, of course, she's also in a 'very agitated state'?'

Dr Norman frowns at him, then picks up the phone.

11.41 a.m.
Counselling Room, Fletcher Ward

Dr Norman shows DS Thompson into a small, freshly painted room in pale lilac and green and leaves. There are three chairs and a small coffee table. On the windowsill is a dehydrated spider plant, which he itches to water.

Sue arrives carrying a painting, with Grace in tow. Grace is looking nervously around and is reassured several times by Sue. Eventually she sits down and Sue introduces her to DS Thompson.

'I've some very good news Grace. I can call you Grace, can't I?' he asks.

Grace nods and he continues, 'Adam's been found and is in hospital.'

Grace buries her face in her hands for a few seconds then looks up and asks, 'How is he?'

'He's not too well at the moment, but he's responding to treatment and the doctors are very optimistic about his recovery.' DS Thompson watches Grace intently. Sue circles a protective arm around her as Grace puts a hand to her mouth and tries to prevent small sobs from escaping.

DS Thompson continues, 'The problem is, Grace, the man who took him is still at large and we need your help to try to find him. Is there anything you can tell me?'

Grace shakes her head and Sue prompts her. 'What about your dream, Grace? Tell the sergeant about your dream and the picture.'

Grace takes a deep breath and without looking up starts to tell the officer about her dreams and visions of Adam…

1.00 p.m.
Dr Norman's room

Hilary Norman re-reads the report in front of her then puts it down on her desk. Outside she can hear the patients chatter as they leave the dining room and return to the lounge. She contemplates a course of action for a few minutes then rises and opens the door. Sue is waiting in the corridor so Dr Norman asks her to come in.

'Sit down Sue,' she asks formally, once Sue is inside the room.

Sue waits apprehensively for what Dr Norman has to say. 'I've read your report about the course of action you took regarding Grace Watson but I'd like to know why.'

Sue weighs her options then goes for the truth, hoping that will reduce the gravity of the situation. She doesn't want lies to compound her actions. 'Because I believed her, once I'd checked her house for the other picture—I'm sorry, but I thought it would help'

Dr Norman sits and shakes her head. 'That was completely unprofessional of you. Not only do you steal keys from a patient, break into her house, break patient confidentiality—'

Sue tries to interrupt, 'I had her permission—'

'—but you act in direct opposition to what I instructed you to do.'

'I know that,' Sue agrees rather sheepishly, 'but it seemed important at the time. It might have helped find Adam.'

'And just how did you figure that one out? Did it have map locations? Grid references? No? Then how was it supposed to help?'

'I just thought—'

'No, Sue, you didn't think. Did it help them find him?'

'No,' Sue confirms, miserably.

'I'm sorry, Sue, but this is out of my hands now. You're in severe breach of your contract and there'll need to be a disciplinary hearing.'

'If it makes it any easier, I'll resign,' Sue offers miserably.

'I think it will probably come to that anyway. What on earth were you thinking? I can't believe you'd do something so stupid!'

Both women are silent for a minute then Sue says in a small voice, 'I think it's best if I just resign and go now, don't you? I don't feel I'm cut out for this anymore. I've been thinking I need a change and this seems the ideal—'

'It's hardly ideal! Collect your things, Sue. I'll inform security and they'll escort you off the premises. You're suspended until we receive your written resignation.'

'I'm sorry,' offers Sue.

Dr Norman pauses, looks her directly in the eyes and says quietly, 'Me too.'

Sue leaves the room and Dr Norman picks up the phone.

2.22 p.m.
Coglin Mews

'Hi Cass, It's me. How d'you fancy going on a year's sabbatical, just travelling the world?' Sue's lounging on her settee, travel information printed from the internet strewn on the rug at her feet.

Cass laughs at her friend's suggestion but Sue is insistent.

'I'm serious. I need to get away from everything and decide what I want to do with my life.'

'What about your job?'

'I'm leaving.'

'I still haven't got a proper job—won't it be hard for you to get another when you get back?' Cassie interrupts.

'I may not come back. And if I do, things might have changed by then. Anyway, I might find I want to do a different kind of work.'

'Look Sue, I've got no money. Or has that escaped your notice?' Cassie counters.

Not to be dissuaded Sue suggests, 'How about renting the flats out and just taking off, working our way round the world? If it doesn't work out we can always come back.'

Sue listens, waiting for Cassie's response.

Cassie doesn't reply for a while then says, 'This is absolute madness you know.'

'I know it is. But just think of it as an adventure, Cass.'

'I'll think about it. But I'm not promising anything.'

'Great! I'll get loads of stuff off the internet for us to look at. How about coming over for a meal at, say, seven and we can talk about it more then?'

'Hang on! I need some time to think. It's a big step you know.'

'How will you feel when your grandchildren ask you what you did with your life and you have to tell them you passed up an opportunity to travel the world?'

'The way things are going at the moment there's a distinct possibility I'll never reach the children, let alone grandchildren stage,' Cassie responds.

'My point exactly! Why waste time here when there's a world out there with lots of blokes waiting to be met, places to be seen and experiences to be had?'

There is a silence for a couple of seconds, then Cassie says, 'A meal would be lovely, but I'm still not promising, okay?'

That agreed, Sue goes back to her information, smiling at the prospect of at least a year away and time to re-assess her life, with or without Cassie.

3.45 p.m.
Police HQ

DS Thompson files a report of his interview with Grace. It was a waste of time, really, but you have to follow these things up. He is convinced she believes in her dreams but there was nothing in the painting that someone who has listened to the news couldn't have known about. And as to the standing stones, anyone with knowledge of that area knows you can see those things from miles away. They've got the lad anyway, so no harm done. Now if only they can find the abductor he can finish off all this paperwork…

4.27 p.m.
ICU, Carlisle General Hospital

Adam's eyes flutter open. Jayne sits beside him, still holding his hand, but it takes her a couple of heartbeats to realise he really is awake. She shouts for a nurse and Adam smiles at her. She starts to cry—she never thought she'd see that cheeky grin again.

5.51 p.m.

WDS Sanderson leaves the hospital and phones through to HQ to speak to DS Hedley.

'I've seen the boy, sir, and he wasn't abducted. He ran away from school and apparently became ill and stumbled onto a homeless guy who looked after him. So that lets Hindmarsh off the hook, I suppose.'

DS Hedley sighs. It's been a long day and it's getting longer. 'Thanks Caroline, I'll let DCI Truman know. Have you got the lad's statement?'

'No, sir. He was a bit tired and I didn't stay too long, but I've got the sequence of events as he remembers them. I told his mother I'd be back to take a formal statement from him tomorrow, if he's up to it.'

'Good work. Get back here and write your report up. I'll see what DCI Truman wants to do now.'

Sanderson switches off her mobile and heads towards the car park.

6.50 p.m.
Nenthead

Gary is nervous. He thought about phoning first, but Was afraid Jayne would cut him off. Or not answer at all. It's harder to do when it's face to face…If he can only just touch her, hold her. They had magic between them—surely she can't have forgotten? If only he can get to kiss her, make love to her, it'll be fine. And then there's Adam. She can't have forgotten the bond he had with him before…before all this.

Not sure what to say, he has rehearsed different speeches over and over but none of them say what he wants to say. He can't seem to find the words for that. Hopefully he will be able to improvise when he gets going. It's too soon to tell her he wants to settle down with her, to look after her and Adam, but maybe in time she will see how he's good for her. How they're good for each other. And with Sandy put away…the fucking bastard! He's the one responsible for all this mess! If he could only get his hands on that lying, fucking lump of shite!

He pulls up and parks outside the door. His hands are shaking as he locks the car door and his legs feel soft as walks. He has to take deep breaths to try to calm down as he waits for Jayne to answer the door. She doesn't, it's Lizzie. He is shocked at how she looks. Her hair hasn't been washed, her eyes have black rings round them and she has lost weight. He can't be a much prettier sight after his ordeal but at least he has taken the trouble to shower and shave.

'I'm sorry, Gary, but she's not here.'

'Look, Lizzie. I've been banged up in police cells, interrogated, accused of…..please, let me see her.'

Lizzie falters, then holds the door open for him. He follows her into the lounge and checks around. Satisfied Jayne is not there he asks, 'How's Adam?'

Lizzie picks up a bag she has packed. 'He's still at the hospital. He's been poisoned—'

'Poisoned?'

'From eating mushrooms apparently. There's some liver damage but he's responding to treatment. I've been picking up a few things and am just on my way back over. Jayne's staying with him.'

Lizzie is exhausted. He can hear it in her voice, see it in her eyes.

'I need to see her,' he insists.

'Now's not the right time, Gary. Surely you should know that. Hasn't she gone through enough?' Anger sparks in her then. 'This isn't about you. She's lost a daughter and very nearly Adam too.'

Gary looks at his feet, ashamed. 'I know that, but I want to help.'

'Well leave her alone. That's the only way to help right now.' Checking her watch he says, 'Look, I've got to go.' She moves towards the door and Gary reluctantly follows her and they leave together.

'I'll give you a lift,' he offers, 'it'll save Derek and I want to see Jayne.'

Lizzie is too tired to argue.

7.30 p.m.
Carlisle General Hospital, Waiting Area
Lizzie leaves Gary downstairs while she takes the bag up to Jayne and to let her know Gary wants to see her. She returns ten minutes later with Jayne and discreetly moves away from them and sits on a plastic chair near the entrance. Jayne approaches Gary.

'Why did you come?' she asks.

Gary stands up to embrace her but she folds her arms in front of her chest and he backs off. Her face is drawn and she's wearing an old tracksuit he hasn't seen before.

Gary keeps eye contact with her and replies softly, 'Jayne, I care about you, about Adam…'

Jayne throws her arms up into the air in exasperation, 'Gary, I can't do this right now.' Seeing his hurt expression she tries again. 'Look, you're a nice lad—'

'Lad? Nice lad? What're you talking about?' He's on his feet and all the pent-up anger at the police and Sandy rises to the surface. He is unable to help himself and yells, 'Have you any idea what I've been through? Have you?' Suddenly he realises where he is and sits down, deflated.

Jayne sighs, wearily, and sits next to him. When she speaks, it's as if she is explaining something to a little boy. 'Gary, we had fun, I enjoyed your company. But right now I haven't got time for myself let alone you. I nearly lost it, so I have to keep myself together for Adam's sake. That's all I want to think about.'

'Okay, I'll give you space—'

She stands up. 'No, Gary. I don't want to see you again. There's been too much…just go. Please, just go.' She moves past him and starts to climb the stairs

He grasps at straws. 'Maybe in a few weeks. When you've had time—'

Without turning she says, 'It's over, Gary. Go home.'

He stands up to leave, feeling the injustice of it all…

8.10 p.m.
Police HQ
DS Thompson and DS Hedley squash into DCI

Truman's room. There is only one seat and Thompson plonks himself down into it. Hedley rests against a filing cabinet behind him.

Truman is the first to speak.

'I've thought about all the angles and I think we need to bring this investigation to a close. Medhurst can be indicted for several offences—wasting police time, attempting to pervert the course of justice, even assault—but the amount of money spent on man hours to find him quite frankly isn't worth it. I've spoken to the CPS and they've advised us that even if we caught him the chances of getting a conviction are slim. There'll still be an outstanding warrant for his arrest should he surface in the future, but it's time to stand down and get the paperwork up to date…

10.00 p.m.
Merry Farm

Gary sits on the floor in the dark as he dials the number.

'Hello, Dad. It's me. I thought I'd let you know I've been thinking about your offer. It'll take me a while to wind up things here, to finish the work I've made a commitment to—'

'That's great, son,' he shouts, ' Joyce, it's Gary. He's coming over.'

'Dad, don't get carried away, there's still a lot to look at before I make the final decision—'

There is a scuffle at the other end then his mam interrupts, 'Eee, pet, is that right? You're coming over,'

'I told dad I'm thinking about it. I thought I'd come for a long holiday first, to see what it's like.'

'That's wonderful. You'll love it. They've got girls here too you know.'

He is unable to hide the bitterness in is voice. 'I'm sure they have, but right now I've had enough of girls.'

His mother's voice has a smug tone to it now. 'What's happened? You've fallen out?'

'No, Mam. I just… it didn't work out. There's been some… oh, never mind. I miss you, so thought I'd look at the practicalities. It may come to nothing, but—'

'Jason!' Joyce shouts to his brother, 'Gary's coming to join the business! Isn't that wonderful!'

'Put him on, Mam,' asks Gary.

There's more scuffling and sounds of excitement until his brother takes over.

'Hiya. What's this then?' Jason asks.

'Jace, I'm looking at it. That's all. You know what they're like, so try to keep their hopes from running away with them. It's early days and it may not be practical, but I'm certainly looking at it.'

'Understand. But, hey, it'll be good if you do decide to come. There's loads to do here, and the talent…you should see all the beach babes…you'll love it.'

'Yeah, well, okay. There's nothing but the business holding me here, so you never know… Anyway, I've got to go. I'll let you know how I get on.'

'Sure. That's great. See ya,'

''Bye,' his Mam and Dad chorus, then the phone is silent and Gary discovers he's crying again.

Friday 5 September

9.45 a.m.
St Julian's Hospital

The leaves have started to change colour as Jayne drives into the hospital grounds. Bronze, orange, red and gold spiral in the wind like confetti, then settle on the newly mown grass. Winding the window up, Jayne opens the car door but doesn't get out straight away. Sitting there, she inhales the burnished scents of late summer, steadying herself for the ordeal to come. A few more breaths then she decides—it's now or never. Adam is back at school. A new term, a new start. Hopefully.

Grace was moved to a different unit in late July and is nearly ready to go home. She has been having intensive therapy and the hospital has arranged a package of care to enable her to live independently. Grace has asked if Jayne would come to one of her therapy sessions, and here she is. She doesn't know whether she is doing the right thing; she has only spoken to Grace a few times by phone, and this is the first time she has seen her since leaving for Paris. She is having her own counselling and this meeting is also part of her own therapy, but she's dreading it, afraid of what she might feel, how she will react, or what she might say.

Her stomach knots as she passes the smokers outside the main entrance. They look normal, anyway. She is not sure what she expected—drooling, lolling tongues, vague expressions?—but is pleased they are not like that. She has never been in a psychiatric hospital before and feels afraid. However, she presses on, along the corridors tastefully decorated in pastel shades, adorned by paintings, until she finds where she is looking for.

She catches the attention of a young woman dressed in jeans with a label hanging round her neck identifying her as Carol Reid, psychiatric nurse.

'Excuse me. I've an appointment with Dr Norman. It's about Grace Watson. I'm her daughter.'

Carol Reid smiles. 'Hello. Grace is expecting you. Can you take a seat because Dr Norman would like to see you before you meet with Grace. I'll just let her know you've arrived.'

She walks off and Jayne sits down. She doesn't have to wait long.

10.00 a.m.

The session takes place in a cool, airy room painted lilac and pale green. The women sit in a circle around a low coffee table and there is a box of tissues on the table alongside a jug of water and three glasses. Jayne and Grace help themselves to water. Dr Norman has already outlined the purpose of the session and the 'rules', which they have agreed to. She then asks Jayne if she wants to be the first to start. Jayne nods.

'Is there something you'd like to ask your mother, Jayne?'

Jayne looks directly at Grace and asks, 'Tell me about my father.' Turning to Dr Norman Jayne says, 'She won't ever tell me about him.'

'Grace, can you tell Jayne about him?' prompts Dr Norman.

Grace finds eye contact with Jayne difficult. She looks at her glass as she responds to Jayne's question. 'What do you want to know?'

Jayne is animated. 'Everything! His name, where you met, if you loved him—everything. I need to know.'

Grace's voice is barely above a whisper. 'Can't you leave the past alone?'

Jayne is persistent 'No. I can't, actually. Because one of the things this has taught me is that nothing is ever really in the past. We live with it day in, day out. And no amount of drink, sex or drugs changes that. It's always there, inside.'

Grace looks into her daughter's face and sees the earnest expression. She drops her eyes and concentrates on pouring more water into the glass, then she replies, 'He was kind and helped me. I loved him and thought he loved me. He did, but not enough. That's all there is to it.'

'No it's not. What's his name?'

Grace shifts uneasily in her chair. She can hear the rise and fall of the other women's breaths. Eventually she answers, 'Brendan.'

Jayne nods to herself, then asks, 'How old was he?'

Grace looks to Dr Norman. 'Do I have to do this?'

'Not if you don't want to. You can stop at any time,' she assures.

Taking a deep breath Grace exhales then continues, 'Twenty-nine.'

'But you were only—'

'I know. Now can we—'

'That's disgusting. Was he married?'

Grace hesitates, then answers, 'In a way. He was married to his job. He went to work abroad and left me.'

'Why? … Because of me?' Jayne asks, fighting down her old fear.

'Is that what you think? No, Jaynie, it wasn't. He was a weak man. A wife and family was,' she struggles to find the words, 'out of the question. Don't ever think it was your fault.'

Jayne bristles a little at the use of that name, but lets it go.

'So what was this job that was so important?'

Grace responds by saying, 'I'm very tired Doctor. Can we do this another time?'

'You always do this,' accuses Jayne.

'What?'

'Opt out. Change the subject. Walk away. You never just sit and talk. You never tell me things, things that are real or matter.'

Dr Norman intervenes at this point and asks Grace, 'How do you feel about what Jayne's just said? Is she right? Do you avoid talking to her?'

Grace is visibly upset but tries to continue, 'It's not that—I don't know what else to do.' She breaks down, her shoulders heaving with suppressed emotion. Then, with an aggression that Jayne has never seen before, Grace turns on her, 'You have no idea! My mother used to beat and torture me… because I was evil. Because I saw and heard things. Brendan saved me. Then he dumped me.'

'You're one to talk about dumping people!' Jayne is furious but looking at Dr Norman reminds her why she is there. In a calmer voice she continues, 'You left me! I had to stay with the Sisters. I cried and cried for you but you never came. They told me what you did, how you tried to kill yourself. You wanted to leave me. How could you do that? I was just a little girl, I needed you.'

Grace is still sobbing but manages to continue. 'It wasn't my choice. I was ill. They took me away and said I'd never get you back. I believed them.' She turns to Dr Norman. 'Tell her what they did to me.'

'Why don't you try to tell her. You're doing really well, Grace'

Grace composes herself then continues, 'They gave me electric treatments, isolation, water therapy. And all the time… I worried about you, if I'd ever see you again.'

The room is eerily silent after the outburst. Dr Norman asks Grace, 'Is there anything you want to ask Jayne?'

Grace shakes her head. She is still crying.

Dr Norman prompts, 'Didn't you want to know if Jayne wanted to be part of your care package for when you go home?'

'How can she? It's all my fault. I'm so sorry.'

'Then tell her.'

Grace looks up. She wipes her eyes on one of the tissues, takes a deep breath and says, 'I'm really, really sorry about Claire. About everything…' Her voice trails off to be replaced by further sobbing.

Jayne starts crying quietly and reaches over to grasp Grace's hand. 'I know, Mam, I know,' she says, her voice thick. Turning to Dr Norman she says, 'What's this care package? Right now I'm only just coping with myself and Adam'

'The details are still to be worked out, but we're putting in place a multi-agency package involving CPN, (that's the Community Psychiatric Nurse), social services, Grace's GP and outpatient services. Grace needs a lot of counselling, but contact with you and Adam will be really beneficial to her.'

'And to Adam,' Jayne admits. Turning to Grace she says softly, 'He's really missed you, Mam.'

Grace's sobbing increases in intensity and Jayne moves closer, putting an arm around her. Dr Norman lets them stay like that for a little while, before summarising, bringing the session to an end and asking if they want to arrange another meeting.

Friday 19 September

1.22 p.m.
The Shambles

It's so good to be home. Jayne brought me back yesterday with Adam. She's got Gary's car and dog—he went to Australia at the beginning of the month for a year's visit and gave them to her as a leaving present. The dog was for Adam.

Adam's so quiet now, compared to last spring, but he's almost normal with the dog, when life creeps back into him. They aren't staying over; Jayne wants to drive back, but they're coming again next month for a visit. Maybe they'll stay then. Maybe not. There are still deep, dark waters between us and sometimes I don't know how to swim.

I went for a walk this morning, along the cycle track to the beach. The wind was strong, tearing at loose rags of cloud, snatching my breath, making my skin burn. Pale ladders of sun escaped the clouds and the morning passed, relaxing yellow. At the harbour a gust of wind spat water in my face and the sea boomed. I felt Claire beside me, clutching at my back, calling my name, her voice changing, dampening. Light wobbled on the surface of the sea, then she was gone. I force myself to remember the last time we were here, and it's like a film, something unreal, that happened to someone else…

The wind had been picking up and crystals of sand snaked across the beach, stinging our eyes and bare legs. The crouching children complained but I wasn't moving, just staring ahead, out to sea, the wet rhythms calling to me.

Adam approached and shook my arm for several seconds. His face was drawn and tight.

'Grandma, the sand hurts.'

'I can smell it,' I replied.

'What?'

'It's coming closer, we have to go.' I got up quickly, turned around and headed off towards the bikes, leaving the children to pack up and follow. I sat astride my bike and waited, sniffing the air. The children looked at each other and mounted their bikes in an uneasy silence.

At the harbour the stiffness between us remained, even when I asked for their order in the chip shop. Adam chose fish but Claire decided on fishcake and they shared a portion of chips. I didn't want anything.

On the pier I kept looking out to sea, aware of the children eating their food from paper trays the colour and texture of egg cartons, using a twin prong spoon to stab the chips and skewer the fish or fish cake. No-one spoke. The bikes were sprawled beside a capstan, which was necklaced with a large, thick rope securing a small boat bobbing on the water beneath. The sea was visible through the gaps in the wooden boards of the pier and Claire knelt down to get a better view. Her little bottom was raised in the air, pink knickers visible underneath her pink summer dress. Adam watched her and smiled.

'Careful the birds don't bite your bum!' he shouted.

Seagulls wheeled overhead and the suddenness of their loud screeches caused Claire to run in panic away from the sound. Adam started to laugh but saw her getting dangerously close to the edge of the pier. He jumped up just as she collided with the bikes and was tipped over into the water along with the red bike, which had become attached to her right foot. Adam grabbed my arm and shook and shook, but I couldn't respond. My eyes were glazed, my whole body rigid, yet my senses expanded, taking me outside myself, hovering in the air, a husk of shadows.

I watched him frantically looking around till he saw someone on a neighbouring pier and shouted for help, waving his arms wildly. The man didn't look up from his nets. I could see Adam as he raced over to the fish and chip shop, grabbing a woman about to enter. He was incoherent. It took the woman several minutes and the help of the shopkeeper to understand what he was saying. They ran to help, leaving him with a shop assistant. Curled up on the floor, hugging himself, he cried and cried. I struggled to stay with him but couldn't. Something drew me back inside myself, wrapped itself around me and kept me there till the ambulance came…

I can never undo what's been done, but in this ebb and flow of life, if I'm lucky, then maybe I can close a circle that was torn open years ago, before I was even born.

Memory is a strange thing. Sometimes a smell, a sound, a touch can catapult me back to the shifting, sighing dark where images and emotions are inseparable and are carved by rusty nails on my imagination. Yet at other times, I struggle to recall faces, days, events. Each day is a gift, whatever it contains, and gradually my days are filling more and more with the slow rhythms of the world and I stretch my fingers to attach myself, to become a part of all that is. It's hard, but I'm alive, in all senses of the word.

Epilogue
Friday 10 May

The Rise

When I sit here by the window I can still see her there, playing with all her toys, running round with Adam, tripping over her feet. I can hear the intake of breath and count the seconds before she exhales and cries, hear her squeals as he threatens to catch her, tickle her, or squirt her with water. But then the darkness comes and I hear the terror. I can see her screaming and struggling in the water, feel her lungs filling up, and watch the life trickle out of her as she drifts to the bottom. The nightmares are worse.

Sometimes I can hear Claire at night, knocking on the walls, crying to be let in. I look and look for her but she's always just out of reach. And then I find my mind going blank and I panic.

These days I don't see her as clearly as I used to. Every now and again my memory fades and I see shadows around her, like the ghosting of a television screen. I used to know every inch of her little body, its smell, its touch, its feel, but now and again there are gaps when I try to visualise her. That's when I have to get the photos out, to stop the memories eroding. And to assuage the guilt that there's a single second I'm not thinking about her.

I never understood why my mother kept looking at old photos so much while we were in Ireland; now I do. She used to get them out in the evening sitting in front of the fire in winter or in her chair in the garden in summer and just sit there, motionless. She'd drift off into that world of hers and nothing I said or did could shake her out of it. What if I end up like her? Sandy used to goad me into a fight by saying, 'You're just like your mother.' But I am, in lots and lots of ways. Gary used to say it was a good thing to be like one of your parents, but he didn't have mine.

I didn't think I would, but I miss Gary. He has the kind of lopsided smile that makes you want to kiss it into a straight line. And when he laughs he just throws his head back and guffaws. I never knew what that word meant, guffaw, or the sound it was supposed to be, until I met him. It describes him perfectly. He took such pleasure in being alive, in the simple things around him; it scared me. Then there was Claire's accident and I couldn't look at him without being reminded of her. He's met someone else now and decided to settle in Australia, so I wish him well. He deserves that much, at least.

It's been a year since the funeral. I don't remember much at all except a tiny coffin and the smell of flowers. Claire would have loved them. She always picked buttercups and never tired of holding them under our chins to see if we liked butter. Or making daisy chains with Adam. Well, he made them, she wore them. Maybe we should make some daisy chains to put on her grave? Adam's never been to the grave since the funeral. Nor have I. I feel closer to her here, in the garden. When I get better maybe, I'll take Adam to her grave. And Mam. She's doing quite well as long as she takes her medication. We're all having counselling and it helps. Adam, being young, has the best chance. There are parts of all of us that are completely broken and I don't know if anything will ever heal them, but for all our sakes, and to honour the memory of Claire, we have to try. Sometimes, that's all anyone can do, and sometimes, like the wondrous birth of a child, we see miracles hidden in the bare bones of ordinary life. That gives me hope.

Acknowledgements

I would like to thank the many people who helped me with the research for this story; Brian Marshall for army information and search and rescue procedures; Cumbria Police; and the NHS for medical advice. Any errors are my own.

Thanks also to Mary Smith for reading the novel and offering invaluable advice, to Renita Boyle for her unconditional support and unstinting belief in me, and to my family and friends who have encouraged and prodded me.

All characters in this story are fictional and bear no relation to any individual, alive or dead. I have also taken great liberties with the geography of the settings, mixing real place names with fictional ones, so I apologize to any purists out there.

Photograph of the author by Kim Ayres
www.kimayres.co.uk